Montana
★ MAVERICKS

Welcome to Montana—the home of bold men and daring women, where more than fifty tales of passion, adventure and intrigue unfold beneath the Big Sky. Don't miss a single one!

Montana
★ MAVERICKS™

LAURIE PAIGE
Father Found

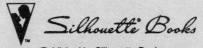

Silhouette Books

Published by Silhouette Books
America's Publisher of Contemporary Romance

Special thanks and acknowledgment to Laurie Paige
for her contribution to the Montana Mavericks series.

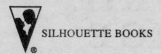

SILHOUETTE BOOKS

ISBN-13: 978-0-373-31031-9
ISBN-10:   0-373-31031-5

Recycling programs
for this product may
not exist in your area.

FATHER FOUND

Visit Silhouette Books at www.eHarlequin.com

Printed in U.S.A.

LAURIE PAIGE

says, "One of the nicest things about writing romances is researching locales, careers and ideas. In the interest of authenticity, most writers will try anything…once." Along with her writing adventures, Laurie has been a NASA engineer, a past president of the Romance Writers of America (twice!), a mother and a grandmother (twice, also!). She was a Romance Writers of America RITA® Award finalist for Best Traditional Romance two times, and has won awards from *Romantic Times BOOKreviews* for Best Silhouette Special Edition and Best Silhouette Book. She has also been presented with *Affaire de Coeur*'s Readers' Choice Silver Pen Award for Favorite Contemporary Author. Currently settled in Northern California, Laurie is looking forward to whatever experiences her next novel will bring.

One

Moriah Gilmore let herself into the apartment. Silence greeted her. With a frown, she went into the kitchen and deposited the heavy grocery bag on the counter. Her arm trembled with the effort. She sighed and looked for a note on the refrigerator.

> Mom, I'm at Jessy's. We're studying for a big test.
> Her mom said I could have dinner with them. Okay?
> Love, Melanie

Moriah smiled. Yes, it was okay. Jessy and Melanie were both A students, merit society and all that. They also worked on the school paper, an honor because only two juniors were chosen for this job each year. They would be co-editors their senior year. Moriah was proud of both girls.

After pausing to stretch her tired back, she put the groceries away, prepared a grilled-cheese sandwich and, because she felt a little lonely without Melanie's bright chatter, treated herself to three bread-and-butter pickle slices.

"Some treat," she muttered. She ate a bite of sandwich and popped a pickle into her mouth. Sitting at the breakfast bar on a tall stool, she looked out the window toward the south.

Clouds, dark and sullen, hovered on the far horizon. It was raining down that way, she supposed. Here in Great Falls it was partly cloudy, humid and growing cold. She was glad she didn't have to dash out to a class.

When she'd finished the summer term, she'd decided to take a break until after Christmas. It would be a relief not to have to worry about grades and tests and attending courses for a while.

When she finished night school and got her degree, she'd be a paralegal. Only one year to go!

With the experience she was gaining as a receptionist-typist at a local law firm, she should be able to land a good position next year. And an interesting one, she hoped. Maybe in the same firm. She'd been there almost five years—

Her thoughts were interrupted by the telephone.

Probably Melanie. Moriah answered it with a quip: "What did you forget that you can't live without?"

Silence greeted her. Moriah realized she'd surprised someone on the other end of the line...and it wasn't her daughter.

"Sorry, I was expecting someone else," she said. She slipped into the crisp but friendly manner she used at the office. "This is the Gilmore residence. How may I help you?"

"Moriah?"

Her heart stopped. It had been sixteen, almost seventeen years since she'd heard this particular masculine baritone, the unique timbre of which reminded her of a mountain lion's purr. Not that she'd personally heard one of the big cats purr, but she imagined it would sound the way this man did—smooth and rough at the same time. His was unlike any other voice. She recognized it at once.

Heat swept through her. She felt disoriented, as if in an instant she'd been catapulted back in time, to a distant past in which this same voice had whispered the loveliest of love words in her ear as they lay together, their hearts beating as one.

She ran a trembling hand through her hair and immediately recalled other hands doing that. Kane had loved her hair, had loved to smooth a strand and watch the curl bounce back when he released it. He'd liked to tickle her neck and her breasts, using a lock of her hair like an artist's brush, his touch sure and gentle, so very gentle.

"It's like holding fire," he'd murmured, nuzzling his nose along her temple, kissing and biting at her ear. He'd dropped his hand lower, touching the auburn hair at the joining of her legs. "There's fire here, too," he'd said, teasing her, loving her, making her feel beautiful and *wanted,* which was something more than desired, although that was there, too.

Oh, God, she'd been so young. Seventeen…

She closed her eyes and drew a deep breath, seeking the calm center in the hurricane of emotion his voice induced. Like a drowning person, she pressed a hand to her throat, needing air and unable to get enough of it.

"Moriah?" Kane Hunter said again.

She had to answer, but only one thought—one illogical, stubborn thought—swirled in her head. *Kane. Her first love. Her lover. Her betrayer.*

"Yes?" She forced the word from her parched throat. Her voice came out husky, cautious. Perhaps this wasn't

Kane. It could be a salesman. One who called her by her first name with that oddly intimate note of past knowledge in it? No, the man on the other end of the line was no stranger.

Her heart beat furiously, loud and frantic in her ears. She glanced around the small, neat kitchen as if looking for a place to escape the memories this voice conjured up.

"This is Kane. Kane Hunter," he clarified. "This *is* Moriah Gilmore, isn't it?"

"Yes."

The drowning sensation became stronger. Once she had thought she would die of ecstasy in his arms, he'd brought her such bliss. He'd liked to watch her take pleasure from his touch. And she had. So much pleasure. And later, he'd caused so much pain.

She swallowed as emotion balled in her throat, and forced herself to respond like a normal person rather than like the loving, trusting teenager she'd once been.

"Kane," she managed to say without gasping. "This is a surprise."

"I'll bet." His tone was sardonic. "I'm calling about your father," he continued, without giving her a chance to speak again. "The police have been looking for him—"

"What police?" she interrupted, unable to take all this in at once—that Kane was calling like a ghost out of the past and that he wanted to talk about her father, who had abandoned her and her mother years ago.

"The Whitehorn police," Kane replied caustically. "You know, the ones in the town where you used to live?"

He spoke as if she were dimwitted. Which was how she felt. She ignored his nasty crack and assumed the cool, controlled manner she'd learned years ago in order to cope with life. "Why were the police looking for my father?"

"That's what I'm trying to explain to you."

She could almost see him forcing the words out, the muscles in his jaw like steel ropes under his smooth, swarthy skin. A picture came to mind of her stroking along his whipcord-lean body, down the rippling contours of his chest and torso, along his thighs, feeling the powerful muscles tense beneath her touch. He'd been incredibly strong from his years of ranch work, his body hard…all over.

She freed the image from her mind with a violent toss of her head. "Then please do," she requested, after a sizzling pause.

"I went up to his cabin—"

"My father has a cabin?" She'd wondered about him over the years, of course. She'd even sent a Christmas card to their old address a couple of years after she and her mother left. Her father hadn't answered. "He doesn't have the house?"

"Not anymore," Kane said.

Moriah could hear the forced patience in his voice. The Kane she'd once known had been infinitely patient with her. And tender. The most considerate of lovers.

That tenderness was gone. And so was the house where they'd shared their love during the snowy afternoons of that magical Christmas holiday. Gone like the lovely snowflakes that had whispered so softly against her bedroom window while she and Kane murmured their hopes and dreams for the future.

Foolish, ridiculous tears burned behind her eyes. She realized that someplace inside her she still mourned the loss of that innocence, that sublime belief in life that only fools and children have.

She clutched the telephone as pain she'd thought long dead and forgotten coursed through her. She'd trusted Kane, and for a while, he'd given her bliss and a sense of wholeness, of freedom…and oh, so many wonderful things.

"So he lives in this cabin?" she prompted when the silence stretched to unbearable lengths. She wondered if Kane was remembering, too. She sighed and focused on the present. Her father was in trouble. She'd better listen.

"Yes. Anyway, I went up there a couple of weeks ago. He and I were supposed to go fishing. He didn't show up. Then Rafe Rawlings spoke to me about him—"

"Rafe Rawlings?"

"A cop in Whitehorn. If you'll let me finish…"

She stilled the questions that rose in her.

"Your father is missing," Kane said bluntly after the taut silence. "He's been gone two weeks that we know of."

She started to ask him how he knew and if he was sure of the length of time her father had been missing, but decided against it. He'd only snap at her.

"Rafe and I searched, but we didn't find any signs of the old codg—uh, Homer. That was this past weekend. I was up there the weekend before. So that makes two weeks we know he's been gone. And he's missed two appointments he knew about."

"Is that unusual?" She was in her office mode now, asking questions, taking down information from the clients who called, assessing their needs.

"Yes. Homer is a bit…um, eccentric, but he's usually reliable. Skipping out isn't like him."

A lot Kane knew, she thought, calling on cynicism to stop the hurt from long ago. Her father hadn't been there when she'd needed him. *When she'd been pregnant and desperate and afraid.*

Only her mother had stood by her. Men slipped out the back when trouble walked in the front, as her mom had often stated.

Moriah knew that for a fact. Moreover, men followed their own dreams, heedless of others' wishes, then blamed the woman when things didn't pan out. Oh, yes, she knew how reliable men were.

"Let me get this straight," she said. "My father lives in a cabin in Whitehorn. He's been gone somewhere for two weeks. You and some local cop searched but couldn't find him. Is that right?"

"Actually, Homer lives in a line shack on the old Baxter place. It's owned by the Kincaids now, but they've let him use it for the past ten or fifteen years, I think."

"I remember it," she said.

"It isn't the same one we used that time," Kane informed her, his tone as chilling as a north wind.

Wild heat ran into her face at his reference to the cabin where they'd once taken refuge in a snowstorm. They'd made love by the fire while the wind raged outside, heaping snow against the side of the tiny hut. Inside, she'd been warm and cozy, locked in Kane's embrace, covered by his kisses.

Her body reacted with another surge of heat, becoming soft and liquid, ready to receive him…. She gripped the counter edge until her knuckles turned white.

"I didn't mean… I wasn't talking about…" She drew a calming breath. "My father used to take me prospecting with him. We stayed at a cabin in the heart of the old mining country. It was near the Baxter ranch road."

"Yeah, that's probably the one." His tone was flat, without any emotion that she could detect. "You need to file a Missing Person's Report. Rafe and I are afraid something serious has happened to him."

"Do you think he's lost in the mountains?"

"I wish I knew. There's no evidence of foul play, but I have a gut feeling that all isn't well. Homer needs help. You'll have to come home."

Her mouth dropped open at this imperious order. There

was no mistaking Kane's attitude. He expected her to rush right down to Whitehorn and find her missing parent.

"I can't. Why should I?" she added defensively.

"Because he's your father and I'm damned tired of being responsible for him. If you don't care, then he'll probably die, perhaps trapped in a cave-in somewhere."

His angry voice beat at her through the telephone. Her own temper mounted. "I recognize a guilt trip when I hear one." She was as cold as he was. "It won't wash. My father abandoned me years ago—"

"That's a damned lie!"

She stopped, stunned by Kane's vehemence. "It's true," she insisted. "He deserted us. My mom and I had to leave and make our way alone in the world."

"Save the sad tale for someone who'll fall for it. I won't." His disgust hit her like a whiplash.

"I wouldn't expect sympathy from *you*." She banged the receiver onto the wall receptacle and tried to calm the tremors that rushed through her.

Taking her plate, she tossed the sandwich, which had only one bite out of it, and the other two pickle slices down the drain and hit the switch, letting the grinder run until her anger cooled.

She didn't know what was going on, but she wasn't going to become involved in it. If Kane expected her to drop everything—her life, her job—to go on some wild-goose chase, he could think again. Her father had always headed into the mountains every chance he got. There was nothing unusual in that.

Go back to Whitehorn?

Never!

Dr. Kane Hunter observed the birth in progress with both professional and personal interest—professional because Lori Bains, the midwife, had asked him to stand by in case a Caesarian section became necessary; personal because the parents were Native Americans from the Laughing Horse Reservation and were known to him. He, too, had grown up on the res.

Kane found his own muscles clenching, working with the mother as she struggled to bring new life into the world. He'd delivered hundreds of babies, both on the res and in the small town of Whitehorn, but it never failed to move him.

This was Day One in the life of the child. He thought of all the days that would follow, and the growing and learning needed to make it in this world. He studied the new father, who stood by his wife's side, her hand clutched in his.

The silent, earnest young man was eighteen.

The same age he'd been when he'd met his first love….

The memory leapt into his mind with the hot insistence of a branding iron. He frowned, angry but not surprised by it.

Since he'd talked to Moriah about her father on Monday, bits and pieces of the past had floated into his consciousness at odd moments. For a second, tired from too much work and too little sleep, he let the memory have its way.

When he and Moriah Gilmore had been lovers, he'd thought the world was his. He'd had a scholarship for college, all the way through medical school, one based on brains, not his athletic ability. And then, the first day of his first Christmas home from classes, he'd met her.

Sure, he'd known her before. She'd been a year behind him in high school, but they hadn't spoken more than a dozen times during his sojourn at Whitehorn High. Certainly it had never occurred to him to ask her for a date.

The Indian kids had been bussed in from the res, and he
hadn't had a car. Besides, town girls didn't date res guys.

Their meeting had been an accident. He'd walked out
of the diner and bumped into her. Christmas packages had
tumbled into the fluffy snow that was falling, driven by a
northwest wind.

"Sorry," he'd said, recognizing her at once. "Here, let
me help you."

She'd looked up at him, laughter in her eyes, which
were large and golden brown like a doe's. "That's okay. I
wasn't watching where I was going. I had my head down."

She'd been walking into the fierce wind. Her hair—a
dark auburn so rich and warm he'd wanted to hold out his
hands to it the way he would warm them before a fire—had
been sprinkled with snow. A white knit toboggan hat had
been pulled down to cover her ears from the freezing blasts.

He'd fallen in love with her in that instant.

"Are you going to your car?" he'd asked politely,
warmth spreading through him, blocking the freezing cold
of the wintry day as they talked. "I'll carry these for you."

He gathered the packages, wanting an excuse to stay
with her for a little while longer. He'd known even then
that he was crazy, that nothing could ever come of it, but...

She'd studied him for a second, then with an impish
smile, she'd nodded and allowed him to carry her
things...two blocks down the street to her home.

There, she'd invited him into the neat, snug house set
back from the street among tall oak and pine trees. She'd
had him put the gift-wrapped presents on her bed.

Being in her bedroom had made him jumpy, as if her
father might show up and accuse him of something vile.
Maybe guilt played a role in his case of nerves, too. He'd been
thinking every erotic thought he'd ever dreamed of as he'd
glanced at that bed with the girlish pile of dolls on the pillow.

"Would you like some hot chocolate?" she'd asked, pulling off her coat and hat and mittens.

He'd spent the rest of the afternoon with her, not leaving until her parents came home from work. Mrs. Gilmore hadn't liked him being there, but Homer hadn't minded....

"Okay, once more," Lori instructed her patient. They clearly didn't need him now, but Kane lingered to make sure the child was going to be okay.

The young wife pushed, delivering her baby seconds later. "What is it?" she asked at once, her breath a gasp.

Lori held the boy up so the parents could see. Tears spurted from the mother's eyes. The father rubbed vigorously at his brow, effectively hiding his face for a minute. The child yelled at the indignity of being displayed.

"He's beautiful," Lori said sincerely. She placed the squalling bit of humanity on the mother's abdomen while she readied the pan for the afterbirth.

Kane's eyes stung. He blinked a couple of times to dispel the intense emotion. When he glanced up, Lori grinned at him. She'd often teased him about being an "old softy."

"See you later," he murmured, able to leave now that baby and mother were both fine.

"Have a nice day. Relax." It was an order.

"Yes, ma'am," he said. After a glance at the couple, who were completely absorbed in their child, he nodded to the girl's mother, who'd stood by without saying a word during the entire procedure, and left the birthing room.

When he stepped outside, the crisp autumn breeze ruffled his hair. The sun was coming up over the horizon.

Babies had their own schedules, he thought as he walked to his four-wheel-drive utility vehicle. For the next few months, the parents would be at the child's beck and call, anxiously answering his every cry. They would join the ranks of the most sleep-deprived people in the world, especially the mother. But she was young, barely eighteen. She'd cope.

Kane felt infinitely old all at once. He'd had a birthday a few months ago. Thirty-five. Not so old, but not young, either. The notion came to him that if he was going to have a family, it was time to start.

Unbidden, the earlier memory returned. He'd thought, that snowy Christmas almost seventeen years ago, that his world was complete. He and Moriah would marry, have children, grow old together here in Whitehorn. A fool's dream.

The anger simmered in him. He didn't understand it. Why get worked up over a past that was long gone? It made no sense.

But then, nothing about his brief fling with Moriah had. The first meeting had been accidental. Their first kiss was the same. He'd helped her collect toys for the church, whose members would fix them up and give them away along with food boxes and clothes.

Taking a shortcut through a back lane, he'd slipped and crashed to the ground. Moriah had bent over him anxiously.

"Kane, are you all right?" she'd asked. "Did you hit your head? Say something!" she'd demanded when he'd remained quiet, enjoying her concern for him.

He'd snaked one hand behind her head and pulled her mouth down to his. Instead of pulling away, slapping his face and stalking off—which he'd half expected—she'd made a crooning sound and bent closer, her hands slipping under his head to hold it off the cold ground. It had been bliss.

She'd taken his kisses and returned them tenfold. She'd accepted his caresses, each one bolder than the last, overcoming her shyness and his own fears until finally there had been neither shyness nor fear between them. He'd given her everything he had to give—his love, his dreams, his future.

He shook his head slightly, trying to shed the memory. His first encounter with love had been a real lesson—a painful one he'd not forgotten. It had been almost seventeen years ago, but he remembered the raw ache as if it were yesterday.

The wind caressed his face with tentative, probing fingers—the way Moriah had once touched him, shyly, hesitantly, a look of wonder on her face....

Moriah. She'd been the love of his life, he'd thought then. When she'd left town without a word the following spring, he'd been confused, hurt and finally angry. His letters had been returned by the post office. No Forwarding Address had been printed on them in big red letters. He'd never heard what had happened to her.

A shiver ran down his spine. He realized he was standing there staring into space while the cold October wind whistled down the neck of his shirt. He climbed in the ute and headed home to change clothes.

It was Wednesday. He had the day off and he was going to enjoy it, by damn! He'd go to the house he was building and work on it. Sawing lumber and driving nails soothed his soul.

However, an hour later he bumped over a logging road and into the narrow clearing in front of the log cabin where he was to have met Homer Gilmore for the fishing trip. His conscience had demanded that he check for the old man once more. He jumped out of the ute and went to the door.

No one answered his knock.

"Homer?" he called, heading around back, repeating the pattern of his earlier visit. The old man wasn't at the woodpile.

Returning to the front door, Kane went inside. The place was the same as it had been two weeks ago. He frowned as he glanced around.

The cabin was messy. Newspapers were strewn on the floor. A tablet and several pens had fallen onto the chair by the table. Another chair was pushed into the middle of the room. Dust covered the few pieces of furniture. It looked as if the old codger had deserted the place.

Worry ate at Kane. Though Homer was usually a fanatic about neatness, Kane knew the old man didn't take proper care of himself.

Homer was in his early sixties, but he looked older. He lived on Social Security and the handouts Kane and Rafe Rawlings, a local police officer, provided. Between them, they'd looked after the eccentric recluse for years.

Kane felt the familiar anger harden in him. Homer Gilmore was Moriah's father. She'd never returned to see about the old man, not once in sixteen years. Even if she never wanted to see *him* again, she could have at least checked on her father.

Ah, God, why was he dredging up the past? Those were ancient times. With a curse, Kane bent and picked up the scattered papers. He straightened up the cabin and wiped the dust off the furniture with a damp bandanna.

He lifted a sheet of paper from the table and read again the letter from the detective agency. On it was written Moriah's address. That was how he'd known to reach her in Great Falls. Homer had had his daughter traced.

A jolt of emotion Kane couldn't identify ran through him. He scowled as he looked at the letter, which was over a year old. He wondered why Homer had bothered. Moriah didn't give a damn about her father.

Hell, it was no business of his. He put the brief note with the tablet, placed both on a low shelf Homer had attached to the wall and anchored them down with an arrowhead.

Kane studied the artifact for a minute. Made of black flint, the arrowhead was finely crafted. For a second, he was seized with a longing for a time when life had been simpler. Or had it ever been? Maybe he'd seen too many movies.

With a cynical smile, he straightened. He brought in the supplies from the ute and started a pot of soup for supper, in case Homer showed up.

Eating crackers with peanut butter and a banana for lunch, he sat on the porch and pondered the last couple of weeks. The old prospector had known Kane was coming for the fishing trip two weeks ago. Kane distinctly remembered telling him so last month when Homer had shown up at his office with his hand festering from an embedded thorn.

Last week, Homer was supposed to meet some Park Service people to map the local terrain, which was full of abandoned mines and air shafts, a danger to man and beast. He hadn't shown up for that, either. Half of another week was gone and there was still no sign of the old man.

The chill October wind hurled down the hillside. Kane stared out at the mountains, his thoughts shifting from the father to the daughter.

Moriah had loved the mountains. On their frequent hikes through the woods and glens surrounding White-horn, she'd played hide-and-seek with him among the trees. Laughing, she'd let him catch her, a woods elf, spirited and free. Then he would claim his reward—a kiss—then another....

Heat attacked his insides until he felt like melting wax. Just looking at her had burned a hole straight to his heart. When they'd made love, her fire had engulfed him. Each time, he'd felt reborn, like the Phoenix rising from its ashes.

She'd liked to stand on a high ledge, her arms outstretched to embrace the world, the wind off the jagged peaks stirring her hair until it looked like living flames blowing about her face and shoulders. He'd loved to touch her hair—such fiery glory!—and bury his face in it, in the soft, silken textures of her body....

Together, they'd decorated her home with cedar and pine branches until the whole house smelled like a forest. They'd made cookies, eating and kissing and exchanging bites.

Longing grabbed him and wouldn't let go. He'd loved her, his sylvan beauty, but he hadn't been able to hold her.

He surged to his feet, his emotions in a tumult. He wasn't here to think about Moriah and their past. Homer was the problem.

There were no signs of foul play, but the cabin didn't feel right to him.

Something rotten in Montana as well as Denmark?

He smiled grimly and headed for the path into the woods.

Two

"Hi, Mom!" The door slammed behind the teenager as she dashed into the house at her usual breakneck speed.

Moriah glanced up from the table where, as usual on Friday, she was writing checks to pay the bills. She smiled at her daughter, feeling a sweet, possessive pride in the girl.

"Hi, Melanie, how's it going?"

"*Really* bad."

Moriah grimaced at the current saying among the younger crowd. "Really bad" meant really good, but then so did "super." It was hard to keep up with what meant what these days.

She watched the dark, almost-straight hair bounce against Melanie's back as she raced to her bedroom. In two minutes her daughter returned in jeans and a sweat shirt and started rummaging through the refrigerator like someone who'd spent a month in the desert without food.

"Want me to fix you a sandwich?" Melanie asked. She turned toward Moriah, her eyebrows raised.

"No, thanks. Don't ruin your appetite. We're having ham and pineapple tonight."

"Oh, my *fav*," Melanie cried. Her black eyes sparkled like large, shiny agates. "But I have a date tonight." She waved her hand airily, then lost her cool and covered her mouth as giggles erupted.

Moriah's heart gave a hard *thump*. "Who with?" she asked. At Melanie's impish grin, she clutched her hands to her bosom like a Victorian heroine about to swoon. "Not—not...The Hunk?"

Melanie hugged herself and danced around the kitchen. "Yes. Yes. *Yes!*"

Moriah laughed at the display. Sometimes she wondered how this child, this wonderful, delightful being, had come to be hers.

Melanie had seemed to spring to life on her own, tossed by fairies into Moriah's waiting arms. Her personality had gleamed like the rarest of gemstones from the first. Her temper was sunny, her laughter frequent. Moriah had seen people stop and smile when they heard the girl laugh.

Melanie loved everyone and everyone loved her.

Where Moriah was reserved, her daughter was exuberant. Moriah had always had to study hard to make her grades; Melanie breezed through school, not on charm, although she had plenty of that, but because she had a brilliant mind and was a respectful student besides. No parent could ask for a more-loving child.

Where had she come from—this sweet changeling who had made life worth living when Moriah had felt it wasn't?

When Melanie rushed into her bedroom to bathe and dress, Moriah finished the bills, pleased that the two of them were doing well financially. Refilling her coffee cup, she found her thoughts being drawn to the past, as they'd been every night that week since Kane Hunter had called and demanded she return home and do something about her father.

What did he expect her to do—drop everything and camp out in the hills until she found him? Or until some hikers found her shriveled up into a little mummy?

She shook her head angrily, as if arguing with some unseen foe. Her life was good. Her mother, Joleen, lived near enough that they could visit, but not right on top of them. Moriah finally had a job that allowed her to pay the bills with ease. The future looked rosy, with not a cloud on the horizon. Until Kane had called.

After Melanie was born, Moriah had finished high school by taking the GED exams. She'd worked as a waitress, so Joleen could watch the baby when she wasn't at her job in a big department store.

Later, Moriah had been employed by her mother at the discount dress shop she had opened in a nearby mall. Melanie had been in first grade by then and came to the store after school each day. That had worked for a few years.

Realizing her mom was taking complete control of her and Melanie's lives—with Melanie fighting every step of the way—Moriah had moved them out of the house and into this apartment five years ago. Joleen had been furious, but Moriah knew it had been a wise decision. She and Melanie had gone through the girl's "difficult years" without a cross word…well, hardly any.

Melanie would have a two-day break from classes next week. If Moriah hadn't had to work, they could have done something special together. They both liked to hike and explore the rugged Montana countryside.

Schools hadn't had teachers' work days when she'd attended, Moriah reflected. But they'd had holidays off, such as Christmas.

She laid a hand over her heart as old but not-forgotten pain seized her. She'd met Kane during Christmas break. In one short week, they'd become lovers....

She tried to close out the memory before it formed. Not that one. She didn't want to remember how foolish she'd been.

Moriah let her anger grow as she recalled Kane's expectation that she would drop everything and rush down to Whitehorn on his say-so. She wouldn't.

However, driven by the guilt he'd fostered in her, she had called and talked to Rafe Rawlings at the police station. He had confirmed what Kane had said.

She chewed her lip, wondering what she should do.

Homer wasn't her responsibility.

But he was her father.

He'd abandoned her and her mother to go off prospecting like he did every spring...at a time when she'd needed him....

She returned to the table and put the cup down before she dropped it. She was shaking, she realized.

"What do you think, Mom?" Melanie whirled into the room. "Too much?"

Moriah forced herself to check her daughter's outfit. She wore a spring suit of apple green with a—correction, with *her* pink silk blouse. Melanie's hair and eyes came from her father, but her skin, naturally rosy, came from Moriah. Except her daughter didn't freckle in the bargain. Instead, she tanned easily, so that her complexion had a slightly dusky bloom to it. Like a rose.

A voice from Moriah's past intruded. *You look like a rose, one of those pink-and-white ones that Winona Cobbs raises.* Kane had once told her that, lying on her bed one snowy afternoon.

"*Mom?*" Melanie wailed, wanting an answer.

Moriah returned to the present. "You look perfect, good enough for dinner at the family mansion."

"That's where it is. A sit-down dinner with silver and napkins and everything. Don't worry—I'll chew with my mouth closed," she teased. "Oh, do you mind about the blouse? I had absolutely nothing—"

"I would have insisted you wear it."

Melanie gave her a hug and spun away. "Oh, you are the best mom in the world!"

Moriah had to smile at her daughter's exuberance.

The doorbell rang. Melanie's smile disappeared. Her eyes widened. "There he is," she whispered, looking ready to flee.

"Invite him in so we can get the interrogation over," Moriah suggested dryly. She always vetted Melanie's friends. Sometimes that had caused difficulties between them, but when she had made it clear that that was the rule, things had smoothed out.

Melanie wrinkled her nose. "Please don't use the bludgeon," she begged dramatically. She ran off to answer the door when the bell rang again.

He was an impatient young man, Moriah thought with a frown of disapproval. If young Lochinvar thought he was God's gift to women, she would soon put him straight.

"Mom? You'd better come here. It's some guy…um, man, who says he knows you."

Puzzled, Moriah rose and went to the door.

"Hello, Moriah," Kane Hunter said.

Mom. The word exploded in Kane's brain like an unseen land mine. Moriah had a daughter. Did she also have a husband?

He realized he hadn't even considered that possibility. She'd answered the phone with her maiden name, hadn't she? Yes, but women didn't always take their husband's name these days.

Her eyes—those same large, golden eyes that reminded him of a startled doe—widened in surprise as she realized who he was, then an odd expression crossed her face. Shock? More like panic. As a doctor, he'd learned to observe his patients' emotions for clues to their health.

He also noticed she was as beautiful as ever and that he was reacting to her as he had that first time they'd run into each other. His heart beat hard, then seemed to skip about before it got into a regular rhythm again. Heat speared through him.

"Come in, Kane," she said. She still spoke softly, not breathlessly or anything, but low, so a person had to pay attention to hear the words. She was smiling now, acting the gracious hostess, so he must have been mistaken about the surge of emotion.

Why should she have any reaction to seeing him again? After sharing the most incredible lovemaking, she'd left him without a backward glance all those years ago. She'd taken his heart and his soul and never looked back.

He quit that line of thought. He wasn't here to discuss the past. He was still uneasy about her father. He thought Homer was in trouble. As a doctor, he felt an obligation. Homer had come to him for the few medical needs he'd had.

If Moriah had an ounce of compassion, she'd do something about the old man. Homer needed help.

"Whatever are you doing here?" she asked.

She made a vague gesture to indicate her home, the city and the area in general. Her hands were shaking.

Well, at least she wasn't indifferent to his presence. He himself was still having heart palpitations at seeing her. The daughter, the possibility of a husband—these had thrown him off-balance. He tried to recall the speech he'd planned during the drive from the airport.

"Mom," a younger voice chimed in, demanding to be noticed.

Kane swung his gaze to the girl who'd let him in. He could see curiosity in her eyes as she assessed every inch of him. She looked to be about sixteen, maybe seventeen.

No, she couldn't be that old. It had been sixteen years ago last April that Moriah and her mother had packed up and skipped town without a word. They'd left during spring break.

The irony of the situation hit him anew. He'd saved every spare penny so he could come home to the great love of his life. He hadn't gotten a glimpse of Moriah. Her mom had intercepted his call and told him to stay away or else.

This time Moriah was the mother, but the tone of voice was the same, making it clear he wasn't wanted. Glancing at the youngster, he admitted he was curious about her…and the man who had taken his place in her mother's bed.

Her hair was darker than brown, but not quite black. Here and there the overhead light picked out glints of red, like banked embers, in the thick dark strands. It hung down her back and was clipped behind her ears with two sparkly barrettes.

The girl had eyes as dark as her hair. Like her mother, her skin tones were pink, but she was tanned a tawny gold.

He looked back at Moriah. She still had that shy, vulnerable aura about her. Dressed in a pale blue jogging outfit, her face bare of makeup, she looked as young and innocent as the girl.

It was her eyes, he decided. They held a wariness in their lucid depths like that of a young deer afraid to come too close.

That wary vulnerability had attracted him years ago. It had made him feel protective toward her. He was amazed to find it affected him the same way after all these years. He was definitely going soft, he decided wryly, stifling the ridiculous emotion.

The silence stretched a fraction too long before she began to speak. He realized she didn't want him to meet her family.

"Kane, this is my daughter, Melanie—"

The doorbell rang again. All three turned. Melanie opened the door. A young man in a suit and tie stood there. The scent of his after-shave wafted pleasantly into the tiny entrance hall where they all stood like figures in a wax museum.

Melanie took over the social functions, introducing her date to her mother and then saying with an impish grin, "This is my mom's boyfriend. Do you think we should stay here to chaperon them for the evening?"

The young man looked disconcerted.

"Melanie," her mother protested, a flush running up her neck and into her cheeks.

An image came to Kane...of Moriah with her soft, smooth skin flushed in passion, her hair spread over the pillow like strands of dark fire, his body meshed with hers. Dark and light they'd been. Sunshine and shadow. After making love, she'd wanted him to stay inside her.

An ache settled deep within him where no amount of reasoning or ridicule could reach. She had been his first love. He'd put all his dreams into her hands, had bared his heart to her, trusted her. She'd become the very center of those dreams. Then she'd left. Without a word. No explanation, no letter...nothing.

He forced his thoughts to the present.

"What time do you plan to bring Melanie home?" Moriah was asking her daughter's date.

Kane listened with reluctant admiration while she made the young man responsible for the outcome of the evening and for her daughter's safety. He hid a smile when Melanie caught his eye, rolled hers toward heaven, indicating this was a familiar ritual, then subsided until the interview was finished.

When the couple left, Moriah stood at the door, watching them go down the sidewalk to the kid's car at the curb. She had a curious expression on her face—as if she was looking into some distant future that was bleak. There was an air of loneliness about her.

Oh, hell, next he'd be seeing visions the way Winona Cobbs, the psychic back in Whitehorn, sometimes did.

"You handled that very well," Kane said sincerely, picking a safe subject to start the conversation.

She glanced at him, looked back at the kids, then closed the door. "What are you doing here?" she asked, all signs of friendliness gone now that they were alone.

So much for the niceties.

"I think we need to make some decisions about your father," he said in his best professional style.

She pushed a hand into her hair. It was still the same shade of auburn. It still looked warm and inviting. He still wanted to hold his hands out to it…. Ah, God!

"Did you find him?"

Kane was surprised at the anxiety in the question. Well, perhaps she did care. A smidgen. Not enough to come down.

"No. I don't think he's dead," he added, when she lifted a hand to her throat as if distressed.

"Why?"

"A feeling." He didn't really believe in intuition, but he didn't discount it, either. "I think he'll show up eventually. He took his backpack with him, so he planned on being in the field for a few days. Maybe he met someone and decided to visit."

She looked doubtful.

"Do you think we could sit down? I had an emergency surgery early this morning. It's been a hectic day."

She led the way into the living room and indicated the sofa. He sat on it. The room was decorated in pleasant shades of beige and green, the latter being her favorite color. Her bedroom had been white and green. He forced his mind to the business at hand.

Moriah perched on a chair like a sparrow entertaining a falcon. It irritated him.

"Relax," he advised. "I'm not going to attack." Yet, he added silently. He felt an almost overwhelming urge to do something drastic to shock her out of the cool control that was at odds with the tension he could sense in her.

One of those hot, melting kisses they had once shared would do the trick— He broke off the thought abruptly. What the hell was the matter with him? This was strictly a professional call.

Her chin lifted a notch. Her tone was defensive when she answered, "I never thought you were."

"You resent like hell my being here," he said, deciding to come right out and say what was on his mind. "Too bad. Your father needs help. I'm speaking as his doctor," he continued, when she stiffened even more.

She considered and obviously decided to hear him out. "All right. What's wrong with him?"

"I think he's schizophrenic. It's a mild case, but there are signs. He hears voices and thinks he's a medium to the spirit world. He thinks he saved the world from aliens—"

She made a choked sound, but didn't say anything.

"He needs a thorough medical evaluation, physical and

mental. There are medicines available that can help his condition. I can recommend a local clinic, if you like."

She stood and paced to the window before facing him. "If you're suggesting I sign some papers to have him locked up, I won't do it. I think that's wrong. If he's not hurting anyone, then why can't he be left alone?"

Kane stood. "You don't give a damn about him, do you?" He headed for the door. "This trip was a waste of time."

"I could have told you that when you called." She followed him into the tiny entrance hall.

He let his gaze slide slowly over her, past the generous curve of her breasts, down the narrow waist, over the flare of her hips. He realized she was in her socks. It added to her vulnerable appeal. He hardened his heart.

"Once," he murmured, his hand on the door, "there was a compassionate woman in that gorgeous body. What happened to her?"

He walked out and closed the door, needing to get away from her before his anger exploded, before the feelings left over from years ago forced him into words or actions he'd regret later.

The door opened behind him.

"She learned not to let it show," Moriah called after him. "Only fools do that." She slammed the door.

"Mom?"

Moriah pushed the cool washcloth off her eyes. "Yeah, punkin?" She hoped it wasn't anything important.

"Head still hurting?"

"Like you-know-what." She managed a faint smile.

Melanie sat on the side of the bed, causing Moriah to wince as the mattress jostled. "I'll rub your temples," the teenager offered, and proceeded to do so.

Moriah tried to will the migraine away. It was no use.

"Who was that man last night? Kane somebody. You never did introduce us."

On purpose, Moriah admitted to herself. She'd been very glad when Melanie's date had shown up. It had given her a few minutes to regain her composure. It had also distracted Melanie from being her usual inquisitive self. No such luck today.

"He was someone I knew a long time ago. In high school," she added, hoping that would be enough.

"So he *was* your boyfriend." Melanie pounced on this tidbit like a robin on a night crawler.

Moriah tried to think. It caused the little bolts of colored lights behind her eyelids to increase. She'd never lied to Melanie in her life. Like her mother had done with her, Moriah tried to answer her daughter's questions with total honesty.

"For a month," she managed to say without bitterness.

One month. She'd thought he was her gift, her special reward for all the lonely years she'd spent waiting for her parents' marriage to finish falling apart.

"Did he know my father?"

For a minute, Moriah couldn't draw a breath. Her body simply stopped working. Melanie hadn't asked about her father in years, and she wasn't prepared for the question.

Joleen had tried to cover for Moriah's foolish mistake in trusting Kane by telling Melanie, when she'd been much younger, that her father had died in an accident. But Moriah had sat her daughter down and told her the truth.

He didn't want us. I called, but he didn't call back. So we moved away, Grandma and I, and started a new life. When you came, I was very happy.

She tried to answer with the truth now, but no words came to mind. "Yes," she finally said, her voice raspy with pain.

"Is he coming back?"

Oh, God, I hope not. "I don't know. I don't think so."

"I wish he would. I'd like to ask him…would it hurt you if I asked him about my father?"

Moriah opened her eyes. Melanie's face hovered over hers in the dim room, her expression so concerned, so earnest, that Moriah nearly cried out. *Yes, it would hurt. I don't want you to know him. You might choose him over me.*

She gasped when she realized what she was thinking. In that moment, she faced a hard truth about herself: she was afraid for Melanie to know Kane and always had been.

Kane Hunter was handsome. Charismatic. Dynamic. Charming. Intelligent. All of the above.

"Kane doesn't know the man was your father. It wasn't something I announced." Closing her eyes, she pressed the damp cloth to them to stop the burning sensation behind her eyelids.

"Where is Kane from?"

"Melanie, please, not now," Moriah said with an edge in her voice. "Later. I'll tell you later. When my head stops hurting."

"Sure, Mom. Sorry. I was just…curious."

"I know. Remind me tomorrow. We'll discuss it then."

If she were lucky, tomorrow would never come.

Kane climbed the stairs, stripped and headed for the shower. It had been a busy day here at his office in town. Tomorrow, at the clinic on the reservation, would be just as bad.

He couldn't remember a time when he'd been as tired. Yes, he could. Back in college, when one of the girls at the restaurant where he worked had been in a car wreck, he'd taken on two shifts for a while. He'd wanted the money so he could go home at Easter, to see Moriah.

With a violent curse, he finished his shave, dressed in comfortable sweats and went down to the kitchen. Later, after eating a low-fat, low-salt, low-calorie frozen dinner, he flipped on the TV, more for the noise than because he was interested in the shows. That insight gave him pause.

Turning the TV off, he listened to the silence inside the house. Only the creak of wood in the old Victorian he'd bought and remodeled into a combination home and office greeted his ears.

It was the sound of his life. A lonely sound. An empty sound. He grimaced. He'd devoted his life to medicine after he got his degree. He'd once thought it would be enough. He'd *told* himself that it was. But it wasn't. It hadn't been enough in a long time.

Restless, he reached for the phone and dialed Lori's number. He got her answering machine. He left a message that he was home, then rose from the recliner and paced the narrow room.

The silence became a roar in his ears, growing louder and louder until it made his head hurt. He thought of the recent birth he'd observed and of the young couple's joy in their child.

A family, that's what he needed. Someone to come home to at the end of a hard day; someone who'd understand the demands made on a doctor; someone to share the joys and sorrows.

Lori? Was she that person?

Who knew better than a busy nurse-midwife the rigors of the medical profession? With her to share his life, things would be different. He and Lori were compatible, in temperament and work habits. After all, they'd been working together for more than a year, on several different pregnancy cases, and had been seeing each other on a casual basis for three months.

Yeah, it was time to settle down. He'd ask her to marry him. Soon. He'd make it special. Dinner. Candlelight. Wine. A ring and the old-fashioned, on-his-knees stuff. Yeah.

With that thought in mind, he locked up and went to bed, expecting his sleep to be deep and untroubled now that he'd resolved his future. But it was as restless as it had been the night before, and the night before that....

Patients were already lining up at the clinic when Kane arrived at the reservation at seven. He grimaced, recalling his recent spate of restless nights.

Lori hadn't returned his call. She'd probably worked all weekend and into the wee hours of the morning. Babies often arrived at the most inopportune times.

The second patient he saw that morning was Maggie Hawk. Her husband, Jackson, was the tribal attorney and de facto chairman, since the old chieftain had suffered a series of heart attacks during the last couple of years.

"Maggie, how are you feeling?" he asked. He'd come to like Jackson's wife as much as he did his friend and cousin.

"Large," she replied with a rueful grin.

He looked at her mounded abdomen, ripe with the child she carried. A harsh twinge of envy shot through him. He wanted what Jackson had—a wife, a home and now a child.

Kane smiled grimly and set about the examination. Everyone was pregnant these days, it seemed. He tried to remember what had happened last winter to produce so many babies this fall. Usually, high births followed severe weather that kept everyone indoors. The winter hadn't been that harsh.

He bent and listened to the baby's heartbeat. Strong and

steady. He lingered for a few more seconds, thinking of the pain ahead for Maggie, which she would never begrudge the child nor hold against the man who'd helped her start this new life.

The miracle of life. Would he ever know this gift? The restlessness, like a roaring wind, momentarily filled his ears. A family of his own was definitely what he needed.

His own parents had been caught in the cycle of alcohol and despair that afflicted so many people. They'd died of exposure one winter night when they'd driven directly into a ten-foot snowbank coming home from a bar. He'd been raised by his grandmother from the time he was seven.

"Well?" Maggie asked when he straightened.

"It sounds fine." Kane knew the child was a boy, but the couple didn't want to know, so he used the gender-neutral pronoun.

"Good." She sat up with a grunt of effort, then laughed. "I feel like the Goodyear blimp on a windy day."

"All pregnant women feel that way," he assured her, smiling with genuine pleasure for her and Jackson, the inexplicable envy washed away by his affection for them. "You look beautiful."

Maggie's eyes softened. "You and Jackson," she murmured. "You both know how to make a woman feel special." She studied Kane while he looked over her chart. "We just need to find you the right woman…." Her voice trailed off thoughtfully.

Kane glanced up. "I think I can handle that."

"Are you trying to tell me something? Have you and Lori made a decision?"

He shook his head. "Not yet," he heard himself say. But his intention was implied, he realized.

Instead of a big grin, Maggie gave him a troubled frown.

"Why the long face?" he demanded. Maggie was a friend whose opinion he trusted.

"Don't do anything rash," she suggested.

"I'm thirty-five, long past the rashness of youth."

An immediate picture came to mind—pale rose skin against his own darker tones. "You're like a flower," he'd said to Moriah.

She'd looked him over with those big, brown eyes. "And you're like the earth. A person could grow deep roots in this soil."

And she'd run her hands over him, her gaze adoring and trusting, making him want to move mountains for her.

Only for her.

With a start, he realized he'd never felt that way about any woman he'd known since Moriah…not the girl he'd finally gone steady with in college, until she'd discovered he'd meant it when he said he was returning to his tribal home to help his people; not the Cheyenne teacher he'd met soon after returning to the area to take up his practice.

He said goodbye to Maggie and went to the next patient, putting his personal life on hold and concentrating completely on the task before him. It was this trait of his that had driven the final wedge between him and the teacher. He tended to miss dates when he was involved in medicine.

Well, Lori would understand that side of him. She was the same. In fact, she hadn't called him back yet. When he did that to a woman, she got mad. But he understood. Lori had six women due within two days of each other.

What the hell *had* happened last year to produce so many kids this year? He'd ask his grandmother when she returned from her trek into the mountains to gather herbs. She knew the old ways.

Maybe he should go on a vision quest, he thought later

that day, letting himself out the side door of the clinic. Or maybe he needed a real vacation. His grandmother would tell him he needed a healing. Perhaps she was right. Maybe he was sick in his soul.

Or his head, where thoughts of Moriah lingered like a faint whiff of some tantalizing perfume he couldn't identify.

He climbed into the ute and sat there for a minute, feeling the utter weariness of having been twelve hours on his feet. He'd had ten cases of cold and flu and one broken wrist. He'd removed two sets of tonsils, checked six babies and found them healthy and normal, treated a dozen minor complaints and told an old man his wife of sixty years had inoperable cancer.

A feeling of helplessness hit Kane as he recalled the man's face. One might have thought the old Indian didn't hear the words, he'd sat so still after the medical explanation, but Kane had seen the man's eyes and the way his hand trembled when he opened the door on his way out.

Damnation, Kane groused at himself. He was turning into an old woman. If every birth and death affected him like this at thirty-five, he'd be a basket case by the time he hit forty.

With a grimace, he started the vehicle and headed for town.

He noticed a police vehicle ahead of him and recognized Rafe Rawlings at the wheel. There had been an epidemic of nuptials as well as babies the past year or two, especially among the justice-department people, Kane recalled.

First the chief detective had married. Then the sheriff had remarried his first wife. Rafe had married the public defender. Even the local judge, Kate Randall, had recently married.

Maybe he'd better ask his grandmother about those signs. It seemed a propitious time for marriage and all the things that went with it. He should strike while the iron was hot, as the saying went. He would do it. Definitely.

Kane followed the police cruiser into town. At his house, he tried Lori again. This time she'd added a message for him on her answering-machine tape.

"Kane, I'm camping out at the clinic. Babies are coming faster than we can change the sheets. I'll call you."

He opened a can of pork and beans, one of applesauce and one of carrots. That, with a slice of bread, was his supper. Too tired to think, he changed to sweats and slumped in his easy chair while he looked through the mail. Nothing of interest.

He thought of the detective agency's letter with Moriah's address and wondered how long she'd lived in Great Falls. She hadn't waited very long after their affair to marry and have a family. She must have met someone as soon as she graduated from school to have a teenage daughter. Melanie was the girl's name. She'd seemed like a nice kid. Where was the husband?

Moriah hadn't worn a wedding band and she still went by the name Gilmore. Did that mean she was divorced? He realized he knew next to nothing of her life after she'd left Whitehorn.

Another family now lived in the cottage where he and Moriah had spent a month of glorious afternoons, exploring each other in every sense of the word. He closed his eyes and leaned his head back, unable to stop the memories.

The surprising thing had been the depth of her passion. He'd thought making love with her would be a quiet, delicate thing—and sometimes it had been. But more often it had been so wildly erotic, he'd nearly exploded as the hunger rose higher and higher, urged on by her ecstatic cries, her hands, which had touched him everywhere... *everywhere*....

He brought his fist down on the chair arm, angry that

he couldn't seem to control his thoughts. He hardened his resolve and thought of the present.

It was one thing for Moriah not to care enough to contact him, but didn't she have a shred of decency regarding her own father?

He stormed up from the chair and paced the room, anger roiling in him. He felt hard and cold and aching with the need to do something.

A tree branch scraped against the house, startling him. He went to the window and watched the play of lightning along the mountain peaks. The last rays of the sun lit the underside of the black clouds, painting a surrealistic portrait of land and sky.

It was raining in the mountains. For some reason, the thought filled him with nostalgia and yearning, and other emotions too tangled to figure out. Unbidden, another memory surfaced.

He and Moriah had gone hiking through the snow, gathering mistletoe from the oak trees on the reservation. A storm had come up. They'd taken shelter in a cabin. There, the world had been theirs…for a little while. Until they'd had to return to town in the pickup he'd borrowed from a friend. He'd sold the mistletoe through an arrangement with the local gift shop and earned enough to buy a Christmas present for Moriah.

He'd given her a necklace, fourteen-carat gold. Twenty-five dollars on a special deal from Old Man Mason, whose son now owned the jewelry store. It wasn't until years later that Kane had realized the necklace was worth four times that much.

Unlike the necklace, Moriah's love hadn't been solid, but thinly plated. It had worn off soon enough.

Three

Moriah took her foot off the accelerator at the city-limit sign and let the car slow to thirty-five miles per hour.

"Whitehorn." Melanie read the sign aloud.

Moriah ignored the excitement in her daughter at their arrival in the town she herself had hoped never to see again. Her own attitude was one of fatalistic calm. She had a sense of marching forward to some destiny she didn't want to meet but couldn't avoid.

Well, whatever happened, she'd had to come. Her conscience wouldn't rest until she checked on her father.

During the past week, she'd been haunted by memories of her early life. As a child, she'd adored her father. He'd been the one to comfort her when she cried. He'd delighted her with bird's nests and secret things in nature. Her mother had been the brisk, pragmatic one, making sure homework and chores were done, looking out after her health and such, but it had been her father who'd lifted her high on his shoulders and taught her joy.

She swallowed hard as other memories returned with each block she passed. As she'd grown older, her father had retreated more and more frequently to the woods.

Schizophrenic, Kane had said.

Reading up on the disease, she'd found it could be controlled by drugs such as lithium. She had to help her father if she could. Once he had shown her the world could be a place of wonder.

She'd missed him, she realized. She regretted that Melanie hadn't had a chance to know and love him. Moriah doubted he'd ever known he had a granddaughter....

"Where shall we stay?" Melanie asked, a worry line puckering her smooth brow. "I don't see any motels."

"There used to be some boardinghouses in town. One was a big old Victorian mansion." She turned onto Center Avenue and drove through the heart of town, which was about two blocks long. "There it is," she said. She pulled into the drive. "Oh," she murmured, startled as she read the sign by the door.

The Victorian was now a medical office. Kane Hunter, M.D., was the name on the shingle. She'd known that Kane had made it through medical school and that his office was in Whitehorn. Once, out of idle curiosity, she'd dialed information in Whitehorn and asked if Dr. Kane Hunter was listed. He had been.

"Look, Mom, that sign has Kane Hunter on it. Is that your Kane, the one who came to our place in Great Falls?"

"Yes," Moriah said shortly.

"Did you know he was a doctor?"

"Yes."

"Heavy!" Melanie said, a note of awe in her voice.

Moriah flinched from the hero worship evident in her daughter. She wondered for the hundredth time since starting out that morning if she'd totally lost her mind.

With an inward sigh, she admitted fate had conspired against her. When she'd talked to her boss about her father, he'd given her the rest of the week off—his niece was looking for a temporary job, so it had been no problem for her to fill in for Moriah—and told her she should take as much time as she needed.

That worried her. She didn't want to lose her job. It was the best one she'd ever had.

"I think I'd like to be a nurse," Melanie mused aloud.

"Why not be a doctor? That way, you get to be boss."

"Medical school costs a lot."

"You'll easily qualify for a scholarship, and your grandmother and I will help you all we can. You know that."

"A scholarship. I never thought of applying for one. I thought they were for, you know, really poor people."

Moriah was touched by Melanie's assumption that they were firmly grounded in the middle class. She'd never seemed to notice that she had less than her friend Jessy.

"Kane went to school on a scholarship," Moriah said, then wished she could have taken back the words. She didn't need to give her daughter any more reason to think he was wonderful.

"Did he? For football, I'll bet. With those shoulders…" Melanie giggled as she let the thought trail off suggestively.

"For brains. Kane is very intelligent," Moriah informed the girl. "An honor student like yourself."

She found herself irritated, the way she'd been years ago when her mother had expressed the same view of Kane. Most people seemed to think Native Americans were physically but not mentally endowed. It had bothered her then. It did now. She shrugged the odd emotion aside.

"Smart and handsome, too. Wow! Is he married?"

Moriah felt her heart take a swan dive toward her toes. "I don't know." She'd never thought of him that way.

"He must be. No sane woman would let a man like that walk around free. Where's that boardinghouse you mentioned? Let's get settled. I'm starving."

"This was it. I suppose we can drive around town and see if we can find something else."

"Yeah, that should take maybe five minutes," Melanie quipped. "I didn't realize the place was Hicksville."

Moriah smiled. "Don't be so superior. This was my hometown, you know. Your roots come from here."

"Yeah," Melanie said, a quieter note in her voice.

Moriah grimaced. She prepared to back up and craned around to see if anyone was coming down the street. One car. She waited for it to pass.

"Mom, there's Kane…Dr. Hunter!" Melanie exclaimed. "He sees us." She waved to him.

Moriah jerked around. Sure enough, Kane was coming along the sidewalk. He stopped by the car. She rolled the window down.

"Hello, Moriah." He bent over and peered into the vehicle. "Melanie, isn't it?"

"Yes," Melanie answered, very much at ease. "I didn't know you were a doctor."

Moriah met his dark eyes and looked away. An unexpected pang struck her in the chest. Smart and handsome? Oh, yes.

"I don't suppose your mother had any reason to mention it. Are you two down for the day?"

"For the rest of the week, maybe more," Melanie cheerfully explained. "We're looking for a place to stay. Any suggestions?"

"The Amity Boardinghouse on Cascade, near the intersection of Mountain Pass. Do you remember it?" he asked Moriah.

"Yes, I think so." She met his gaze, now past her first

nervous quiver at seeing him. "Well, we'd better get with it. I want to talk to the police about my father."

"I spoke with Rafe yesterday. He's letting the ranchers know to keep an eye out for Homer. Listen, I was just going to lunch. If you want to join me, I'll fill you in."

Moriah tried to think of a reason to refuse. By the time she did, she realized it was too late. The silence had already become awkward. "I...I suppose we can."

She saw his eyes narrow slightly, as if her reluctance angered him. He glanced at Melanie, then back to her. His smile was sardonic. "Fine. You can leave your car here. It's a short walk to the café."

When he opened the door, she had no choice but to turn off the engine and remove the key from the ignition. Melanie hopped out of her side of the car and went around to stand by Kane. Moriah reached for her purse, then joined them.

"Shall we go?" Kane held out an arm to Melanie. She laughed and tucked her hand into the crook of his elbow. He turned to Moriah and did the same, a challenge in his manner as he waited to see if she would follow her daughter's lead.

She declined. "You two go on. I'll bring up the rear. The sidewalk isn't wide enough for three abreast."

They started out that way, but soon Melanie had let go of Kane's arm and rushed ahead to peer into a store window. Kane dropped back to walk with Moriah.

"She's a lovely girl," he said.

Moriah's heart clenched into a tiny ball. "Yes."

"You don't wear a ring." He caught her left hand and lifted it to study her ringless fingers.

"I'm not married," she said stiffly, removing her hand from his. "Not now." There, that wasn't a total lie. It implied she had been married in the past, of course, but she wasn't responsible for his interpretation.

"I see. Does Melanie's father live in Great Falls?"

"No." At Kane's sharp glance, she added, "I don't know where he is." The lie emerged thick and cloying from her throat.

"Is that where you met him?" Kane was watching Melanie as she pressed her forehead against a store window to survey the merchandise displayed. His eyes were narrowed…against the sun's glare or in suspicion? Did he suspect she was his?

"No, it was…we lived someplace else before we moved there." At least that much was true.

Moriah felt the same fear she'd experienced when Melanie had questioned her about the past after meeting Kane—the fear that her child would choose Kane over her.

If Kane knew the truth, what would he do? He was obviously wealthy and successful now. He had money and resources. If he wanted his daughter, he could put up a good case for custody. She knew that much from her law-office job.

"How old is Melanie?"

The question came quick and sharp, but Moriah was on guard. "Fifteen. She turned fifteen last month." She waited for the heavens to open and strike her dumb for the lie.

"Fifteen," he repeated thoughtfully.

Moriah could almost hear him mentally tallying the years since she'd lived there and they'd been lovers. She risked a glance at him. His expression didn't give her a clue to his thoughts.

Melanie turned to them when they caught up with her. "Isn't that red dress the neatest thing? It would be perfect for the Christmas dance. Maybe we could stop in and look at it after lunch." She cast a pleading glance at her mother.

Moriah didn't want to remind the girl of their limited finances in front of Kane. "Perhaps. We have to find a room first, though."

They paused briefly in front of the plate-glass window. The glass reflected the three of them standing in the noonday sun.

Moriah's breath caught in her throat. Oh, God, why hadn't she seen it before? Kane and Melanie…their thick dark hair, their ebony eyes, the tawny shades of their skin—their similarities were so apparent next to her auburn fairness.

"We'd better hurry," she said. Her voice quavered. She covered it by clearing her throat and hurried down the street.

Kane swung into step with her while Melanie followed. He kept giving Moriah little quizzical glances.

She felt sick, feverish, foolish. No one knew anything about her daughter, she reminded herself. No one would have reason to suspect Kane. No one but her mother knew they'd even dated.

"Here it is," Kane announced. He held open the door to the small café and let the two females enter first.

The place was busy. One table stood empty near the back. They threaded their way among the crowded diners.

"Kane, hello," one woman called as they passed. She was an older woman, her hair an improbable shade of red-gold. Beaded earrings of an Indian design swung from her ears and almost touched her shoulders. "Does Lori know about this harem you've got?" she teased, openly curious about the two women with him.

Moriah saw a flicker of impatience dart through Kane's eyes, then it was gone. "Hello, Lily Mae. This is Moriah Gilmore and her daughter, Melanie—"

"Gilmore," the woman said, breaking in. Her eyes lit with renewed interest. "Homer Gilmore's girl?"

"Yes, Homer is my father," Moriah confirmed.

"Has he turned up yet? I thought he was still missing."

"He is." Kane gave her a quelling frown.

Which didn't daunt the woman at all, Moriah noted. She vaguely recalled Lily Mae…as the town gossip. Yes. Joleen had been terrified Lily Mae would find out about the coming child and broadcast it to the county.

"Well, it's good that you've come home to see about him," Lily Mae said, nodding her approval. "Where's your mother these days?"

Moriah explained about the discount store in the mall.

"Well, maybe she's found her place in life. She sure didn't like it here. Seemed to think we were a bunch of hicks."

Melanie spluttered with laughter, tried to hide it behind a cough, choked up and went into a real coughing fit. Moriah patted her daughter on the back. She had to smile. Lily Mae apparently had known Joleen Gilmore well, for that had been her attitude toward Whitehorn and its inhabitants. She'd said as much when Moriah had told her she and Melanie planned to visit here. Lily Mae, fortunately, seemed to feel no rancor at being so classified.

"A dress shop, huh? Well, your mom was always ambitious. I don't know why she ever married Homer in the first place—"

"Our table is ready," Kane put in hurriedly. He ushered them past the talkative woman.

"Goodbye, Mrs., uh…" Moriah was trying to recall the woman's last name as Kane urged her toward the back.

"Wheeler, dearie," Lily Mae called out. "I'm widowed now. James passed on some years ago."

"She's been married and divorced twice since then," Kane muttered, holding a chair for Moriah when they reached the table in the back corner, "but she still calls herself a widow."

"It sounds nicer than being divorced," Melanie told him. "My grandmother hates to be reminded that she's a divorcée. She said it sounds so middle class."

He flicked a glance at Moriah. She could see the questions in his eyes regarding her own circumstances. She picked up a menu and studied it, saying, "We'd better hurry. We still have to get settled."

"There's plenty of room at my place," he informed her. "In case the boardinghouse is booked up."

Melanie's face lit up. Moriah spoke before the impulsive teenager could leap upon Kane's offer, if that's what it was. "No, thanks. I'm sure we can find something."

She gave her order as soon as the waitress appeared. While Melanie was asking about an item on the menu, Moriah thought of the conversation with Lily Mae.

The widow had mentioned someone named Lori. Moriah wondered who she was. Kane's wife? Girlfriend? She glanced at his hands, holding the menu. No rings. Not that that meant anything.

When the waitress left, she assumed a casual air. "Is Lori your wife?"

"No." His smile became softer, different from any he'd given her since this ill-fated encounter began. "Lori is a nurse-midwife. We work together at the local hospital."

"Are you dating her?" Melanie put in.

Moriah wanted to tell her daughter not to wear her heart on her sleeve. Not that Melanie didn't know Kane wasn't available for her, but Moriah feared she'd picked him out for *her*. The girl was an incurable matchmaker. She'd tried very hard to marry her mom off to her first-grade teacher, no matter that the poor man had had a wife and three kids. And she hadn't let up since.

Moriah gave her daughter a warning glance. Melanie returned it with an innocent look.

Kane didn't miss the byplay, Moriah noted. "We're friends," he said easily, which could have meant anything. He spoke to Moriah. "You might remember her. Lori

Parker was her maiden name. She married Travis Bains right out of high school. They were a couple of years behind you, I think."

"Oh, yes, Lori Parker. I remember her...vaguely."

"She's married?" Melanie asked.

"Not now," he replied. He flicked a rapier glance at Moriah, tossing her earlier answer back at her.

She knew then that he was seeing Lori...dating her. Suddenly, to her utter consternation, an abyss of pain opened inside her. All the frightened, lonely nights she'd spent since he'd left her to go back to college years ago returned to haunt her.

The fear, the humiliation, the self-recrimination when she'd realized he'd never meant any of the things he'd said rose again, making her feel vulnerable and desperate and incredibly naive.

"Excuse me," she murmured. She stood and left the table.

In the rest room, she dampened a paper towel, locked herself in a booth and placed the towel against her throat, cooling the blood that was pounding into her head. She didn't want another migraine. She had too much to do.

She took deep breaths until she felt in control again. Seeing Kane was more unsettling than she'd thought it would be. He was as wildly attractive as ever. The thought that he might find out Melanie was his daughter terrified her. She knew, on some instinctive level, that he would be furious.

He'd told her that he wanted a big family. An orphan, raised alone by his maternal grandmother, he'd envied his cousins their families. He'd been included in their holidays and activities, of course, but it wasn't the same. He'd wanted his own family.

So had she. The life of an only child was lonely, too.

A longing ran through her, unbidden and unwanted. She'd wanted his children. Fresh pain reverberated through her head.

Forget the past, she ordered herself. Forget what had been between them…as he had. He'd gone back to college without a thought of her. He hadn't cared that she might be in trouble. He probably wouldn't care if he found out about Melanie.

But if he did…if he wanted his daughter… No! He had someone. He could marry and have children with her. Melanie was *her* child, all she would likely ever have.

Why did life have to be so hard? Hadn't she paid for her sins? Hearing about his midwife girlfriend reminded her all too clearly of her shortcomings. She was so *ordinary*.

When Kane had gone back to school, she'd let herself dream of getting a scholarship and becoming a nurse. She'd had visions of them working together, doing great and wonderful things with his tribe, saving them from disease and alcohol…oh, God, such dreams!

The counselor at school had advised her, in kind tones, that she wasn't really college material. Her grades were average. She had no particular talents that anyone could discern. It would be very hard to find a scholarship for her.

Then she'd realized she was pregnant, and her dreams had changed. She saw herself and Kane as a young couple living in college housing, having impromptu picnics with other couples in like circumstances.

It had taken a while, but finally she'd faced reality. When Kane came home at Easter vacation and didn't call her, the final dream had died.

Knowing she had to go back to the table, she removed the towel and left the booth. She freshened her lipstick and ran a comb through her hair. The strands crackled with static electricity and followed the comb. She wet her hands and ran them lightly through her hair to neutralize the charge, then finished combing it into place.

Melanie bounced in. "Mom, we were getting worried. Are you okay? Is your headache coming back?"

"No, I'm fine," Moriah assured her. "I was just coming."

"Isn't Kane super?" Melanie gave her a conspiratorial wink. "I'll bet you're prettier than any old midwife."

"Melanie, if you're bent on one of your matchmaking schemes, please recall those of the past."

"Come on, Mom, I didn't realize my first-grade teacher couldn't have another wife. I thought we'd round out his family nicely. As for the banker—how could I have known he was skimming a few thousand here and there? I'm just a kid."

"Right. So keep your nose out of grown-up affairs."

"Huh! You don't even have those," Melanie reminded her.

Moriah put her comb away. They returned to the table together. She was aware of Kane's inscrutable gaze upon them every step of the way. She prayed he wouldn't ask any more questions. She didn't think she could make up any convincing lies off the top of her head, not with Melanie listening to every word.

"Are you all right?" he asked when they were seated. "Melanie said you'd had a migraine over the weekend."

"I'm fine." She didn't want to discuss the state of her health, or anything else, with Kane Hunter. She didn't know what she was doing here, in this town, at this table, with this man.

"I think my mom's afraid of men," Melanie announced with a wicked grin. "As a doctor, do you have any advice?"

Moriah wanted to throttle her mouthy daughter. A wave of uneasiness washed over her. She should never have come back here. She wasn't responsible for her father. He was a grown man. He'd made his decisions in life long ago. She didn't owe him anything.

She didn't owe Kane Hunter anything, either. He had no reason to know anything about her. He'd opted out sixteen years ago.

Kane was aware of Moriah in every nerve in his body. She wore a blue two-piece outfit that went well with her auburn hair and fair skin. At thirty-four, she was incredibly beautiful.

She'd always been that, he admitted mockingly. And she was still a good listener.

That first afternoon at her house, he'd talked for hours, he recalled, telling her things he'd never told another person. He'd stayed so late he'd almost missed hitching a ride back to the res. People didn't stop for hitchhikers after dark, and only Indians stopped for Indians. It had been a real challenge getting to town to see her that month.

"Mom says you got a scholarship to college. I'm thinking of going into medicine," Moriah's daughter told him. "Are medical scholarships hard to get?"

He studied the girl while they talked. Her father must have dark hair and eyes. Homer had been a redhead like Moriah. Mrs. Gilmore's hair had been a russet brown. Homer's eyes were blue, his former wife's light brown, sort of golden, like Moriah's. Melanie's were very dark brown.

"Well, the one I received was available for a member of my tribe," he answered. "They needed a doctor on the res. That made it easier."

"But your office is in town," the teenager pointed out.

"I found it takes money to run a practice. You whites have more than us Indians, so..." He shrugged.

"Good thinking," Melanie said with a laugh.

At that moment, Rafe Rawlings came in. Kane invited the local police officer to join them.

"Have you found out anything more on my father?" Moriah asked.

Kane scoffed silently at her anxious air. She hadn't seen the man in sixteen years and all of a sudden she was worried? Ha!

He realized he resented the way she'd sat there so far without contributing a word. While he enjoyed the talkative teenager, it was the woman he was interested in....

Fury rose in him when he realized what he was thinking. He was curious about Moriah, that was all. Certainly he wasn't interested in her in a man-woman sense.

"Not a thing, I'm sorry to report," Rafe was saying. "I've put out the word to the ranchers so they can watch out for him. Kane alerted the tribal police."

"The fact that he's been gone this long is troubling. However, he might have gone off prospecting on a hot tip from an old book," Kane said. "He reads journals about the area during the winter and plans his spring expeditions accordingly."

"Yeah," Rafe agreed. "He probably forgot about the geology people he was supposed to guide."

"But what man would forget a fishing trip?" Moriah questioned.

Kane was surprised at the distress in her expression. So maybe she wasn't entirely coldhearted, after all. He glanced at her hair, remembering how warm it had been when he'd run his fingers into the long, silky strands. Warm hair, cold heart wasn't exactly the saying, but it was close enough.

"Homer's getting on in years," Rafe said. "He might be, uh, forgetful." He shot Moriah an apologetic glance for mentioning her father's possible decline.

"Aren't we all?" She gave a rueful laugh.

The musical sound jumped right into Kane's nervous system, stirring things he didn't want disturbed. She'd laughed in his arms once and told him she hadn't known before what it meant to be happy, truly happy. Her eyes had glowed as if twin suns burned in her soul.

He'd wanted to put her in his pocket and keep her there forever like a good-luck charm…. God, what a sucker he'd been for her sweet lies.

Never again. He'd been a boy then, ready to believe whatever his heart wanted to hear. He was a man now. He'd put away childish things long ago.

"When you have time, you should stop by the station and file an official report. The state and county officials didn't want to do much on my say-so," Rafe advised. "With the query coming from a relative, they might agree to a real search effort. Although, without evidence that something's wrong, they probably won't," he added.

"I thought I would look myself," Moriah said.

"What?" Kane said, taken by surprise.

She gave him a defensive glance, then ignored him while she talked to the local cop. "I used to explore the mountains with my father every spring and summer. I think I'll remember—"

"After sixteen years? Hardly," Kane interrupted. He gave her a stern glance, effectively telling her not to be a fool. If he and Rafe hadn't been able to find the man, she sure as hell wouldn't.

For a moment, she looked like an enraged cat, then all emotion left her face. He was taken aback by the display. He'd never seen a show of temper from her.

During the wild, sweet month of passion, she'd been all soft, responsive woman, answering his passion with her own. When he'd had to return to school, she hadn't wept

or made impossible demands. She'd simply whispered,
"Write when you have time."

He paused, thinking about that. Maybe she'd already
been tired of him. He shook his head slightly and forced
himself to concentrate on the conversation. When their
food arrived, he ate automatically and didn't let his mind
roam to the past.

"This is neat," Melanie said, approving the Amity
Boardinghouse, which was another old Victorian built
during the mining boom of the 1800s. It was pink with
white trim.

Moriah nodded absently. "Let's see if they have a
room." She led the way into the three-story structure.

A woman about her age greeted her from behind a delicately scrolled desk of a bygone era. "Actually, we have
small suites," she said in answer to Moriah's query. "We
have one with twin beds you might like. I'll give you a key
so you can look at it." She removed a key from a hook and
told them the suite was on the second floor, facing the front.

Moriah and Melanie went up the stairs. The railing was
hand-carved mahogany. Lighter wood was inlaid in fleur-
de-lis cutouts.

"I would love a house like this," Melanie exclaimed.
"Isn't it wonderful? I'll bet it's just full of interesting
nooks and crannies. I wonder if Kane's is like this."

Moriah ignored the bright chatter. Opening the door to
the suite, she walked into a room filled with light and
warmth.

"Look, we can see the mountains," Melanie pointed out,
going to the tall windows, which reached almost to the
ceiling.

The walls were so thick that each window embrasure
formed a natural window seat. The teenager found a door

in the side wall and stepped outside onto a small, private balcony, from which one could watch the sunset, the hills or the street below.

Moriah approved of the room, too. There were two alcoves, each with its own twin bed, table and lamp. Maple shelves over the beds held a variety of books, appropriate to the era.

Good, she thought. They would each have privacy at night. To her surprise, another door disclosed a private bath. She'd assumed they would have to share, for the price of the minisuite was quite modest. In an armoire across from the lyre-back sofa, she found a small television. All the comforts of home.

"I think this will do," she said.

Melanie came in and closed the door. "Um-hmm."

They traipsed downstairs, paid for four nights and went out to collect their bags. Milly, who was running the place while the owner was on a trip, explained about breakfast when they came in.

"It's served in the dining room. This way." She led them to a large, comfortable room that had once been a porch. It was now glassed in and filled with tables and padded chairs. "From six until ten, there will be muffins, cereal, fruit and juice here on the sideboard. The refrigerator is here." She opened a door and showed them. "Help yourself."

"Thank you."

"If you want to join us for supper around six, let me know in the morning so I can put on more stuff. We keep it simple—chili or soup or stew."

"That sounds nice."

They carried their bags up to the suite and unpacked. An hour later, they were settled in.

"What's next?" Melanie demanded.

"I think I'll lie down," Moriah said. "I'd like to rest before we have dinner."

"Are we going to eat downstairs?"

She didn't feel up to making any more decisions that day. "I suppose. We'll have to ask Milly."

"I will. Is it okay if I take a walk?"

"Yes. But don't go far."

Melanie laughed. "In this town? There's no place very far to go to."

After she left, Moriah was too restless to sleep. She finally sat in one of the deep window seats and stared out at the mountains to the west of town.

The day had been incredibly difficult. During lunch, she'd been a bundle of nerves, afraid that Melanie was going to bring up the subject of her father to Kane.

She pushed her hands into her hair in despair. She had to keep those two apart. Melanie already had a crush on Kane.

Who could blame her? At thirty-five, he was success-ful, confident and self-assured. He'd achieved all his goals, running an office in town and a clinic on the reservation, she'd gathered from the conversation over lunch.

A quiver ran through Moriah as she envisioned Kane's hands during the meal. He'd sometimes gestured with his fork, making a point as he answered her daughter's myriad questions.

Kane's hands. His fingers were long and slender. They'd looked capable and skillful. Steady. Unlike hers, which had had a tendency to tremble while she'd tried to appear calm and only mildly interested in his replies to Melanie.

Unable to suppress the memories, she let them rush over her, destroying the barriers she'd put in place years ago.

Kane's hands. Once they'd touched her with such exquisite tenderness. He'd explored her body and discovered the passion that had lain hidden, like a secret gift, inside her.

She'd done the same with him. They'd held nothing back from each other.

Closing her eyes, she moaned softly. Watching him talk to her daughter, remembering the past, Moriah had sensed the danger in being near him. To her utter dismay, she'd realized how very attractive he was—more so as a man than he'd been as a boy—and she knew that she wanted him still.

Four

"We got the report on Homer," Judd Hensley, the county sheriff, told Moriah the next morning. "Rafe Rawlings has been pestering us about him for most of this month. The problem is we have no indication of anything wrong. Your father has been a recluse for years. His going off to prospect is nothing new."

"I know." Moriah liked the sheriff. He seemed kind. Like many big men, he had a gentleness about him that was reassuring.

Like Kane.

She thrust the troubling thought aside.

"If you find evidence of foul play, then we'll investigate, of course. Otherwise, I'm afraid we just don't have the resources to put behind Kane's sense that something isn't right."

"Oh, did he tell you that?"

"Yeah, he's been a pain in the…neck, too."

Moriah smiled at the sheriff's obvious change in his

choice of words. It gave her a warm feeling to know others were concerned enough for her father to speak to the authorities. The residents of small towns might be nosy, but they were caring, too. She'd missed that in Great Falls.

"With your report—" he indicated the Missing Person's Report she'd filled out "—this makes the case official. It'll go out on the state-wide police net so that the highway patrols know to keep an eye out for him."

"Good." She stood. "Thank you very much for your advice and your help."

"Wish we had better news for you." He walked her to the door and saw her out.

Moriah emerged from the police station and stood on the steps, letting her gaze drift over the landscape. Across the busy street, several children played in the sandbar of the city park while their mothers sat on benches and chatted.

There was a nice feeling to the town, she thought. It was peaceful. Quiet. A good place to grow up. She'd liked living there, she recalled. It had been home. She hadn't appreciated it at the time, but now...well, the city was lonely.

She crossed the street to the dress shop. Melanie was waiting for her, ensconced in the red silk party frock. She'd pulled her hair up on top of her head and had pinned it in place. The teenager looked so grown up, so mature and sophisticated, Moriah felt a jolt of fear run through her heart.

Not yet, she cried silently. She wasn't ready for it. She wanted her laughing, darling little girl. She wasn't ready for Melanie to face the heartaches of being a woman, of falling in love and learning that life isn't perfect....

"Isn't it beautiful, Mom?" Melanie spun around in her bare feet, interrupting the disturbing thoughts. "Isn't it perfect?"

"Um, yes. How much is it?"

Melanie wrinkled her nose and looked apprehensive. She held out the price tag.

"Oh," Moriah said when she saw it. "Melanie—"

"I know. It's too much." She sighed, then brightened. "Maybe I can get a job after school. That way, I could pay you back."

"What about your work on the paper?"

"I don't have to be the senior editor." She walked back to the changing booth. "But I know you want me to be."

"I thought that's what you wanted. You and Jessy were going to be famous reporters, exposing graft and crooks in high places."

"Yeah, well, maybe I'll be something else. A doctor, maybe."

Moriah knew what—or rather, who—had brought on this change of heart. Kane Hunter already had a profound influence on her daughter. It worried her. She had a feeling she should grab Melanie and run back to Great Falls as fast as possible.

"Shall I put the dress on layaway for you?" the clerk offered when Melanie came out of the dressing room.

Moriah gave Melanie a regretful glance. She didn't have the money for the dress and wouldn't for the foreseeable future.

"No, thanks," Melanie said to the woman with a resigned air.

"I thought we might have a picnic for lunch," Moriah said on a bright note as they left the store. "There's a park just down the block."

"Sure."

Moriah mentally went over their finances while they bought fruit, rolls and cheese at the grocery. There was no way. She couldn't dig up the money for the dress.

Resentment washed through her. Just one time, she'd like to give her daughter something that wasn't homemade or left over from a sale at Joleen's dress shop. Melanie asked for so little in material things. But this dress was so expensive.

They selected bottled drinks, paid for their food and went to the park across from the police department. They found a table in the dappled shade of an old oak tree.

"Tell me about growing up here," Melanie requested. "Did you play in the park?"

"A few times. I had a lot of chores to do, so I had to go straight home from school."

"Because Grandma had to work?"

"Yes. I kept house and started supper."

"What did my grandfather do?"

"He worked at the lumber mill when it was open. Each spring he got restless and went off exploring. I used to go with him when I could."

"Grandma let you?"

Moriah considered the past. "Well, she didn't like it, but during spring break and summer vacation, it kept me out of her hair. My father was fun to be with…."

Her voice trailed off as she realized this was true. Her father had been very patient with her, teaching her woodlore and camping skills. Basically a solitary person, she'd loved being out in the wilds, the same as he did.

"That was a long time ago," she ended.

"There's Dr. Hunter," Melanie said suddenly. "Hi, Dr. Hunter!"

Moriah stiffened, then forced herself to relax.

"Call me Kane," he said, arriving at their table. "Mmm, an old-fashioned picnic. Looks good. I didn't get time for lunch."

"Join us," Melanie invited. "There's plenty."

She moved over, making room for Kane on the bench. He sat down. Moriah stared across the table at them, fear clenching at her as she was forced once again into an awareness of how much alike they were. Their hair, their eyes...

With a start, she realized those two things were the only real similarities. Melanie's features came from her side of the family.

The teenager had a round, soft face, where Kane's was all hard planes and angles. Melanie's hair gleamed with auburn highlights in the sun. Kane's hair was pure black, with no traces of red or blond in the thick, shiny strands.

Relief made her light-headed. No one knew about her and Kane. No one would suspect—

"Do you mind?" he asked, turning to her rather belatedly, since he was already seated.

"No, of course not."

"Would you like something to drink? I'll go get it," Melanie volunteered.

He dug some change out of his pocket and handed it over. "An iced tea. Sugar, no lemon."

"Right." She swung her legs over the bench and dashed off.

"She's a charming person," he said. "Are her grades high?"

"Yes. She's an honor student."

"Umm, too bad she isn't at least a quarter Native American. There's a tribal scholarship in medicine that she could probably get, if she's really interested."

Moriah nibbled on a piece of string cheese, her thoughts flying in several directions. She wondered if it would be possible to get a scholarship without disclosing who Melanie's father was.

"I don't suppose her father was Indian?" he continued.

Moriah's newfound confidence faded. She licked her lips nervously. "He might be…partly."

"Don't you know?"

She felt like a person standing on a bridge that suddenly starts to crumble. She didn't know whether to go forward or run back. "I think he once said something about it. I…didn't pay much attention. It didn't seem important at the time."

"You could ask him. I'd be glad to write a recommendation for her to the tribal council."

He knew…he must know. Or else why… No, no, he couldn't. "Wh-why would you do that?" She hoped he didn't hear the quaver of fear in her voice.

"She's bright, friendly and seems mature for her age." He smiled. "I like her. You've done a good job raising her."

"Thank you."

He sighed, then pressed his lips into a thin line. "If you'd rather, I can leave. You can tell your daughter I had an emergency I had to take care of."

Moriah stared at him, not comprehending his meaning.

"You look like I'm Jack the Ripper every time I come near you and your daughter. What the hell do you think I'm going to do—tell her that her mother had a mad fling with an Indian years ago?"

A gasp escaped her at his stark accusation. "I…no, I don't think that. It's just…" She could hardly confess the truth. "It's harder to face the past than I thought it would be."

He nodded and bit into a roll, taking some of his anger out on it. "Are you ashamed of what happened between us?" he finally asked, after swallowing.

Heat rushed into her face, then receded, leaving her feeling chilled and pale. She stared at the roll and cheese she'd been eating and tried to think of an answer that gave nothing away.

"Not when it happened," she whispered through an aching throat. "But…" She couldn't tell him how stupid she'd felt when her mother had pointed out the cold, hard facts to her.

"But you were later," he concluded. A muscle worked in the side of his jaw.

She watched his slender, graceful fingers rip a piece from the French roll and press it into a ball. He tossed the dough ball at a fat gray squirrel that was sneaking toward them, its nose twitching busily. The nosy creature grabbed the bread and rushed up a tree, to perch on a limb before examining the treat.

"Yes, later, when you didn't return my call."

His head jerked up. "During Easter break? Is that when you mean?"

She nodded. Tremors rushed along her body like tiny earthquakes. She couldn't control them. For years she'd wanted to ask him if it had all been a joke, something to amuse him during Christmas vacation because he'd had nothing better to do. Now she knew. He hadn't cared.

"I did call," he told her.

She hated it that he lied. She'd stayed at home every single day, waiting….

"Your mother said you didn't want to see me."

She shook her head, denying his words. Her mother had known how desperately she'd needed Kane. Joleen had been furious, yet surprisingly sympathetic when she'd confessed her pregnancy. "She didn't. She wouldn't have said that."

His eyes speared into hers like icicles. "She told me she'd have me arrested if I didn't leave you alone." He gave a brief, bitter laugh. "I was a slow learner. I came out to your house the next day, determined to make you tell me to my face that you didn't want to see me again. You were gone."

Moriah's breath came in gasps. She didn't believe him.

She couldn't. "My mother wouldn't lie. She knew…how I felt."

"How?" he demanded, pouncing on the word. "Tell *me*. Make *me* see how it was, how you could leave without a backward glance after all that happened between us."

She recalled how anxious her mother had been to get away before anyone found out about her condition. Joleen had pointed out that Kane would lose his scholarship if he was forced to marry her, that he would end up hating her and the child.

In the end, that's why she'd left. She couldn't bear the thought of his hating her and their baby.

"You never called before that," she reminded him defensively. "After the Christmas holidays, you didn't contact me."

"I wrote, but you didn't reply. Then I worked two shifts for a while so I'd have money to come home at the Easter break. So we could be together," he added, his gaze impassive now, the fierce emotion of a moment ago swept away by his iron control.

"I didn't get a letter," she told him. "At Easter, I saw your cousin. He said you'd arrived home the day before. Why didn't you call me then?"

"It was late. The next morning, I had to report to the tribal council about my scholarship. That's where I was when your call came in. I phoned back as soon as I was free."

"That's when my mother threatened you?"

"Yes."

"I see." She stared into his eyes, trying to figure out the truth. She couldn't believe her mother had lied, yet Kane was looking at her with a steady, unwavering gaze.

Dizziness rushed over her. She felt as if she were drowning in the dark, intense stare he directed at her. She wanted to believe him, she realized, so much that it hurt.

He muttered a curse. "You don't believe me, do you?

You wouldn't have believed me then, either. I guess that tells me where I stood with you."

"What do you mean?"

"If you love a person, it seems reasonable that you would believe him before anybody else."

She looked away from his accusing glance. Confused and uncertain, she tried to sort through the facts. "I wrote you. Later. After we moved to Great Falls," she told him.

"I didn't get any letters. I wrote you, too, at your old address here. Twice. My letters came back. You and your mother hadn't left a forwarding address." His voice had dropped to a low, throbbing drone, edged with bitterness.

Moriah's entire being seemed to stop functioning while they locked eyes and probed each other's souls. She was mesmerized by the intensity she saw in him.

The way she'd been long ago when he'd talked of the future, when he'd said "we" and included her in his plans, she realized, trying to break the contact, but unable to do so.

The moment shifted, and other feelings came into play. A hint of puzzlement appeared in his eyes, as if he didn't understand what was happening between them. She thought she did, and it frightened her. Desire wasn't part of her plans.

His gaze intensified. The air shimmered like a bright curtain around them, enclosing them in a veil of longing and accusation. In that instant, she found herself wanting to believe him, to have that once-perfect faith restored… but she couldn't.

Her mother had never lied to her. She'd told her the truth and made her see that Kane had used her.

At her continued silence, he shrugged and turned away, to throw another crumb to the squirrel. "I figured, what the hell. The lady isn't interested. So I got on with my life. As you obviously did." He nodded at a point behind her. "Your daughter is lovely."

She glanced around and saw Melanie crossing the grass.

"Here's your drink," the teenager said, taking her place beside him again. She glanced from Kane to her mother. "Did you two fight while I was gone?"

Melanie saw far too much. And had no qualms about commenting on her observations. Moriah forced a smile. "Of course not." She gestured down the street. "I was noticing the changes in town. There's a new grocery on the corner. I can't remember what was there before."

"An abandoned livery stable," Kane supplied.

"Oh, yes."

"It probably had one stall," Melanie quipped. At Kane's questioning look, she explained. "Well, for a one-horse town…"

"You only need a one-stall stable," Kane concluded with a chuckle, which sounded only a little forced to Moriah's ears.

She listened quietly while the other two talked like old friends who'd been apart for a while, yet had no awkwardness when they met again. It was troubling, the way they took to each other.

Even more troubling was the way she felt. Sitting across the table from Kane, watching him and her—their—daughter charm each other, she, too, was charmed.

Her gaze fastened on his mouth as he talked. When he smiled, his teeth were brilliantly white against his deep tan. He looked as if he worked outdoors rather than inside.

When he saw her looking at him, he paused fractionally in some anecdote he was telling Melanie. Their eyes met. His went darker, deeper, drawing her into those fascinating depths. She wondered if anyone else had ever noticed that the outer edge of his irises was forest green, very dark, very enticing.

She felt the heat pool in her abdomen, in that secret place where life began....

She looked down, startled by the direction her thoughts had taken. He continued his story with barely a pause.

It had all happened in the space between one heartbeat and the next, and yet she felt as if she'd lived an aeon in a second. For a moment a door had opened, and light and warmth had flowed into her, thawing all the cold, lonely places she'd hidden for years.

She stood abruptly. She'd had enough of the impromptu picnic. She had to get away...to shore up her defenses. "If you want that red dress, we can put it on layaway—"

"Mom!" Melanie squealed. "Do you mean it?"

"You'll have to help pay for it."

"I'll get a job, I promise. I'll even baby-sit."

Moriah had to smile. Her daughter had developed a dislike of baby-sitting after keeping a preacher's kids one summer. They had been the proverbial brats.

"I wish you lived here," Kane commented. "I could use someone in the office. My secretary married and left town all of a sudden. The nurse and I can't find a thing."

"Mom's a wonderful secretary," Melanie chimed in. "You should hire her."

"I have a job," Moriah quickly stated. "My boss was very nice about letting me off, but I have to be back on Monday."

"Yeah, she does." Melanie subsided, but Moriah could see the scheming going on behind the innocent smile. She would have to speak sternly to her daughter about embarrassing her in front of others. This ridiculous matchmaking had to be nipped in the bud.

"What are your plans while you're here?" Kane asked.

"I thought we would go out to the cabin tomorrow."

He nodded thoughtfully. "There's a dance at the reservation tomorrow night, a money raiser for the tribe's education fund. Would you like to go?"

"I don't think so."

"Mom, I've never been to an Indian dance," Melanie put in, giving her an appealing look.

Kane tossed Moriah a challenging glance. "There'll be lots of interesting things to do…educational, even."

Melanie sighed and pushed her hair behind her ear. "It really sounds like fun."

Moriah knew she was being manipulated, but she couldn't think of a graceful way out of it. "I suppose we can go."

"I'll pick you up at six," Kane said. He rose, drained the last sip from the bottle of iced tea and started off.

"I have my car," Moriah called after him. "You needn't bother stopping for us."

"It's no bother." He dropped the bottle in a recycling bin and headed down the street to his office.

"Wow," Melanie said, "he is so cool."

Moriah gave her daughter a firm glance and began the lecture she should have delivered earlier about matchmaking and other embarrassing tactics.

"I feel like the white captive in a movie," Melanie whispered to Kane and Moriah as they approached the circle of dancers. Kane had picked them up as promised and brought them to the reservation.

"There're plenty of whites here," he pointed out.

"I thought Indians—uh, Native Americans—didn't like others to see their ceremonial dances."

Kane grinned. "Well, we Indians found out you whites will pay good money to see us stomping around in a bunch of feathers. This dance is mostly for show, not a real ceremony."

"It's probably a dance to put a curse on all of us whites—like give us warts or hives."

"Hmm, maybe I'll mention that at the next tribal council."

Moriah was amazed at the companionable teasing between the two. Kane and Melanie got along well. They seemed to have a similar sense of humor. She sighed and wished the evening was over. This trip had been a mistake from the start.

"There's the sheriff and his wife," Kane said.

Moriah recognized Judd Hensley. The woman clinging to his arm must be his wife. She was far along in pregnancy and moving rather slowly. Her hair was also red, but of a much-lighter shade than Moriah's own deep auburn. Her skin was fair and tended to freckle. Moriah felt an immediate kinship.

Kane made the introductions, then spoke to the mother-to-be. "Tracy, how are you feeling?"

"Large, impatient, ready to pop. Pick one," she said with a rueful grin.

"Maggie Hawk is the same," Kane assured her. "Jackson says she's impossible to live with."

"Yeah? I didn't see him out looking for rocky road ice cream at two in the morning last Sunday," the sheriff complained, his dark eyes twinkling. "Maggie doesn't have anything over Tracy when it comes to impossible. And you're no help."

"My patients must be indulged," Kane said solemnly. "The ice cream might have some ingredient she particularly needs."

"Huh!"

Moriah found herself laughing with Tracy Hensley as Judd scoffed at the doctor's statement. Later, while the men were on another topic, Tracy confided she'd had a miscarriage the previous year and that this time her husband and the doctor were acting like a couple of mother hens.

"There's Maggie and Jackson Hawk. And Winona. Have you met Winona Cobbs?" Tracy asked. "She's our local psychic."

She waved at a couple and an older woman across the way, while Melanie absorbed the information with avid interest.

They hurried over. Kane introduced Moriah and Melanie to his cousin—the tribal lawyer wore his hair in two braids tied with rawhide, which impressed Melanie—and to Jackson's pregnant wife, then to the psychic, a short, plump woman of uncertain age, whose gray hair was braided and coiled about her head.

Moriah remembered her. In school, a common taunt had been the threat of buying a hex from Winona to put on an enemy.

"You're Homer's daughter, aren't you?" the psychic asked.

Moriah said she was.

"And this is…" Winona stopped. She looked confused all of a sudden. She looked at Melanie, then at Kane, then back at the girl. She laid a hand at her throat, as if experiencing some emotion too strong to be ignored.

Moriah felt her heart start pounding. It beat so hard it caused tremors through her entire body.

"Winona?" The sheriff's wife took the old woman's arm.

"I'm all right. It was just…for a second I thought…but never mind," she finished.

Moriah had the oddest sensation that the woman knew exactly who Melanie was. Fear ate into her. Every day that she stayed in Whitehorn increased the chances of the truth coming out. And yet she couldn't just go home and forget her father, either. She felt trapped by a fate she couldn't ignore.

"Did you see something about Moriah's father?" Tracy Hensley asked. "Did you get a vision?"

"No, nothing that strong." Winona studied Moriah, then spoke to her. "Why don't you come out to my place for lunch tomorrow? I'd like to talk to you."

"Melanie and I are going to look for my father tomorrow," she said, declining the invitation. "We have to return to Great Falls on Sunday. I have a job and she has school."

"I thought you went out this morning," Kane put in.

"We did." Melanie glanced away from the dancers she'd been watching. "We explored all around the cabin, but we didn't find any signs of my grandfather. My mom knows how to track," she added, a proud note in her voice.

Moriah had impressed her daughter when she'd taught her how to discern a set of prints and other telltale signs of humans having been in the area. For a few hours it seemed like old times, with them doing a task together, enjoying each other's company. Those times came less frequently as Melanie grew older.

"My aunt is cooking fry bread over at the booth," Jackson Hawk told them. "I'll treat."

"Fry bread!" Tracy exclaimed. "I've been dying for some."

"You'd better get it now," the sheriff advised. "I'm not coming out at two in the morning looking for the stuff."

Laughing, the two couples, along with Winona, Kane, Moriah and Melanie, carried paper plates of fry bread, dripping with honey or sweetened berries, over to a table under an oak tree.

"This is wonderful," Melanie said, closing her eyes in delight while she licked her fingers clean.

Moriah watched Kane skillfully roll his piece up and eat it without dripping honey down his chin. She did the same.

An image from long ago came to her—of Kane's hands

caressing her, his skin dark next to the pale tones of her abdomen. He'd touched her with awe and reverence, his eyes closed as if she were a sight too wonderful to behold. He'd made her feel so special, so loved. She looked quickly away from him.

Her gaze met that of the psychic. The woman's expression was sympathetic. It was as if she knew what had transpired in the past and knew of Moriah's agony and the sense of betrayal she'd felt when she'd realized Kane wasn't going to rescue her.

Tracy Hensley sat next to Winona. It was obvious they were special friends, almost like mother and daughter.

Moriah considered her relationship to her own mother. She'd never felt close to her, she realized. They hadn't formed the bonds that she sometimes felt with Melanie. She wondered why. Her mother had been there for her when she'd needed help, but there had been no special sense of affection between them.

A flutter under Tracy's maternity blouse caught her eye. The baby was moving. The sheriff saw it, too. He laid his hand on his wife's side and rubbed gently at the spot, soothing the child. His gentleness did things to Moriah's insides.

A wave of longing washed over her. To be cared for like that would be the most wonderful thing in the world. To share the magic of creation with the right person must be heaven on earth.

She'd thought she had that with Kane. A foolish dream on her part. No one had ever needed or wanted her very much—except her child, and that would soon be past. Melanie was growing up. Moriah sighed and turned to watch the dance that was starting.

The Indian women wore bright cotton skirts that twirled around their ankles as they circled with their partners. The men wore cotton shirts, mostly of floral prints, with a few solid reds or blues here and there, and well-worn jeans and boots. A few wore moccasins and fringed buckskins, but not many.

She and Melanie had worn summer slacks, hers green, Melanie's yellow, with matching cotton peasant blouses of white with lace around the gathered necklines.

Melanie clutched her arm. "Mom, look, he's coming this way."

Moriah glanced at her daughter and followed her line of sight to a young man dressed in slim jeans tucked into cowboy boots and a plaid shirt with mother-of-pearl snap fasteners. He had dark blue eyes and dark hair, partially hidden by a white cowboy hat. He was in his twenties, too old for Melanie.

He came to them and stopped in front of the girl. "Would you like to try the dance?" he asked. He had a nice smile.

Melanie looked at Moriah. Her sparkling eyes told Moriah that she wanted to. Moriah hesitated.

"I can vouch for him," Judd Hensley said. "This is Keith Colson, a fine, upstanding citizen. Keith works at one of the local ranches and will be heading off to college in the spring."

Moriah was surprised. He looked older than a recent high school graduate. There was an air of maturity about him, as if he'd been on his own a long time.

"All right," she murmured. Melanie leapt to her feet. She put her hand in the cowboy's, and they joined the dancers.

"Come on, Winona," Jackson Hawk invited. "I'll twirl you around. Maggie's moving too slow these days to dance."

"We can try it, too, if you'd like," Kane volunteered. He stood and held out his hand.

Getting to her feet, Moriah laid her hand in his. His

fingers closed about hers. Tiny currents raced along her arm to nestle in some hidden place in her body.

They took their positions in the loosely defined circle and, still holding hands, moved in time to the insistent beat of the drum.

The tempo picked up. The dancers whirled faster, the women's skirts flying out as they were turned by their partners. Moriah found the dance easy to follow. Step, step, turn, turn, then sidestep and turn, then move forward around the circle. It was a round dance performed to tom-toms, shakers and tambourines.

After a bit, she looked up to find Kane studying her with a half smile on his face. She returned it without thinking.

The drums invaded her body. Each beat was a separate throb through each vein, each nerve ending. Tilting her head, she listened to the music, sensed it through the earth under her feet and slowly, slowly felt herself coming alive.

For an instant, the rhythm faltered, then it became faster still, until they danced as if they were racing the wind. Her hair shook free of the combs that held it back at the sides. Kane reached out and took them, slipping them into his shirt pocket. Her hair sprang wild and free about her face.

He watched her without speaking, rarely blinking, his dark eyes steady on her. Near them, she heard her daughter's laughter, heard it catch on a quickly-drawn breath as the young cowboy swung her around, lifting her from the ground.

Then a rush of sound, of wind or music or her heart, drowned out all others as Kane lifted her, his hands strong and sure at her waist, bringing her up close, so that her thighs rested against his chest as he held her up, her head higher than his. Slowly, he let her down, her body pressed to his as the music ended abruptly in a flurry of drums.

Her breasts rose and fell against his chest. He was panting, too—lightly, like a mountain cat after a brief chase. His hair tumbled attractively over his forehead. He looked young, reminding her of the youth she'd fallen in love with so long ago.

No, no, not again. She wouldn't fall under his spell a second time. She pulled away and smoothed her hair back with nervous hands. "My combs," she murmured.

He gave them to her. After she'd fixed them in place, he guided her to one of the booths and ordered a beer for himself, then looked at her.

"A soda," she said, not needing anything to make her dizzy. She already felt that way.

"You still like to dance," he said softly. He took a drink, watching her over the rim of the paper cup as he did.

"Yes." She looked away with an effort. They had danced many times, waltzing naked around her bedroom, lost in the music of love, their hearts keeping the beat....

Only with Kane, she thought. He was the only man she'd ever been natural and free and happy with. She'd tried to be that way with another man once, after she and Melanie had moved to their own place, but it hadn't worked. She would never be that young and carefree and trusting again.

"Why didn't you ever come back?" he asked.

"I couldn't."

He nodded as if he understood, although she knew he didn't. What would he have done had he known about Melanie? Would he have grown to hate her, as her mother had said he would, for holding him back from his dreams? Or would they have made it?

She looked at the milling crowd, talking and eating and making merry. *Gather ye rosebuds while ye may...*

They had done that. Her lovely daughter had been the result. She'd be more careful in the future. She'd learned her lesson.

Five

Moriah was acutely aware of Kane's hand on the small of her back as they returned to their table and joined the other two couples. She tried not to notice that Maggie Hawk and Tracy Hensley were very pregnant...and very happy.

She looked around for Melanie and spotted her daughter a few feet away, talking quietly with the young cowboy. Her heart jerked like a fish out of water at the tender look they exchanged. She knew that look, that shy meeting of the eyes, the glancing away, then back as if drawn by an irresistible force.

Oh, yes, she recognized the signs and knew exactly what they meant. Fear ate at her. Her little girl was growing up and falling in love.

She scolded herself for overreacting. Melanie was barely sixteen, a long way from serious attachments. Soon they would be back in Great Falls. Then everything would be fine.

She let her breath out in a weary sigh. Winona returned

to the table, looking attractively flushed from her exertion. "Ah, here's Lori," she said.

Moriah looked around. Her heart did a nosedive. Yes, indeed, she remembered Lori Parker. Lori had been a cheerleader, a freshman when Moriah was a senior at Whitehorn High. Moreover, she was the paradigm of the American girl—blond, blue-eyed, slender but with a wonderful figure and a perfect complexion.

Smart, too. A midwife, which was almost the same as a doctor. Like Kane.

She swallowed past a sudden blockage in her throat as Kane stood and took a few steps forward. Lori stretched out her hand to him. He used it to pull her against him. They kissed, nothing heavy or embarrassing, but telling in the very ease with which it was accomplished.

If she hadn't known before, she'd have realized it now. They were *very* good friends...and had been for a long time.

She looked away and met the understanding gaze of Winona Cobbs. Moriah wished she could talk to the older woman. She needed someone who would listen without saying "I told you so" or giving any of the unhelpful advice people offered.

"Did all the babies get here okay?" Maggie Hawk asked, a note of wry laughter in her voice.

"Yes, thank goodness," Lori said, shaking her hair back from her face with a graceful gesture. "Now it's a race between you and Tracy." She grinned at the two pregnant women.

"I want to be next," Tracy declared.

Maggie nodded. "Me, too."

"Babies have their own schedules," Kane advised.

Lori made a playful face at him. "I thought you'd be at the hospital." She smiled at the others. "Kane loves babies. I can hardly get rid of him when I have a delivery. He takes a personal interest in every child in the county."

He laughed, but didn't deny the charge, then gestured toward Moriah. "Lori, do you remember Moriah Gilmore? She used to live in Whitehorn and attended high school here. She was ahead of you by a couple of years."

"Three, actually," Moriah said, forcing a bright smile.

Lori studied Moriah, then grinned. "Of course. You used to work in the school office while the secretary went to lunch. You were the only student ever entrusted to do that. I was terribly jealous and crushed that I wasn't asked."

"You were jealous?" Moriah managed to return the teasing remark. "You were the only freshman to make the cheerleader team. All the boys in school drooled over you while all of us girls quietly turned green with envy."

"That's Melanie, Moriah's daughter, over there with Keith," Kane pointed out when the laughter faded. He held a chair for Lori, seating her between him and Winona.

"She's lovely," Lori said, sounding totally sincere.

"Thank you," Moriah said.

After that, the conversation became general. Moriah listened while they discussed the weather and the price of beef and corn and alfalfa. Tourism was up, it seemed, while agriculture was down.

She didn't pay much attention. When Kane got up to dance with Lori, the other two couples went, too. Moriah noticed Melanie and Keith were dancing again.

"Your daughter is quite beautiful," Winona Cobbs said. "I can see the affection between the two of you. It's nice to see a mother and daughter who get along."

Moriah smiled. "Sometimes I think she was given to me by mistake. The fairies got mixed up or something."

The psychic watched the couples dancing to a slow

tune. A regular band had joined the drums and tambourines, and they were playing popular songs now.

"If we all viewed our children as wonderful gifts, I wonder what the world would be like?" she mused.

Moriah looked at the mountains, which were outlined by the soft light of sunset in brilliant fuchsia. "Filled with spoiled adults, I imagine. Do you have children?"

"No. I never had that privilege." She was silent for a minute, watching the dancers. "Does Kane know?"

Moriah froze for an instant. "Know what?"

"About his daughter."

Clasping both hands against her chest, Moriah looked at the older woman with despair. "How did you know?" she whispered. "Do you think...does anyone else..."

"No, no," Winona assured her. "It's just me. Sometimes I get these...vibes, I guess you'd call them. When I looked at Kane and your daughter, I could see a bond between them, as if they were wrapped in the same aura. I saw them joined by a common thread."

"We were so young," Moriah explained. "I was in high school. He was in his first year of college."

"So your mother took you away," Winona concluded.

"Yes. We thought it for the best."

Winona shook her head. "You should have allowed Kane in on that decision. He would have claimed his own. He'll be furious when he finds out—"

"He won't find out," Moriah interrupted. "We're leaving soon. And I won't bring Melanie back."

The old woman closed her eyes. "No," she said. "Your father needs you. You must stay."

Chill bumps climbed Moriah's neck at the portentous words.

Winona opened her eyes and laid a hand on Moriah's

arm. "You must. Your future lies here. You refused to face it once. You must do it now."

"What—what do you mean?"

"I don't know," the psychic confessed. "It's just something I feel. It will hurt, but you must stay." She removed her hand and tucked a strand of hair back into a braid. "You must."

Moriah put her own hand to her forehead. She was torn by her duties—those of a daughter to her father, those of a mother to her daughter. She didn't know where she belonged.

When Kane and Lori returned to the table, they were laughing. "How about something to drink?" he asked, glancing around at the others as they seated themselves.

"Yes, something cool. Lemonade," Tracy requested.

Everyone echoed the request. Moriah wanted to go home, but now she'd have to wait until they'd had their drinks. She looked around for Melanie and the cowboy.

"Relax," Kane advised. "They're at the drinks counter."

"I'll help you carry ours," Moriah volunteered, getting up.

"I'll go," Lori said. "You're a guest."

The impact of that statement, spoken cordially and without guile, as far as she could tell, made Moriah feel like an outsider. She sat down abruptly. Fortunately, no one noticed.

She raged at her stupidity for coming with Kane, for not driving her own car. Now she was trapped. Unless she used the oldest excuse in history to get out of an awkward situation.

When the other two returned with the lemonade, she forced herself to drink some. The drink was too sweet, too tart. She gave up on it and sat quietly, waiting for a chance to escape.

When Kane finished his drink and asked her to dance again, she shook her head. "I'd really like to go home. My head is…it aches." Her excuse sounded flimsy to her own ears.

She saw a muscle tighten in Kane's jaw, but he nodded. "When this song is over, I'll get your daughter," he promised.

Finally, the music ended and the band took a break. Kane signaled Keith, who brought Melanie to them at once. "We have to go," he said to the couple. "Melanie's mother has a headache."

"I'd be glad to drive Melanie home after the dance," Keith volunteered. "It's over at midnight," he added. "I'll have her in at twelve-thirty."

Melanie cast Moriah a pleading glance, then stared at the ground without saying anything.

Silence fell on the group. Everyone waited for Moriah to speak. She frowned as she realized she was being put on the spot. No one believed she had a headache. If she insisted Melanie leave, she would seem like an ogre.

"Keith is a careful driver," Kane said.

"Yes, ma'am," the cowboy agreed, so quickly it caused a titter of laughter among the others.

"All right," Moriah said, defeated by her own anxiety to leave and sympathy with the young people's desire to stay.

"Thanks, Mom." Melanie kissed her cheek. "I'm sorry about your headache. Don't worry about me. I'll be in on time."

Kane touched Lori's shoulder. "I'll see you later."

She nodded, then smiled at Moriah. "Welcome back to Whitehorn," she said.

Moriah thanked her and said good-night to the group. She walked toward the parking lot, aware of eyes on her back and of Kane beside her as they wound their way through the crowd.

"Do you get migraines often?" Kane asked once they were in his car and on the road.

"No. It seems to happen in spells. I'll have several in a row, then they'll quit for a while."

"Hmm, sounds stress related, although hormones can trigger them, too."

She hated his acting like a doctor with her. She wasn't his patient, and she didn't want his advice or concern. "Actually, I don't have a headache. I wanted to leave," she admitted.

"I see." He sounded surprised by her bluntness.

"It's rather awkward being the fifth wheel at a social function." A rush of humiliation swept over her. She lifted her chin. It had been stupid to go to the dance with him, to let herself know the joy of being in his arms again….

"Lori's arrival," he murmured. "You felt you were the odd man out. Yes, I see."

Moriah was taken aback by his understanding. A flush stole over her face, and she was glad of the dark.

"I wasn't expecting her," he said softly.

"That makes it sound worse, as if we were carrying on behind her back," she said tersely.

"Lori wouldn't think that. She knows me."

The statement hung between them. Lori trusted him to be honorable while Moriah hadn't, was the unspoken thought behind it. He'd only asked them because he liked Melanie and thought she would be interested, a one-time thing while his girlfriend was busy.

Sitting up straight, Moriah stared through the darkness at the road in front of the sports ute's lights. The moon was up, edging the rim of the mountains in dull silver and creating a magical illusion around them, as if they rode in a crystal ball.

She needed one, she admitted with a quiet sigh. The future was dark and dangerous, full of pitfalls she couldn't see. She needed to guard her tongue around Kane, or else she might blare out the truth in a moment of anger—that her trust had been destroyed when he'd left her, alone and pregnant, those many years ago.

And if he knew *that*, he'd figure out the whole truth, then what would he do? Take Melanie away from her, came the answer.

"You need to watch your attitude with Melanie," he said, slowing down when they passed the city-limit sign.

"What do you mean?"

"You seem possessive, as if you don't want her around us locals. Like your mother was with you."

Outrage stiffened her back. He knew nothing of her life, yet he obviously felt quite comfortable giving her advice. "I don't know what you're talking about," she said coldly.

"Didn't you ever wonder why Joleen kept you so busy? You had very little spare time from your chores to make friends or indulge in school activities. You were under her thumb."

"That may have been true once, but no more." When Melanie had grown old enough to start talking back to her grandmother, Moriah had realized how much Joleen bossed people and structured their lives. That's when she'd moved out on her own with her daughter. "However, Melanie has a mind of her own and often gets her way. More than she should, according to my mother."

"I'll bet," he said in a dry tone. "I'll keep an eye on the youngsters at the dance and remind Keith to bring your daughter straight home, okay?"

"Yes. Thank you," she added belatedly. She realized he meant to return to the dance. To be with Lori.

When he pulled into the driveway of the boarding-house, she jumped out of the car before he had a chance to open his door.

His apology stopped her. "I'm sorry about tonight. I didn't think how it would be for you if Lori showed up."

She opened her mouth, closed it, then tried again. "It doesn't matter," she finally said. "She was very nice."

"Yes," he said, with an oddly quiet note in his voice, "she is."

She thanked him for bringing her home and hurried into the house. The clock on the stairs showed the time to be a little after nine. Three hours before the dance would be over.

In her room, she dropped her purse and jacket on a chair and went to one of the deep window seats. Kane's vehicle was still in the drive. She could see his silhouette against the glow from the streetlight, which was on the corner behind him.

He was leaning forward, his hands clasped on the steering wheel while he gazed at the house. Even without seeing his expression, she knew he wore a grim look on his face. He was trying to figure her out, she thought. Trying to find what made her tick.

She shook her head slowly from side to side. He would never know, she vowed. He'd never know how much she had loved him, so much she'd given up her dreams so that he could have his. She'd been afraid he wouldn't finish school and get his medical degree, that it would be too hard for him to study and care for a family.

Kane loves babies.

Lori's statement rang in her heart. She wondered if she'd made the wrong decision those many years ago.

Melanie came around the cabin. "No sign of Grandfather," she announced. She stuck her hands in her hip pockets and drew a deep breath of pine-scented air. "I love the smell of the woods."

"Yes," Moriah said absently.

"I really like it here, Mom."

Moriah glanced at her daughter, then away.

"What if we stayed here?" Melanie continued. She was like a bulldog once she got an idea in her head.

"We can't stay here. You have—"

"School," she finished. "And you have a job." She kicked at a rock. "You could work for Kane. He needs someone."

Just for a second, during the brief time it took to go from hope to despair, Moriah let herself think about it— her running the office smoothly and efficiently for Kane, then sharing the end of the day, living together, loving….

"Melanie, please." She let the anger rise in her voice.

"All right. But it would be super. I could go to school in Whitehorn just as well as Great Falls. I like it here better."

"For now," Moriah pointed out. "While you have a crush on Keith Colson. What if he gets a better job somewhere else?"

"He's taking math courses for another semester. He wants to go to college and study range management, but he has to get his SAT scores up. He'll work for the state agriculture service some day and advise ranchers on their cattle operations."

"I see." Moriah walked to a rocky ledge and looked out over the broad valley that encompassed the Kincaid ranch, the biggest spread in the county. "Where is my father?" she asked the sky, the land, the whispering trees.

There was no answer.

She sat on a rock. "I don't know what to do."

"Stay," Melanie said. "Call your boss. I'll bet his niece can work longer."

"That's what I'm afraid of." Moriah sighed moodily. Life was conspiring against her. Being here opened all the wounds from her youth. And maybe added a few new ones.

Melanie wasn't the only one who was attracted to Kane. After he'd driven away last night, Moriah had sat in the window seat and watched the stars for a long time. The loneliness had been devastating.

She sometimes felt that she'd be alone all her life, that she'd never have the home and family she longed for.

Unlike her mother, she wanted to stay home. She wanted to plant a garden, to strip and repaint furniture, to take care of a home for her husband and children. That was where her talents and interests lay. It was just that no one had ever wanted her for those particular things. Except Kane. Once. Long ago.

"Mom? Are you crying?" Melanie knelt beside her and looked at her in real concern.

Moriah blinked the moisture from her eyes. "No, of course not. It's just that I'm worried."

"Call the law office," Melanie advised. "You haven't taken your vacation yet. You know you won't rest until you find Grandfather, so you may as well take the time and look for him."

"Maybe I will. We'll see," she added hurriedly, when Melanie looked as if she would leap on this morsel.

They spent the rest of the day hiking the area. Moriah found that she remembered the old landmarks easily, as if she carried a map in her head. There had been some logging and a few cave-ins around the area, but mostly it was the same.

"These enduring hills," she said aloud, remembering it as a line or title from a book. She felt tied to the land in ways she couldn't explain or even comprehend. This was home. It was where she belonged.

Melanie turned to her in question.

"I'll call my boss when we get back to our room."

A smile broke over her daughter's face. "Super," she said.

"You'll have to stay with your grandmother and go to school."

That wiped out the smile. For a split second. "Christmas isn't so far off," Melanie mused. "And I can come down for the weekends. This is going to work out. I just know it!"

"It's only for two weeks," Moriah stated firmly.

Moriah wished she felt as sure about how things were going to turn out as her daughter did, she reflected as she placed her suitcases on the floor beside the bunk bed.

She had driven them to Great Falls on Sunday afternoon. Melanie had moved in with Joleen—after promising faithfully to obey her grandmother for the time she was there—and Moriah had packed extra clothes to bring back to Whitehorn with her.

Her boss had given her the vacation without a fuss so that she could search for her missing parent. In some hidden part of her mind, she wondered if she would return to Great Falls.

More and more, her conscience nagged her about withholding the truth. With fatalistic insight, she knew that when Kane found out about Melanie, he'd want his daughter with him, and Melanie would want to get to know her father.

It was something she would have to face. If she had a job in town, she could stay close to the girl.

She sighed and looked around the small room. She had decided to stay at her father's cabin. The ranch owners didn't mind Homer living there; surely they wouldn't object to her staying while she looked for him.

Besides, that would save her a lot of money on rent at the boardinghouse. She had the red dress to pay for and get out of layaway before the holidays, so Melanie could have it for the big dance of the school year.

Moriah wondered if she had let herself be rushed into this decision by Melanie's eagerness to return to the area. Or was it her own desire to return? What were her feelings toward Kane?

He was very attractive, and she was attracted. There, she admitted it. Being around him make her edgy, nervous, excited. For the first time in years, she felt…alive.

When he looked at her, his eyes changed, becoming darker and more inscrutable than the Sphinx, and yet there were crosscurrents that flowed like wildfire between them. She'd felt them. She was sure he had, too.

Saturday night, when they'd danced, his breath had quickened. He'd held her against him, just for an instant, before setting her down. The flames had leapt between them, not those called forth by memories, but new ones of the present, hot and demanding.

He was seeing another woman, she reminded herself.

Yes. But…

She was crazy to be thinking about it, to be dreaming of them as a family. Whatever she and Kane had shared was gone. Old memories might stir, but they couldn't rekindle the embers of a lost love.

Picking up her sleeping bag, she spread it over a bunk after pushing one suitcase and a smaller bag under the bed. She cleaned up the cabin, sweeping and dusting and washing the small windows set in each of the four walls. But other than some basic cleaning, she didn't look at her father's possessions. Going through his things would mean she didn't expect him back.

After bringing in four sacks of groceries, mostly soup

and cereal, canned milk and crackers, she cleaned out the
iron stove that was used for cooking as well as heating and
checked the woodpile. Enough wood for a year or more
was stacked behind the cabin. She found an outhouse
hidden among the fir trees.

Further up, she discovered a tiny spring flowing out of
the rocky cliff. Homer, or someone, had built a dam to
form a pool and had lined it with rocks. She remembered
a bucket in the cabin.

Returning with it, she filled it to the brim and carried
the cold, clear water inside and set it on the pine table.
Dishes of blue porcelain were arranged on a shelf above
it. She found clothing, all neatly folded, in the four oak
drawers.

Her father had always been a tidy person, she recalled.
He'd kept their yard immaculate at the house in town.
There'd been flowers from spring into fall, then bushes
with red berries to add color in the winter. Her father had
loved working outdoors.

Perhaps he should have been a cowboy. No. Her mother
would have hated that. If they couldn't own a ranch, then
Joleen wanted no part of the land.

During her early adolescent years, Moriah had
wondered why her parents ever married. At sixteen, she'd
realized the answer. Her birthday was seven months after
their wedding anniversary.

Grabbing a banana and a peanut-butter granola bar, she
went out on the front porch and sat with her feet on the
step made of two flat rocks with a board laid across them.

It was unfair, she mused while she ate her lunch, for
people to be attracted to the wrong person. Things should
have been planned better, so that only the right people
wanted each other.

She sighed in frustration. Restless, she finished her

meal and strolled about the clearing, then decided to go for a walk. She collected a water bottle, snapped it onto her waistband, stuck a pack of trail mix in her jacket pocket and struck out.

An hour later she came out on a high ridge, higher than the one at the cabin. From here she could see the church spire at Whitehorn and make out the courthouse in the center of town, which was about twenty miles away, she guessed.

Dotted hither and yon around the landscape were ranch houses and barns. A logging operation was five miles north of her. She could see in the valley the road leading to the Kincaid place. The house there was hardly a ranch house, more like a mansion. It was hidden among the trees, except for two chimneys that embraced the house like twin bookends.

A wave of loneliness engulfed her.

Don't feel sorry for yourself, she scolded inwardly, but she couldn't seem to drive the feeling away. She was lonely. She'd never had Melanie's penchant for making friends. She didn't feel at ease the way her daughter seemed to in a crowd.

Like father, like daughter?

Yes, Kane, too, had the capacity, self-confidence, whatever, to feel comfortable no matter where he was.

Even her mother liked to be around people. She loved chatting and advising her clients at the store. And they liked her, too.

Why couldn't *she,* at thirty-four, be easy and companionable with others? Only with Kane had she—

She blocked the rest of that thought. With Kane, she'd been foolish and naive. He'd released some wild, unpredictable element in her that she needed to control.

A low rumble of thunder startled her. She glanced over

her shoulder. A storm had gathered on the mountains behind her. She'd better get back to the cabin.

She hurried, but the storm beat her. It dropped over the peaks and down into the valley, bringing a torrent of rain that soon had her drenched.

Once she stopped and raised her face to the rain, feeling each drop splash against her skin like a tiny caress.

The trail came out on the ridge close to the cabin. Instead of running for shelter, she stopped and spread her arms wide as if to embrace the storm, as if the rain were her lover.

Throwing her coat off, she faced the wind that poured down the mountain and felt the cool rain against her hot body. She stared at the clouds, at the mountains shrouded with rain, at the wide valley with its neat fields and pastures, far below.

For that instant, she forgot herself, forgot who she was, forgot the problems that waited like a dark fate for her. She wanted only to remember the moment, the beauty of it as the rain raced across the valley like a silken veil.

And with the unbearable beauty came the unbearable pain—the filled-to-the-brim ache of life, the painful wonder of it. It surrounded her, reached for her, called to her....

She couldn't breathe. She panted, a light flurry of air moving in and out of her trembling body. It wasn't enough. Nothing was enough. She wanted to fly, to soar, to be one with creation....

Only once had she felt like that. Once, for a month, the world had been hers...hers and his.

Time stood still, and she didn't know how long she stayed there, feeling a part of the earth and air, sky and rain, but finally she became aware of the shivers that ran through her.

With a final look, she ducked her head, picked up her jacket and fled into the house, running from the girl who had once loved Kane Hunter with all that was in her.

Six

Kane had a light schedule at the reservation clinic on Tuesday. At one, he secured the final bandage and left the examining room. He ate lunch with his cousin, checked on four post-surgical patients, then headed to town. He might work on the new house he was building for the rest of the day.

After changing into casual clothes, he paused. Moriah was back, living in Homer's cabin and looking for her father. He went to the telephone and called the Kincaid ranch.

A few minutes later he was on his way. When he arrived at the ranch, Dugin Kincaid had two horses loaded into a trailer and a ranch hand at the wheel of the pickup, ready to do his bidding.

Dugin's wife stood on the patio, dressed in a frilly outfit that didn't seem very practical for a ranch. She wore high-heeled sandals and a wide-brimmed hat.

"Thanks, Kincaid," Kane said, shaking hands with Dugin. "I appreciate your help."

"No problem."

Mary Jo crossed the lawn and joined them. Dugin dropped an arm across his wife's shoulders.

"Hello, Mary Jo," Kane greeted her.

"Kane, how lovely to see you." She held out her hand in such a way that Kane wasn't sure if he was supposed to shake it or kiss it.

He opted for a brief shake. "Nice to see you again," he said, realizing how insincere the words were.

Fluttery women got on his nerves. Lori and Moriah—the second name slipped into his mind before he could stop it—were smart, practical females who weren't afraid of work. They didn't worry about mussed hair or having their makeup perfect….

"Don't worry about getting the horses back. I told my man to pick them up tomorrow," Dugin told him.

"Thanks." Kane climbed back in his truck. The driver followed him onto the road. A few minutes later, they arrived at the clearing in front of the cabin.

The place was quiet. He helped the driver unload the animals, which were already saddled.

The cowboy put out a bag of grain. "Give 'em about half this tonight, the rest in the morning. That's Bess. The gelding is Toddy. I'll pick 'em up before noon tomorrow."

"Much obliged," Kane said, nodding.

After the man left, he went to the cabin and knocked on the door, although he was sure Moriah wasn't there. She was probably out searching for Homer on foot.

He looped a canteen over the saddle horn and clipped a fanny pack around his waist. Stooping, he studied the shoe tracks in the dust in front of the cabin and followed them for a ways.

When Kane was sure Moriah had taken the bluff trail, he swung up on the gelding, tied the reins of the mare to his saddle and headed out. An hour later, he found her returning to the main trail from a side path.

She stopped dead in her tracks on seeing him. "What are you doing here?" she demanded. She brushed a tangle of hair from her forehead with her forearm, wiping the sweat away at the same time. She looked tired and irritable.

"Looking for Homer," he replied, keeping his tone neutral. "You seem like you could use a break." He swung down and handed her the canteen.

She hesitated. He thought she was going to refuse, then sense won out over pride. She took the container and drank deeply.

He pulled the pack around, opened it and offered her a sausage biscuit. "Sorry," he said. "It was the best I could do on short notice."

"This is fine." She plopped down on a stump, flung her hat on a bush and unwrapped the sandwich eagerly. "I ate my lunch at midmorning. I've been hungry for hours." Before she took a bite, she looked at him. "Did you really bring the food for me, or am I stealing your lunch?"

"I ate more than an hour ago, but I figured you might get busy and forget, so I stopped at the fast-food place."

"Thanks. It was…thoughtful of you."

He wondered if the words nearly choked her. He brushed aside the cynical notion. He'd come to look for Homer, not to quarrel.

For some reason, he felt obligated to lend a hand after accusing her of being callous toward her father and goading her into coming to Whitehorn. He'd certainly done nothing to help since dumping the problem on her.

"What trails have you covered so far?" he asked.

They discussed the possibilities, then decided to make a circuit along the ridge trail to the west of there. The horses would make it easy to check the entire loop and return to the cabin before dark. They mounted up and rode off.

Moriah let Kane go in front, on the assumption that he was a better tracker than she was. After she managed to relax, she began to enjoy the outing. Their purpose was serious, but it didn't prevent an appreciation of the sights and sounds around her.

Her father had taught her that. The woods had their own special magic. During those years in the city, she'd forgotten what *quiet* sounded like—the faint rustle of the wind through the trees, the occasional snort of her horse, the sleepy afternoon chirp of a bird—without the constant roar of traffic, thumping music from a too-loud stereo or the racket of grocery carts.

And the air…pure elixir.

She drew a deep breath, savoring the fresh scent of pine and fir and a tantalizing whiff of mint as they wound upward beside a tiny creek. She found herself wishing they could keep on going forever. She wished they were just starting out, a man and a woman meeting and falling in love for the first time. She wished…

Closing her eyes, she put the silly dreams behind her. They'd lost their chance long ago. They'd been too young when they met.

At seventeen and eighteen, they'd had very little actual control over their lives and circumstances. That hadn't prevented the love and the passion, but their ages had been a factor in the aftermath, hers especially. Too many other things had interfered. His schooling, for one. Her mother, for another.

"Are you all right?"

She opened her eyes. Kane had stopped his mount and was watching her with concern. It gave her a warm feeling, which she quickly suppressed. He was a doctor. He probably thought she was about to faint and fall off the horse. "Yes, I'm fine."

"We'll stop and let the horses rest at the top of the ridge."

She nodded.

The shadows were long when they reached the crest, where the trail meandered down to the steep ravine on the other side of the mountain from the cabin. They hadn't seen a person or a clue on the trip. She dismounted when Kane did and led her horse to a spring where the creek began.

"Look," he murmured from close beside her. His tone was one of pleasure, his expression tender. He pointed toward the woods. A deer and her fawn stood there, watching them.

Moriah stood very still. The silence surrounded them in a hushed beauty. She felt Kane's shoulder brush hers. She looked at him and smiled her delight. Their eyes met and held. She felt the tenderness in his eyes wash over her.

His smile faded. She saw his gaze roam over her face and settle on her mouth. Warmth seeped into her lips, and they felt full and puffy. The air seemed heavier. She had to open her mouth in order to breathe.

He made a sound deep in his throat, one of protest or anger or perhaps surrender. She couldn't tell.

With one hand, he reached up and touched her face. A shiver raced over her and subsided. She bit her bottom lip to stop the tremor that invaded it. He brushed the captured lip lightly, freeing it, then ran his thumb over it. She closed her eyes.

He probed inside and stroked along the edge of her teeth. Sensation poured along every nerve ending, fleeing to all parts of her body. She heard her breath, then his; her heart…his…

"Moriah," he said, a deep, guttural sound of need.

She opened her eyes with an effort, wanting the moment to never end, but wanting it go forward, too, to some magical joy. She wanted to answer all his needs—

The gelding pushed in beside the mare and drank noisily. The deer and her baby bounded off.

Kane spun from her with a low curse. Without glancing her way, he tied both animals to a tree, then removed the canteen from his saddle. He handed it to her to drink first.

She took a couple of swallows and returned it. She watched his throat move as he drank. An impulse to kiss him there swept over her. It was an insane, intense reaction, utterly foolish, but nearly irresistible. She wanted to continue the interlude of a moment ago. Seeing the loathing in his eyes—for himself more than for her, she thought—she knew it was an impossible wish.

Sighing, she admitted he was the most attractive man she'd ever met. She couldn't figure out why. She'd seen men who were more classically handsome. Kane was rather sharp featured and tended to look stern in repose. But he'd always been her ideal.

He dug into his fanny pack again and handed her another sausage biscuit. He took one for himself this time, his expression savage and remote.

She murmured her thanks. They each chose a rock to sit on and proceeded to eat the meager meal. Finished, she cleared her throat and prepared to be gracious. "I appreciate your bringing the horses and helping me look for my father."

He flicked his dark gaze from a contemplation of the view to her. "My conscience nagged me into it," he confessed.

"Your conscience?"

"Sure. I have one, you know."

She didn't respond to the mocking humor. "Why would

your conscience bother you? From what I've learned, you and Rafe Rawlings have been looking after my father for years."

"Yes, but I'm the one who pushed you into coming here. I wanted to dump the responsibility on someone else. You were the most likely candidate." He plucked a grass stem and rolled it back and forth between his palms. "I didn't realize the disruption it would cause in your life with your daughter and your job. At the moment, I was angry about the situation."

"My father is my responsibility."

"I suspected you'd feel that way," he murmured, surprising her. He met her questioning gaze. "I depended on that fact when I called. You always had an overdeveloped sense of obligation to others, even then."

Except for one snowy month in winter almost seventeen years ago, she thought. For that month, she'd forgotten all sense of responsibility and caution. And look where it had landed her.

Her conscience forced her to admit the truth. That month with Kane stood above all her memories, except those with her daughter. She'd loved him as only the very young, the very trusting, can love, without doubts or fears.

At times during the past week, she'd sometimes dreamed of going back to that innocent age, but she knew it could never be. Too much time had passed. Doubts and fears had invaded their lives. Now she was here for a different purpose. Moreover, Kane had someone else in his life.

With that reminder came an unexpected jab of pain. Kane wasn't hers. She had no right to be hurt. And yet, when she looked into his eyes, she saw the old magic.

"I loved my father," she continued after a moment. "He was wonderful when I was growing up. Before he became...distant." She couldn't bring herself to say "crazy."

"A strange kind of love," Kane murmured. "You never contacted him once in all these years."

"I did," she protested. "He never answered any of the letters or cards I sent. He…he didn't care."

"Oh, yes," Kane insisted. "He cared. I can prove it when we get back to the cabin."

She questioned him, but he told her to wait and he'd show her what he meant. She wondered if her father knew about Melanie. She had written about the birth of his grandchild, but the letter had been returned. There hadn't been a forwarding address.

Night was upon them when the trail opened out in front of the cabin. She invited Kane to supper. He gave her a quizzical look.

"Well, it's the least I can do," she explained casually, while her heart thumped like mad. "For your help."

He nodded. "I'll take care of the horses."

Kane noted the way her hips moved as she walked away, the snug jeans outlining her figure perfectly. For a second he remembered how smooth and pale her skin was. He'd loved to run his hands over her, tickling her a little right below her ribs. Her "tickle spot," as she called it.

At the juncture of her legs, the small thatch of pubic hair was the same dark auburn as that on her head. He'd liked to touch her there, too.

Her weight, like her height, was in the average range. She wasn't slender like Lori. Her curves were softer, her breasts larger. She'd once said she wanted to nurse her children. And that she wanted a large family.

She'd been lonely as an only child, he recalled her telling him. Well, she'd either changed her mind, or she and her husband had divorced before they'd had more children, fortunately.

He was adamantly opposed to divorce when children

were involved. Even in alcoholic families, he'd found, with counseling and lots of encouragement they could usually make it. Family was important to children, the most important thing in their lives.

It occurred to him that he'd never asked Lori about kids…like how many she wanted? If any. That was one thing he was looking forward to. He wanted to have two kids, then maybe adopt a couple…or a dozen.

He and Moriah had talked about everything under the sun when they'd been together. He found he still wanted to tell her things, to share his feelings with her. It was odd.

She'd loved being out today. She loved the land, the seasons, the rugged grace of the mountains as much as he did. He'd seen it in her eyes, had heard it in her soft exclamations at spotting a red bird or an eagle. Once upon a time he'd thought they were two parts of the same soul.

He swore savagely as that strange moment on the ridge returned to haunt him. Against his will, he'd had to touch her, to stroke that rosy, tempting mouth. He'd wanted to lay her in the grass beside the creek and make love to her.

His gaze was drawn to the cabin as he fed and bedded down the horses for the night. He could see her moving about the kitchen, stoking up the embers in the old wood stove to cook them a meal as if she'd been doing exactly that all her life. At seventeen, she'd been just as capable. A strange tenderness for her invaded his consciousness, coming from a vulnerable place he'd closed long ago.

He frowned, wondering if she'd ever had time to be a child. Both her parents had demanded a lot of her, he realized. She'd been a quiet, serious person then. She still was.

After rubbing down the horses, he had nothing else to do. He had to go inside the cabin and eat the meal she'd prepared.

Heat swept through him at the thought. His heart started knocking heavily against his ribs, startling him. If a patient had described the sensation, he'd have diagnosed it as the beginning of an anxiety attack.

Hell, he'd been alone with her all afternoon. What was a quick meal in a cabin?

Except it was dark and they were alone and the cabin was off here in the woods by itself, not a soul within miles.

And he wanted her. It was as simple as that.

Why? He had everything in life a man needed—money in the bank, a nice office with living quarters, plus a house he was building in his spare time on land he'd bought close to the reservation. He knew a special woman who fitted his life perfectly. He didn't need Moriah Gilmore crashing into his plans, stirring up memories, disturbing his libido.

He'd eat, then get the hell out of there.

Moriah checked the beans and found them done. She'd cooked them with a porkchop for flavoring, so Kane could have meat with his meal. There was also a pot of fresh greens she'd picked early that morning while the dew was still on the grass.

She made cornbread in a skillet, fried up some sliced apples and put on a pot of coffee. The dinner was ready.

While waiting for Kane, she washed up and brushed her teeth, then combed her hair and clipped it at the back of her neck. She realized she was nervous.

After setting the table, she stood by the window. October was an unpredictable month. It often snowed in the mountains, a heavy, wet snow, while it rained in the valley. This year the weather had been fairly warm all month. Even the rain the day before hadn't been as cold as she'd expected.

When Kane entered, she felt the rush of cool air as night settled on the mountain. "Supper's ready," she said.

He washed his face and hands in a pan, then took a seat at the table. She placed the food in the center and sat opposite him.

"I wonder when electricity was added to the cabin," she said. "Dad and I used oil lamps when we stayed here."

"Rafe and I strung the wire about five years ago."

"That was nice."

A regular lightbulb was certainly easier on the eyes for reading, she thought as she glanced at the old books and journals her father had collected.

They ate in silence.

Spying an arrowhead on a wall shelf, she nodded toward it. "I had a collection of arrowheads when I was a kid. My father knew how to make them. He showed me one time. At Christmas and my birthday, he always gave me a little animal he had carved."

Kane gave her a long look that she couldn't decipher. Heat collected in her middle as awareness flared between them. She glanced away, frightened by the strength of her feelings.

All afternoon, longing had grown in her. She couldn't figure it out. She wouldn't make the mistake of trusting Kane with her heart again, but when she looked at him, when he spoke, the way he moved…she was drenched with yearning.

It was the past, she told herself, and the memories invoked. The truth asserted itself harshly. Kane was even more attractive now than he'd been years ago. All the fascinating potential she'd sensed in him then had been fulfilled in the man. She was hopelessly attracted to him all over again.

The meal was at last finished. She was relieved. Now

he could go. They'd each played the good-neighbor role and now it could end. "Thank you for your help today," she said formally, rising from the table when he put his fork down.

"I promised to show you something," he said. He went over to the wall shelf and picked up the arrowhead. He lifted a tablet of ruled paper and removed a letter. He handed it to her.

She stared at her name and address. Then she realized her father had hired a private detective to locate her. "I don't understand," she said, puzzled.

"Now do you think he didn't care?" Without waiting for an answer, he went to a small trunk by the wall. He pulled on the padlock. It came open easily. "Look at these."

She walked over slowly, almost afraid of what she'd find. A gasp was torn from her when she saw the contents. With a shaking hand, she picked up an envelope. Across it, in red letters, were the words *No Forwarding Address*.

They were all addressed to her.

Moriah realized the letters were still inside. Looking at the dates, she saw her father had written several times the first year she and her mother had left Whitehorn, then less after that. But always at Christmas and her birthday. She sank to the floor.

Thinking about the past, she recalled that her mother had moved them to Billings first, then, after the baby came, to Great Falls.

Slowly, she opened a letter and read its contents, a single page from her father describing the trees turning red and gold in the fall and the squirrels stashing their nuts.

She put the letter back. In a side pocket of the trunk, she found many of the tiny animals her father used to carve for her from nuts and pieces of wood—squirrels and chipmunks and rabbits, crows and hawks and robins. She counted the items.

Thirty-two. One for each Christmas and birthday since she'd been gone.

Joleen had lied to her. Her father hadn't forgotten her. He did love her, had loved her all those years.

Picking up the letters, she looked at the dates. On one, she recognized her mother's handwriting. *No longer at this address.*

A lie. A blatant lie. Her father must have known it, too.

Tears filled her eyes. She touched each tiny figurine, then put them back in the trunk. Sorrow, regret, a wish to return to the past washed over her. If only she'd known. They could have written to each other.

Despair engulfed her. She clutched the edge of the trunk, feeling seventeen, with her world falling to pieces all over again. Slowly she forced herself to hold back the tears.

Kane was there, watching her, as silent as a statue. She wouldn't let him see her cry. With the back of her hand pressed to her mouth, she stared at the floor and fought for composure.

A violent tremor shook her. The floor creaked. Kane stepped closer to her. He leaned down, took one look at her face and muttered an expletive.

She scrambled to her feet, not sure what to do. She didn't want him there. He shouldn't see her like this, with the stupid, relentless tears filling her eyes.

"You didn't know." He finally believed her.

No words came to her. She pressed both hands to her mouth to stifle the sobs that occasionally shook her. She shook her head.

"You really thought he didn't care."

"Yes," she said, her voice breaking. "I never knew. I

never heard from him after we left. I wrote, but he didn't answer. I thought he didn't answer...." The cruelty of it pierced her heart.

Kane stared at her tear-ravaged face, at the agony she couldn't conceal, and felt his own heart soften. He'd never seen her weep and it tortured him in ways he couldn't explain.

"Don't," he said, reaching out a hand, then letting it drop before he touched her. "Don't cry."

"I can't...h-h-help it." She snuffled like a child, her entire body jerking as she fought for control.

"Ah, God," he whispered, and enclosed her in his arms.

She leaned against him, her tears falling like a hot rain on his shirt, soaking through to his chest. She moved her hands away from her face and clasped the material, desperate in her misery.

He felt her grief as if it were his and knew it was something she'd suppressed until this moment. Sixteen years of grief.

It ripped at him, destroying any sense of self-preservation he'd had before he walked in the door. Her need for comforting was all he could dwell on at the moment...her need to be held...her need for him.

Pressing his face into her hair, he inhaled the sweet scent of her while he fought his own sorrow. After sixteen years, he finally understood her feelings toward her father.

She wasn't indifferent or uncaring. She loved the eccentric old man. Even believing her father had abandoned her, she'd taken the time to come and look for him.

Her sobs gradually died away until they were only jerky breaths once in a while. He rubbed her neck until she calmed, then he handed her his handkerchief.

"Blow," he said, feeling gentle toward her.

She wiped her eyes and blew her nose. He took the

hankie back and tucked it in his pocket, then pulled her against him again, reluctant to give up the closeness.

Leaning her head back, she looked up at him solemnly. "I'm sorry," she said, her voice husky with tears.

He was caught in the golden brown of her eyes. The irises were striated with dark brown ridges. Golden flecks lined the valleys between the brown streaks, like treasure there for the taking.

The tip of her nose was red. Her lips were, too. He could detect the imprint of her teeth in her lower lip, as if she'd tried to hold back the gasping sobs that had shaken her whole body.

"Moriah," he said. He pushed his fingers into the dark auburn waves at her temple and felt the heat underneath the heavy strands.

Moriah.

To hold her was like capturing the wind, a wild, storm wind blowing straight off the mountains…into his arms.

Her lips trembled and her chest lifted, then fell in a shaky sigh. It was more than he could take. He bent his head and sought her lips with his, caught in a trap of tenderness for her.

Her mouth felt soft and puffy. He could taste the tears, a salty warmth, on her lips. He made a sound deep in his throat, one of protest…despair…helplessness, he wasn't sure.

But he couldn't stop.

He kissed her eyes, her temples, her cheeks. He rubbed the back of her head, tangling his fingers in her hair. With the other, he pressed her close. And closer.

He could feel her warmth beneath her clothing. Against his chest, he detected the soft mounds of her breasts, her nipples like small, unopened buds against him.

A shudder went through him. He was filled with needs so long denied that they rushed like an avalanche through his defenses as they broke free at last.

Moriah.

She'd been his first love, his first woman. He'd never gotten over the hunger she'd induced in him. It roared through him now, blocking out the danger signals that might have warned him where this was leading.

He couldn't stop. Not now.

With a throbbing need, he took her mouth, plunging inside to taste the honey, to stroke her tongue with his until she answered his passion, thrust for thrust.

She trembled, then her arms crept around his waist. She let him take more of her weight. He welcomed it, wanted it, loved the feel of her against him.

One step behind him, the bunk beckoned with the promise of fulfillment. He took that step.

When the edge hit the back of his knees, he twisted slightly, pulling her solidly against him as they slipped down on the mattress. He supported their weight on his knee until she lay prone, then he straightened beside her.

She opened her legs. He slipped his thigh between hers and moved slightly, caressing her intimately as he'd done so long ago.

"Kane," she whispered, her eyes closed, her brow furrowed.

Her hands moved over him, exploring as she once had, as if she were blind and had to touch him to know him.

When she opened his shirt, he sucked in his stomach so she could easily slip it from his jeans. Then she slid both hands under the cotton fabric and touched his skin. Wherever her hands grazed, she left a trail of fire behind.

Slipping an arm under her head, he bent close and kissed her again. And again. And again.

"You make me hurt," she said, moving her head restlessly on the pillow. "You make me ache."

"You do the same to me." He gasped when she drew one

finger around his navel, inciting bolts of lightning that seemed to lodge in his loins. His body grew tumescent… demanding relief.

Moriah heard the catch in Kane's breathing and knew she excited him the way he did her. It seemed strange and yet natural to be in his arms. One part of her acknowledged that she'd always belonged to him, from the first moment of the first encounter.

His long, slender fingers searched under her shirt until he touched her bare skin. He caressed along her back from her neck to her waist. Her bra came unfastened as if by magic. It was sheer bliss. Her senses raged as the storm escalated.

"I used to dream of this," he whispered, taking an uneven breath. "For months after you left, I'd wake, hot and aching, wanting you."

"I know," she cried softly. She moved her hands over him, trying to soothe the pain of years past.

"Do you?" He raised his head and looked down at her in the soft light of the wall lamp, his eyes smoldering with equal parts anger and desire.

She stared at him helplessly, wanting to make it all go away, all the hurt, the years of loneliness. Closing her eyes, she planted kisses all over his chest, loving the feel, the taste of him. "Kane, don't," she pleaded. "I can't bear it."

He caught her chin and lifted her face. His mouth touched her forehead, her nose, her chin. "Say it again," he demanded. His hand moved to her side, under her top, then touched her breast.

Her body jerked as if seared with a firebrand. "What?" she murmured, distraught at the storm he induced in her blood.

"My name. Say it. Say it the way you used to, as if your life depended on me, as if your very soul would die if we couldn't be together like this."

Sorrow briefly overshadowed the hunger. "Kane," she said, wanting to please him…and yet, she was afraid. She shook her head a little. "Passion is too easy."

He cupped her breast, molding it in his broad palm as if he were a sculptor and she the clay in his hands.

"Easy? With you, nothing is easy." He flipped the buttons on her top open impatiently and spread it wide. He pushed the bra up and out of the way.

His eyes flashed over her like dark, molten glass, and she felt indescribably beautiful.

"Heaven help me," he muttered hoarsely.

He bent his head and touched her breast, the merest whisper of a caress with his lips, then he looked into her eyes.

She was lost. All sense of self-preservation fled. There was only him. And her. And this ache deep inside.

Sucking in a deep, trembling breath, she involuntarily brushed against him. Her nipples contracted into hard points, so fast it was almost painful. She cried out, a whimper of sound in the silent cabin.

He laughed, an angry chuckle, as if resigned to a fate neither of them could stop. "You want me. I could touch you there—" he blew gently on her breast "—and you'd come apart in my hands."

"No. No."

"Oh, but yes," he contradicted. "It's the same for me with you." He frowned at her. "Only with you."

A thrill went through her at his confession. She was drowning in this stormy passion, and she didn't care. She didn't care!

He touched her again, sliding his hand along her ribs until he outlined her breast with his thumb and forefinger. Watching her face, he squeezed his fingers together, gliding upward to cover her, then trapping her nipple in a tender grip.

Spirals of electricity flowed over her. Hope, fear, bliss churned inside her.

He kissed her eyes so that she had to close them. He swept his tongue over her lashes, measuring them. She felt his chest move against hers when he drew in a deep breath.

"You're trembling," he said.

"I—I know."

"You did the first time we made love, too. Do you remember?"

Remember? How could she forget? "Yes."

"I was, too. I am now." He lifted his hand.

She stared at it, saw the faint tremor he couldn't conceal, then, powerless to do otherwise, gazed into his eyes. He covered her breasts, first one, then the other. Resting on his elbow, his left hand buried in her hair, he watched as he caressed her.

"Light and dark," he mused aloud. "It has never failed to fascinate me…how you can be so fair…with skin as pale as mare's milk. I was almost afraid to kiss you that first time. You looked so pure. You were untouched."

"Kane," she said, a protest. She wanted more than words.

"So was I. We learned of passion together, you and I. Do you remember how it was with us?"

"Yes." She caught his face between her hands and brought him to her. She kissed him. Opening her mouth on his, she took his lower lip between her teeth and stroked it with her tongue.

He shuddered, then he wrapped both arms around her and scooped her against him, her breasts nestled in the wiry hairs that covered his chest. His body was hard and demanding. It felt so right to her.

Their kiss was endless. It was tormenting. It drew the breath right out of her, so that she had to twist away and pull in great gulps of air.

"I remember your passion," he whispered, nuzzling along her neck, then drawing little, meandering trails with his tongue. "I loved to watch you becoming aroused. You flushed a rosy pink all over your chest."

"I wanted to watch you," she reminded him, breathless, her hands restless on him. "I wanted to see you grow big and hard…."

"But I was already that way before I could get my clothes off. Just the thought of you and *poof!*" He laughed against her breast. "I'm that way now."

"Show me." She placed her hands on his belt, then paused.

"Go ahead," he invited. "I'll fly apart, but…"

She unfastened his clothing. He lifted his hips for her to slide the pants down. The faded denim was soft in her hands. He'd worn denim sixteen years ago, too.

He moved his feet off the bed. He removed his boots and socks, the jeans and underclothes. His hands returned to her, stripping off the clothing. He unzipped the sleeping bag and tucked her inside.

For a moment, he stood looking down at her while he shed his shirt. His phallus stood erect, rising from the dark thatch like an ancient symbol of life carved in ivory.

Bending, he retrieved a packet from his wallet. She held her hand out, palm up. He gave the packet to her. She carefully opened it, then laid it against him. His body throbbed against her hand as she guided the condom over him until it was in place. This was something that had been part of their lovemaking long ago.

He heaved out a pent-up breath when she released him and lay back in the sleeping bag. He joined her there.

When he touched her this time, he let his hand glide lower, flowing along her abdomen to the dark auburn curls at her legs. He ran his fingers through them, then dipped lower.

She held her breath as he caressed her intimately, taking a great deal of time, as if exploring a flower one petal at a time.

Heat flowed over her in increasing waves. She writhed against him, aching for his complete touch, her entire body trembling.

"Sweet," Kane murmured. "How can anything be so sweet?"

Her cry stunned him when he delved deeply into her. He paused, but she moved impatiently against him.

"Need you," she whispered, kissing all of his face that she could reach. "I'm burning…oh, please…"

He realized she was caught completely in the passion he'd induced in her. A rush of pride and hunger for her made him dizzy. Stroking her was like stroking rose petals, incredibly smooth, yet hot and wet and sexy. The world spun off its axis.

Her body delighted him, urged him to take her.

Rising over her, he moved between her legs. She opened to him. Her hands on his hips demanded that he come inside.

He did. He closed his eyes and held on while he made the journey into her depths. It was like coming home…a sweet, warm welcome that blew all thoughts of yesterday and tomorrow from him.

She made a little sound, one of discomfort.

When he looked at her, he realized he'd hurt her. He held himself still, then frowned, trying to comprehend how this could be. She'd been ready for him.

"What?" he asked. "Does this hurt?"

She shook her head. "No…not really." She met his eyes. "It's been…" She bit her lip and shrugged slightly.

"A long time?" he finished. "It's been a long time?"

"Yes."

"How long?" He fought for control while his body demanded that he move in those warm, silky depths and find the sweet relief it needed.

"I...years."

He was shocked anew by this confession. It was almost like starting over, like the first time all over again. He experienced a great tenderness for her, one that he'd never felt for any other person in his life. A roaring filled his ears as hunger too long suppressed, too volatile to be contained, rose in him. He held on by a thread, panting with the effort.

One move...

"It's all right," she said. She closed her eyes and pressed her face against his neck. He felt her lips move, kissing him. "I want you. Please."

Her voice, almost a sob, broke the barriers of his restraint. He kissed her hard and passionately. He stroked the swollen bud of her womanhood until she whimpered for more.

Then he let himself move, slowly at first, while she became accustomed to his body, then faster as she rose to meet every slow thrust. It was heaven and hell...and everything in between.

The passion filled his mind like a roaring wind, straight off the tallest mountain peaks, as wild as a spring storm. A Moriah wind, catching him in its wild sweep. He tried to hold back, but she wasn't having any of that.

Wrapping her legs around him, she took him deeper into her, as far as he could go. Her body bucked against his, then she pressed her face into his shoulder. Her teeth sank into the muscle there, not hurting, never that, but needing something to hold on to.

She stiffened. A sound like grief was torn from her as she convulsed around him. He went over the edge, letting his body take its pleasure; the release was so hard it caused an aftershock of pain to course through him.

It didn't matter. Nothing registered but the incredible joining, the sublime moment of climax and the throbbing bliss that had followed. The pleasure-pain receded. He floated in the afterglow, contentment seeping through him like warm honey.

Later—he didn't know how long—he felt her move against him. He heaved a deep breath. It was time to talk.

"Moriah," he said, his voice coming out deep, husky with spent passion, resonant with passion yet to come.

Slowly, she opened her eyes and looked into his. Her head rested on the pillow beside his, so close, so very close.

"Are you all right?" he asked. As a doctor, he knew a woman would experience discomfort if she hadn't been intimate in a year or more. As a man, he hadn't expected it.

"Yes."

He hooked a finger under her chin and tipped it up until he could look into her eyes. She lowered her lashes, effectively shutting him out. Her reluctance to meet his eyes puzzled him.

"We need to talk," he reminded her.

"Not now." She snuggled her head against his chest. "I'm so sleepy." She sighed, her breath warm on his skin.

The tension in her body belied her words. He stroked her hair, suddenly aware of the distance between them. Now that the blazing desire was past, she was slipping away, withdrawing behind the barriers he'd sensed ever since he'd called her about her father.

Anger, familiar and safe, flowed into him. They had shared the most incredible lovemaking he'd ever experienced, and she was turning away from it. He folded his arm under his head and watched her as she pretended to sleep. They lay there for a spell.

"We have to talk," he finally said, and he heard the grim determination in his tone. Raising up on his elbow, Kane gazed at her, soft and vulnerable-looking in the dim light. A wave of tenderness hit him.

"Later. Tomorrow," she promised.

He felt her tighten her internal muscles and felt an answering surge in his own body. He had never been able to resist her, not at eighteen, not at thirty-five. She was his first love…and he'd never forgotten. Never.

He clasped one hand on her thigh, then ran it up and down her hip and leg. He felt her passion stir and smiled. Whatever they shared, she felt it, too. The storm between them was too strong to be denied. But there were other things between them besides passion, he recalled. They had to resolve them.

"Now," he insisted. "There's the future to think of. And Melanie—"

He felt her stiffen. Before he could grasp her intention, she was out of his arms and out of the bed. She pulled on a pair of pajamas, her face averted from him as if she were ashamed of what had happened. With a sinking feeling, he realized it hadn't meant the same to her as it had to him.

He forced himself to face the bleak reality of her rejection. Swinging out of bed, he washed up, removing the evidence of their hour of madness in each other's arms, and dressed, aware of her in every cell in his body.

When he was ready to leave, he faced her. She'd smoothed the sleeping bag and sat Indian-fashion on the bunk, waiting for him to be gone.

He felt trapped by emotions he couldn't define. He'd let himself become lost in her…the same as when he'd been eighteen, filled with all those foolish hopes. This was the woman who'd smashed those hopes to pieces, who'd broken his foolish heart. To let himself fall under her spell again was stupid.

"How can you look so innocent?" he muttered.

She didn't answer. Her cool glance infuriated him.

He paced the floor. "You sit there, looking as young as you did when you were seventeen, your skin all rosy from making love." He fought the need to take her into his arms again. "Yet you walked away as if nothing had happened between us. Not a word in all those years, then you return and..." He gestured toward the bed, unable to find words to begin to describe what they'd shared.

"Perhaps we both were innocent," she suggested.

He gave her a hard, quizzical stare.

"My mother lied about my father. She said he didn't want us, that he didn't care. I didn't believe her at first, but then he never contacted us. I sent him Christmas cards, but he didn't answer." She glanced at the trunk, then back at Kane. "I know now that she returned his letters without my knowledge."

"So you've decided to believe me now instead of her?" he asked, understanding what she was getting at.

She held his gaze. "Yes. I think you did call...like you said. And if you say you wrote, then I'll believe that, too."

"So where does that leave us?"

She looked away. "Nowhere, I think."

He faced reality—she didn't want him in her life. An urge to prick her outward calm hit him. "Yes. It's too late to start over." He walked to the door, then turned and faced her. "I have a future planned...one that doesn't include you."

"I know," she said softly.

He paused, but she said nothing more. He walked out into the night, knowing he'd wanted more from her than calm agreement. The future he'd bragged about seemed infinitely remote and infinitely lonely.

Seven

"You're quiet," Lori said.

Kane stirred from his contemplation of the trees visible from the broad porch that ran across the front of the house and gave his companion an apologetic smile.

It was Wednesday, his half day off, and he'd worked six solid hours on the house he was building. Lori had brought a picnic supper out to him an hour ago. Now they sat on the porch and watched the sky darken in the warm, Indian-summer twilight.

"I should have told you not to come out when you called. I'm not much fun right now, I'm afraid."

"Anything you care to share?" she asked.

The concern in her eyes belied the lightness of her tone. He felt the load of guilt he'd carried around on his shoulders since Tuesday night double in size.

He didn't know what to say. Hurting her was the last thing he wanted to do, but…there was Moriah and what had happened between them. He still couldn't believe he'd been drawn into the maelstrom of passion like that, caught as easily as a mouse in a baited trap. And Moriah had been the irresistible tidbit.

He was a man, not a boy with raging hormones. He should have been able to control himself—

"Kane?" Lori touched his hand.

He heaved a breath and relaxed the fist he'd unconsciously made. He had to say something. Explain himself…

Lori deserved honesty from him, but he didn't know what to say or how to say it. He turned his palm and took her hand. Bringing it to his mouth, he kissed it with great gentleness, then placed it in her lap and let go.

"It's Moriah, isn't it?"

His head snapped around. He realized he'd already hurt Lori, that somehow she already knew, maybe not what had happened, but that something had. He had to explain—

"Do you…are you in love with her?"

He couldn't love Moriah. She'd walked out on him, had believed the worst of him—that he'd taken her, shared a depth of passion he'd never known before or since, then simply dropped her like a used shirt. "No."

But he couldn't forget last night.

He couldn't pretend it hadn't happened, either. He wouldn't tell Lori all that had occurred—that would hurt her too much—but he had to admit his life was in a tangle and he didn't know how to unravel it.

She clasped her hands in her lap. A hint of red bloomed in her cheeks. "Do you realize we've hardly seen each other in ages? Since before that long weekend you took off to go fishing with Homer. I was pretty busy at the time, but later…"

Kane shifted uneasily, feeling her hesitation in bringing up a difficult subject. The load of guilt doubled again.

They had reached a point where it was time for the next step. He wanted to make that step, that commitment to her, but he couldn't. Moriah stood in the way.

"Lori," he murmured, searching for words.

"Were you lovers when she lived here before?" she asked. "Tell me the truth, Kane. We've never had lies between us, at least I don't think we have. I've told you what happened between me and Travis. Don't I deserve the same from you?"

"Yes," he said. But how could he explain a madness beyond comprehension? "We were involved before. My first Christmas home from college, she and I…met."

He couldn't come out and say they'd become lovers. It was something he couldn't share. What had happened between him and Moriah seemed too sacred—a corny idea, but that was how he'd felt at the time…and for all the years after.

"And now? Since she came back?" She turned to him, her eyes intensely blue in the deepening shades of evening.

Are you lovers now?

The question hung in the air between them. He hated what he had to say to her, but he had to say it. "There's an attraction," he admitted, softening the words as much as possible.

Lori's lips trembled ever so slightly, but she nodded as if she understood.

He felt a desperate tenderness toward this woman who had been his best friend for over a year. Why couldn't he feel the reckless passion, the need that had driven him into Moriah's arms without thought to the consequences, for *her?*

More of life's dirty little tricks, he thought with an edge of bitterness toward the whole scheme of things.

"So," she said, watching the lights of a car over on the main road to the reservation, "where do we go from here?"

"I wish I knew. I don't want to hurt you." He laid a hand on her shoulder.

After a moment of hesitation, she reached up and pressed his hand gently, then let go, as he'd done with her a few minutes ago. He drew one leg up and moved his hand to rest across his knee.

"That's not the issue," she told him. "It might be if we were already lovers and you discovered you wanted someone else."

"I wouldn't—"

"Maybe you wouldn't be able to help yourself," she interrupted. She plucked a blade of grass beside the porch and split it into long thin strips with her nails. "Maybe what you feel for her is stronger than you want to admit."

He raked a hand through his hair. "I don't know. I don't want to feel anything for her. Maybe it's just that things were never finished between us. Her mother took her away when she found out Moriah and I were…involved."

Lori gave him a smile that was sad, yet understanding. "Then maybe you'd better try again and see where it goes."

"I can't believe you're giving me that kind of advice. Most women would be coming at me with their claws bared by now."

"Well, I don't feel as calm and logical as I'm trying to sound, but I found out a long time ago it's better to face the truth than live in a vacuum of lies."

His admiration for her increased tenfold. "I don't know what to say. Except that you're one in a million…and you deserve better than you're getting from me."

"Oh, Kane," she scolded, "we can't dictate to our hearts. Haven't you found that out? You're drawn to the woman who I suspect was your first real love. Go to her and see if that love still exists. Date. Go to movies. Kiss. Find out what you really want. If you discover it's me, then come and tell me. I'll listen. We'll start from there and see where we end up, okay?" She jumped to the ground.

He swung down beside her and took her hand. They walked to the compact sedan she drove. He hesitated, then kissed her. It felt like goodbye to him and that hurt, too.

"I'll see you at the hospital," she said. She laughed. "In the delivery room, no doubt."

"No doubt," he echoed.

"Think about what I said," she advised when she was in the car. "Call her...or does she have a phone at Homer's place?"

"No, there's no phone.... How did you know she was staying there?"

"Lily Mae, who else? She also said she thought you two had dated at one time. She saw you together in a pickup truck, apparently."

"She'll have a field day when it's known you and I aren't seeing each other. There'll be gossip." He worried about Lori's feelings.

She shrugged. "They talked when I left Travis. They talked when I came back to town. I'm a big girl, Kane. I can handle it."

He closed the door when she cranked the engine. He felt a sense of loss for what could never be. Their bridges had been burned. He didn't know how he knew that, but he did.

Watching her, he realized something else. She was one hell of a courageous woman.

Moriah stood by the pay telephone outside the Hip Hop Café. She thought of calling her mother and confronting her over the letters she'd found at the cabin. No, that was best left for a face-to-face discussion. Her earlier anger had faded, and now all she felt was a nostalgic grief for what might have been.

And there was the matter of Tuesday night. That had superseded everything else in her thoughts.

Walking on, she mentally counted her money, then went into the boutique and paid off half the bill on Melanie's dress. After checking with the sheriff's office about her father, she returned to the street and stood there, undecided what to do. It was odd to be at loose ends with no demands on her time.

It occurred to her that she hadn't thought of her job and her career-oriented plan of becoming a paralegal since she'd left Great Falls. Nor did she miss it. Maybe she'd chosen the wrong field. Well, she didn't have to think about that at this moment.

Her glance fell on the sign to the café. She'd have a slice of quiche for supper, then go home. That would be a change from canned soup and cereal. She walked the few steps to the café door.

"Hello," a feminine voice called as soon as she stepped inside the place. "Come join me."

The voice belonged to Lily Mae. Didn't the blasted woman have a home to go to?

Moriah swallowed her irritation, pasted on a smile and went over to the table. There was no one else in the café at the moment. Lily Mae was probably lonely. Like her.

Ignoring the thought, she chatted a few minutes about her father and what the local, county and state police were doing.

"Mostly nothing," she admitted. "They say they're keeping an eye out for him." She sighed.

Lily Mae tried to be consoling. "Now, don't get discouraged. He'll turn up, right as rain, one of these days. Say, have you thought of asking Winona Cobbs about him?"

"No," Moriah admitted. She'd avoided the psychic. The woman saw too much.

"Take something of Homer's to her. She might be able

to see where he is. She helped the sheriff and his wife find their little boy when he was lost in the woods. Of course, it was too late. The boy had been shot...by a hunter, everyone supposed."

The widow paused for a moment and looked sad.

"Was he hurt bad?" Moriah asked, her sympathy aroused.

"Yes. He died. It ruined the marriage."

"Oh." Moriah swallowed against the sudden tears that clogged her throat. "But...he and Tracy are expecting... oh, she must be his second wife."

"No, no. They got back together last year."

After Moriah ordered her supper, Lily Mae launched into a convoluted story about Tracy Hensley returning to town to solve a murder case. She and Judd had fallen in love all over again and remarried.

"That's wonderful," Moriah said sincerely.

"Well, the most interesting part..." Lily Mae lowered her voice dramatically. "The most interesting part was the bones."

The hair stood up on Moriah's neck. "Bones?"

"The murdered man," Lily Mae whispered. "The bones turned out to be Charlie Avery. His daughter, Melissa, owns this place. She hired a detective to find out who killed her father."

From there, the story grew more complicated, with more twists and turns than a goat path. Moriah got lost in the maze of people suspected of the murder and the marriages that had taken place among the people involved. She nodded once in a while as Lily Mae rattled on and on.

"It was the Baxter girl that was the cause of it all. Now there was one who had an eye to the main chance."

"Umm," Moriah said, not bothering to ask where the Baxter girl fit in with all this murder and mayhem.

"Some say Ethan Walker—he was arrested for the murder—and Charlie had a fight over Lexine Baxter, and that Ethan killed him. Ethan was released for lack of evidence. I don't think he did it, though, or else it was an accident. Charlie probably fell on his head and broke his fool neck."

Moriah almost laughed at this assessment of the poor man caught in some temptress's clutches. She did feel sorry for Melissa, though. She knew how it felt to think one's father didn't care a damn about his kid.

That reminded her of Kane and Melanie. Her mood became somber. She didn't know what she owed to her child and the child's father in this case. To let her daughter think Kane didn't care about her seemed…unfair. She'd seen enough of the mature Kane to know he'd love his child no matter how he felt about the mother.

Moriah ate mechanically when her meal arrived, not noticing the perfectly baked quiche or the artful arrangement of fruit and vegetables on her plate. She barely heard Lily Mae's chatter.

The door opened. Kane came inside and glanced around.

The rush of blood to Moriah's head was so strong, she thought for a minute she was going to faint. Putting her fork down, she clenched her hands in her lap and held on until her nerves calmed.

"Come on over," Lily Mae invited.

Please say no.

He came over.

"Hello, Lily Mae, Moriah," he said casually.

She marveled that he could be so at ease. But then, why should he be strung out by the situation? Men took their pleasure when and where it occurred. It meant nothing.

"How are things at the hospital?" Lily Mae demanded in her good-natured, but inquisitive manner.

"Quiet...for a change."

"Did Lori get all the babies delivered?"

Moriah was startled at the look of pain that passed through Kane's eyes. She glanced at Lily Mae, but the widow hadn't noticed. Kane didn't realize how sad he'd looked for a minute, she thought, forcing herself to resume eating.

For a half second, she recalled their coming together Tuesday night. For those few minutes, she had felt the way she had the day she'd stood in the rain—as one with the elements, caught up in life and nature in ways she couldn't comprehend. It was something deep within, an instinct she couldn't ignore.

"Yes," he said in answer to Lily Mae's question, "the babies were all fine, four boys and two girls in the last batch."

His smile was easy now, but there was still a great deal of tension in the set of his mouth and in his shoulders.

Laying her fork down and picking up the glass of iced tea, Moriah noticed the fine tremor in her fingers. Kane saw it, too. His mouth thinned. He ordered a cup of coffee.

"I need to talk to you," he said to her, a low note of urgency in his voice, like the deeper notes of a bass viol softly throbbing under the melody of the violins.

Her false calm evaporated. "I really have to get back out to the cabin. I'm going to explore some old mines—"

"Melanie called," he said tersely.

Her heart stopped as alarm filled her. "Melanie? Called you?" She sounded stupid.

"Yes. When you're finished, we'll go over to my office." He glanced at the widow, then back at her.

Lily Mae was taking all this in with avid curiosity. Moriah felt a sigh start in her toes and work its way to her mouth. Life was too hard, too complicated. She should have stayed in Great Falls like any sensible person would in similar circumstances.

"Is she all right?"

"Of course. I'd tell you if it were anything serious. She wants you to call her...something about a project she's working on for school."

"Oh." Moriah's worry turned to anger. She could strangle Melanie for calling Kane. She'd make it very clear to the teenager that she wasn't to do so again.

The quiche, which she'd been looking forward to, felt like a lump of paste in her stomach. She finished it while Kane drank his coffee and chatted with Lily Mae, who'd looked disappointed that the news from Melanie hadn't been more serious. She swallowed the last bite of tender filling and laid her fork aside.

"Finished?" he asked.

She nodded.

He stood and tossed a ten-dollar bill on the table. "That should take care of it. Let's go."

It wasn't until they were outside that Moriah realized he was in much more of a hurry than he'd seemed to be inside the restaurant.

"Melanie is all right, isn't she?" she asked anxiously.

"Yes," he said. "She's had a fight with your mother, but I don't think it was too serious."

"Why did she call you?"

He cast her a glance so hard she would have stopped in her tracks if he hadn't taken her arm and urged her along.

"Who else would she call?" he demanded. "She doesn't know anyone here except Keith, and he's out in the back pastures helping Luke Rivers break a new batch of horses. You don't have any close friends in town."

She thought about what he'd said. It was true. She didn't know anyone in town on a personal basis anymore.

Her best friend from high school had married and moved away. Moriah hadn't written after her own hasty departure; her mother had advised against it. Moriah had been too embarrassed, anyway.

They crossed the lawn to his office. He unlocked the door and flipped on a light. She saw they were in a hall that ran the length of the house. Several doors opened off it. A stairwell halfway down the corridor led to the upper story.

The floors gleamed and the furniture was polished. The house looked well made and well kept. *This could have been mine.*

She didn't know where the traitorous thought sprang from, but she couldn't get it out of her mind as she followed Kane into a pleasant family room that obviously doubled as a study. There was a desk facing the room near one corner, with two tall, glass-fronted bookcases against the wall behind it.

A comfortable sofa and love seat flanked a square table. They were traditional in design and of a medium green that matched one of the shades of green in the oriental carpet. There was a very small stripe of pale beige in the couch material.

The wallpaper was the color and texture of old parchment, with a subtle green plaid in it, a reverse use of the sofa colors. The wainscoting and baseboards were sparkling white.

"It's…this is a charming room," she told him.

"Thanks. Lori helped me with the colors. She did a good job, I think." He pointed to the telephone on the desk and started for the door.

"Yes, she did," Moriah managed to say in a level tone. She went to the telephone and dialed her mother's number. Kane disappeared down the hall.

"Hello?" It was Melanie who answered.

"Melanie, this is Mom. Kane gave me your message."

"Oh, Mom, I have some bad news for you," the teenager said in a tone that was at variance with her words. She sounded quite gleeful, Moriah thought.

"For me? I was under the impression that you and your grandmother were quarreling."

"Oh, we are. As usual. She won't let me go out with the gang from school on Friday night. She says I run around entirely too much. I was just doing my story for the newspaper, but she can't seem to understand that I have to interview people and do research and all that."

Moriah was confused. "What's the bad news? Have you put out a contract on her?"

Melanie trilled her delightful laugh. "Not yet." Her voice became somber. "Your boss called and wanted to talk to you. I explained that you had no phone, and I wasn't sure you had an address, which, if you do, I don't know, anyway."

"What did he want?"

"Well…his niece wants to stay on, and his wife is sort of bugging him to keep her. He said you had sounded unsure about when or if you'd be back. He needs to know. If you quit, he'll pay you to the end of the month and you can draw unemployment after that."

Moriah thought of the rent, food, utility bills; the dress for Melanie that cost a whole week's salary. She was suddenly scared, the way she'd been when she'd moved out of her mother's house to make it on her own.

Yet, as then, she felt an odd sense of relief. She wouldn't have to return to the law office or leave Whitehorn. She realized she didn't want to do either. It was a startling insight.

"Now you can take the job with Kane," Melanie continued happily, so innocently unaware of the problems her mother faced. For her, life was settled. Her mom would have a new job, and she'd be near her new boyfriend.

"Oh, Melanie," Moriah murmured, uncertainty crowding in again.

"I'm sorry, Mom. I know you must be upset, but don't you see—we can both move to Whitehorn now. There's no reason to stay here. By the way, Kane said he would fly up and bring me down this weekend. He has a pilot's license and can borrow a plane from a flight club. They have a four-seater, so you can come up with him. Won't that be fun?"

"Fun," Moriah repeated, the word foreign to her. It had been a long time since life had been fun.

"You aren't really mad, are you, because I called Kane?"

"Yes, I am."

"Well, I didn't know how else to reach you."

"You could have called the sheriff's office and asked someone to give me the message. You could have asked Lily Mae Wheeler to get word to me." Moriah heard the irony in her own voice.

"Kane didn't mind me calling him. He said so."

Moriah closed her eyes and prayed for patience, control and an escape from the fate that was closing in around her.

"And he volunteered to come get me. I didn't ask. I didn't know he had a pilot's license. You never mentioned it."

"I didn't know, either," Moriah admitted. During their month together, they'd talked of many things…wondrous conversations that were serious, playful, so filled with dreams and schemes of great and small things. But they'd never talked of airplanes, that she could remember.

"So can I come down Saturday? He said he needed to pick up some supplies for the clinic, so it wouldn't be a wasted trip."

Moriah gripped the phone and rubbed her temple. What could she say without giving too much away? Nothing. "All right. I'll see you on Saturday. Try not to argue with your grandmother."

"I won't. I'll be so good, I'll drive her crazy."

Moriah's smile was wry. "I'm sure."

"Oh, Mom," Melanie exclaimed, her laughter floating over the phone line. "You know what I mean."

They said goodbye and hung up. Moriah continued sitting there, her mood pensive, but her mind was curiously blank.

She heard footsteps in the hall and steeled herself to face Kane. To thank him for his help. To somehow hang on to her control until she got out of his house. She glanced at the pair of earrings lying on the desk, then at the pleasant room, and thought how lovely the house was…this house he shared with another woman.

Eight

"I have some coffee ready," Kane told her, stopping in the doorway. His hard expression changed to one of concern. He came into the room. "Are you all right?"

The gruff purr of his voice was almost her undoing. She wanted to throw herself into his arms and wail like an infant for all the things that seemed wrong in her life.

She stood. "Yes, of course." She picked up her purse and jacket. "I put the call on my phone card. Thanks for letting me use your phone…and for being kind to Melanie."

"Did you okay my picking her up Saturday?"

Resentment stiffened her backbone. Everything came so easy for him—school, friendship, flying. Whatever he took into his head to do, he did. Now he was taking the one thing she had in life that brought her joy.

No, she admitted, she wasn't being fair. It was just that she was so tired—she'd combed the hills for hours looking for clues to her father. "Yes, I said she could come down. She can take the bus home on Sunday—"

His dark eyebrows lowered ominously. "I'll fly her back to Great Falls Tuesday afternoon."

"School—"

"It's closed for two days. They're having to fumigate the building. Termites are swarming all over the place, Melanie said."

"Oh." It seemed he and Melanie had everything planned. "Well, I'd better go. It's getting dark."

She glanced out the window at the long shadows in the well-kept yard. The sun was setting in a glory of color, backlighting the clouds over the mountains. The beauty of it pulled at her, setting those primitive chords inside her to vibrating.

"We're going to talk," he said firmly. "I was coming out to your place tonight."

She pressed a hand to her temple. She was too unsettled right now to talk to him. Her future hung in the balance. She wasn't sure which way the scales would tip.

"Is your head hurting?"

Kane's voice startled her. It was so much closer. She jerked wildly, as if she were being attacked. He noted the reaction and frowned.

"No," she said. It was, but to confess as much seemed like a weakness. She'd rather die than incur his sympathy. Not that he probably had any for her. With her, he seemed to waver between anger, resignation and an odd tenderness she'd sensed more than once…except when their passion overcame common sense.

"I'll give you something for it."

Before she could protest, he was gone. She followed him across the hall and into the office part of the building.

He unlocked a cabinet and searched around among some pills. "There's a shot I can give you. It's a new medicine and very effective for some people."

"That's okay. Pills are less trouble. Actually, I have some of my own. I'll take one when I return to the cabin."

"We need to plan the weekend…among other things." He turned around and held out a couple of individual packets. "Here, try these. If they don't help, there're others." He gestured toward the cabinet, then closed and locked it again.

Moriah read the instructions on one of the wrappers. "This won't knock me out, will it? I don't want to be unconscious or anything. I have to drive to the cabin."

"It shouldn't." He led the way back into his quarters, down the hall and to the kitchen. He gestured toward the table, to indicate she should have a seat.

She sighed and took a chair. He was determined to talk. "I assumed you and Melanie had worked everything out between you," she said coolly when he returned with two cups of coffee and a plate of cinnamon buns.

His eyes roamed over her. "You're losing weight," he said.

She looked at the steam rising from the cup. She didn't want him to notice anything about her. She didn't want him to be kind. "I'm hiking a lot, checking all the old mines my father and I used to explore."

Kane muttered an expletive. "What if you get caught in a cave-in, or fall and break your ankle? You could die out there in those damned woods and no one would know."

"I won't. I'm careful."

"Huh," he scoffed. "You're as much a recluse as your father," he accused. "You go your own way and everyone else be damned! Heaven help anyone who cares about you. Such as your daughter. She worries, you know."

She opened her mouth, closed it, then simply stared at him.

"Take one of those pills," he added in a snarl.

Her hands shook, but she tore open the foil packet. She couldn't help but remember Tuesday night, when she'd done the same, but the contents had been quite different. A shaft of pain went right through her heart, and she forced the memory aside.

Kane brought her a glass of water and plunked it none too gently on the table. She swallowed the pill.

He took a chair opposite her and sipped at the hot coffee. She wondered what had put him in such a temper. Having to fool with her and her problems, no doubt.

"What time do you want to leave Saturday? I told Melanie we'd be there before noon."

She resented his impatience and irritation with her. "Why ask me when you have it all worked out?"

"I'm trying to be considerate."

He snapped the words so furiously the sentence seemed ludicrous. The asinine humor of the situation hit her. She grinned, obviously startling him. A little geyser of laughter bubbled out of her.

Kane glared at her.

The laughter erupted. She clamped a hand over her mouth. It was all too, too funny. Ridiculous, really. She couldn't stop the convulsions of merriment. Her shoulders heaved, and her control gave way completely. Putting both hands over her face, she laughed until she had the hiccups.

Hands touched her shoulders and began kneading. "It's all right," Kane said. He was soothing instead of angry.

She fought to repress the mirth and finally won. She couldn't look at Kane. She'd break up again.

He continued to massage her shoulders, then slipped his fingers into her hair and rubbed her scalp with firm, circular motions that felt so good.

The wild laughter left her, and she calmed down, feeling as if she'd been crying instead of laughing like a maniac. "Sorry," she said and drew a deep breath. "Don't worry. I'm not going into hysterics. You can stop now."

He didn't. "Shh," was all he said.

His hands smoothed the strands of her hair, then rubbed behind her ears. It sent funny little tingles down her spine.

She sighed in disappointment when he slipped his hands out of her hair. He touched her temples, massaging the skin gently until she relaxed again. She closed her eyes when he stroked lightly across them, then pressed the areas above them.

"I think I've lost my job," she said.

"Melanie told me."

Warmth breezed over her forehead, then she realized he'd bent forward. His breath caressed the top of her head a second before his lips did. She felt them move as he spoke.

"The job here is still open. My nurse is threatening to quit if I don't find someone soon."

Her heart danced, until she remembered the earrings on the desk. "I...I can't." It was difficult to talk. Her tongue felt thick and foreign to her. She seemed to be sinking into a soft, calm darkness that was peaceful and benign.

"Shh." He pressed his fingertips against her eyes for a minute. It seemed to soothe the pain behind them. Then he worked at her temples again. "You can," he said quietly.

She tried to remember all the reasons for avoiding Kane. Melanie. The irresistible wildness of their lovemaking. The insanity of becoming involved with him. There was no future between them. He'd said so.

"Oh, Kane," she whispered. "It's all so hopeless."

"Only if we make it that way."

The tranquilizing touch wiped out all her fears and there was only the darkness, the soft darkness, before her. She felt herself drop into it. She hardly fought at all.

Kane reached over and pushed the coffee cup aside as Moriah's head slumped forward. She was asleep. Good.

Stooping, he slipped one hand under her thighs and the other behind her back. He lifted her into his arms and headed for the stairs.

He was panting slightly by the time he reached the bedroom. She'd lost weight, but she wasn't exactly a featherweight.

Laying her on the bed, he started methodically undressing her. While he did, he wondered what was driving her. She'd been living on the edge of her nerves since she'd arrived in town to look for her father. The possibility of losing her job was the final straw.

The tablet he'd given her should help her rest and get rid of the headache. Then maybe they could talk sensibly about her and her daughter's future. And about the two of them.

He'd meant it about the job. He was growing desperate to find someone qualified, and he was worried about Melanie. The girl was at an age where she needed a father's influence in her life. Being with women all the time, not having a male role model to compare her young men to, she was liable to make some serious mistakes.

The way Moriah had with the man she'd trusted enough to be Melanie's father?

The thought made him angry. He didn't want her to be with other men. She'd been *his* love....

Ah, hell, no use going over that lost ground. Anyway, with her working at the office, she'd be forced into spending time with him. He realized he'd decided to take Lori's advice. He and Moriah had to see where this passion would lead.

He grimaced as he took in the bed and the sleeping woman on it. He had to know if they had more than passion. He finished stripping her, went to his bureau and retrieved a pajama top, which he'd never worn, and put it on her.

Lifting her again, he swept the covers out of the way and placed her in the bed. He frowned. He'd have to sleep in the guest room tonight.

Or he could make up the bed in there, then move Moriah. No, she needed to rest undisturbed. He glanced at his watch. Seven o'clock. She'd probably sleep twelve hours.

After covering her with the sheet, he went down to the study and dropped into the easy chair. Life took strange turns, he mused. He'd never thought to see her again and here she was—in his home, in his bed…. He closed his eyes.

Hell, he wanted to be in bed with her. He wanted her under him, over him, beside him. He wanted to plunge so deeply into her that they'd never come apart—

He cut off the fantasy at once.

No more. He wouldn't fall into her trap again. He wouldn't think he had to have her to be happy. The last sixteen years proved that to be false.

Had he truly been happy?

Slapping his hand down on the arm of the chair, he cursed silently as his thoughts went hither and yon with no direction from him. What was done was done. There was no going back to the youth he'd been when he'd loved her with all his heart. He'd not make that mistake again.

Ah, Lori, what have you done? he questioned. *Was it wise to cut a man loose and tell him to court his old love? I wanted to love you. I wanted my life settled….*

That wasn't a very good reason to marry a woman. Certainly it wasn't good enough for a woman like Lori.

So what did his future hold?

Moriah.

That would be a mistake. He felt it clear to his bones. He'd trusted her once, and she'd left without a backward glance.

So she'd called…one time. And maybe written a couple of letters. So had he. So maybe neither of them had tried hard enough. Anyway, he'd had all he could do to work and get through medical school.

He'd achieved all his goals, he reminded himself.

So why was he lonely as hell? Why did he feel he'd missed out on the most important things in life? Why did he want *her?*

Well, this time would be different. He'd assess the situation between them logically and reasonably, then he'd know if they had anything worth saving. Yeah, that was the thing to do.

He pushed the button to release the foot rest. He slumped into the recliner and let his own weariness sweep over him like a caress.

Kane woke to the sounds of sobbing. He sat up and looked all around, trying to figure out where he was.

Oh, in the study. So who was cry—Moriah!

He leapt to his feet and ran up the steps to his bedroom. His patient was thrashing around, making soft, moaning noises as if she were in terrible pain.

"Moriah, what is it? Where do you hurt?" he asked, dropping to the bed beside her and catching her hands between his.

"Melanie," she whispered. "I've lost her. I can't find her anywhere. Help me. Please. Help me."

"Shh," he murmured, relieved. "You're just having a dream. It's okay. Melanie is fine."

She opened those beautiful eyes that reminded him of

a doe's soft gaze. There was pain in them, as if she were wounded.

"Oh, Kane," she whimpered, "I thought you'd taken her—" She broke off abruptly and stared at him in horror.

"Everything's all right," he murmured. "You were dreaming."

Why did she think him such a monster? He'd offered her a job, he'd looked after her father for years, he was flying up to get her daughter. What more could he do to prove he wasn't an ogre?

She turned her face from him and nodded. "Yes, dreaming, of course," she said.

He could hear the relief in her voice, see it in the way her shoulders relaxed, yet he sensed fear in her. "How's your headache? Is it better?"

Lifting one hand, she touched her temple and considered. "Yes, it's gone." She smiled in wonder. "It is."

"Good."

"That pill I took…"

"A muscle relaxant, actually. You've been on edge for days. Does it disturb you that much to be here in Whitehorn?"

The tension immediately returned. He observed her closely, noting the set of her shoulders as she smoothed the sheet and refused to look at him. There was some mystery here, something more than she'd disclosed. He suddenly wanted her to confide in him.

"No, of course not," she denied. "I'm just worried about my father. And Melanie. And losing my job." She glanced up. Her gaze skittered across his and away. "Isn't that enough to make a person…tense?"

"Maybe." He was silent for a minute. The tick of the hall clock seemed suddenly loud in the quiet room. He became aware of the two of them, alone in his bedroom.

Once he'd dreamed of having their own place, of sleeping with her every night without giving a thought to her harridan of a mother and the woman's opinion of him. A shaft of pleasure-pain hit him as his body reacted to that memory and her closeness.

She was warm and tousled from sleep. She was in his bed. Beyond that, he couldn't think.

He touched her shoulder and felt the heat beneath the cotton pajama top. Her body would be sweet and welcoming. That was the one thing between them that she couldn't deny or make trivial.

"Kane, no," she said.

The protest, low and husky, startled him in the silence of the room. His blood pounded harshly through his body. It pulsed in his nether regions, where he was hard and ready for her.

"Why not? You didn't say no the other night."

"That was…it was…"

He waited, strangely anxious to hear her description of their lovemaking at the cabin.

"It was ill-advised," she finished lamely.

"But good." He leaned closer, inhaling the scent of her. "So damned good."

When he would have kissed her, she turned her head from him. His kiss landed on her cheek, near her ear. He moved over a bit and nibbled on her earlobe.

She laid a hand against his chest. "Don't. I'm not going to make love with you again."

He could seduce her into it. He knew it from the way she sucked in a quick breath as he moved down her neck. He knew it from the tom-tom beat of her pulse against his lips. He knew it from the flush that swept up her neck and into her face.

She'd be rosy all over. He groaned at the picture

that formed in his mind. An intense hunger throbbed through him.

"But you want to," he murmured, drawing back from her.

"I don't."

"Don't lie to me," he said softly, letting the anger rise, hoping it would bury the passion. It didn't.

She flung her head back and glared at him.

For a second, he was overcome by her beauty. She seemed a delicate, ethereal thing, a magical being...like fairies and unicorns. Creatures of dreams and wild imaginings.

He sighed. Where he was concerned, she may as well be one of them. It was back to reality.

"Melanie wants to live here. I think she needs to get away from your mother. The job is still open. Take it."

"I...I can't."

The anger worked this time. He stood and paced the floor. "Why? What's so important that you can't leave a place where your daughter is unhappy and move here? Do you have a lover?"

She gasped.

"No, you don't," he said, answering his own question. During their interlude of passion, she'd reminded him of the virgin she'd been when they'd first made love. His body surged at the thought.

He tamped the wildness down. She didn't want him, not in any permanent way, no matter that they shared an irresistible need.

"Melanie isn't unhappy."

"She isn't happy, either. She needs..." He paused and frowned, as if considering if he should voice his opinion.

"Needs what?" Moriah asked, definitely resentful.

"She needs a man in her life...almost as much as you do."

She visibly recoiled from him.

He gave a disgusted snort. "Look at you—a warm, voluptuous woman, but you're afraid to share anything of yourself with anyone else. It couldn't be just because of our youthful affair. That was over almost before it began."

"Not for me," she said in a low, fierce tone.

She reminded him of an enraged lioness, all ruffled mane and hot fury. His own temper cooled, and the hunger flooded through him again. Heaven help him, but she was beautiful.

He sat down on the bed, his knees going rubbery at the thought of all the things he'd like to do to her.

Moriah closed her eyes against the helplessness that washed over her. How little he knew about it. Their brief affair, which he regarded as unimportant, had changed her life forever. One month and...

She shook her head helplessly. She had Melanie to think of. Her daughter was maybe not exactly unhappy, but dissatisfied. Kane would be good for the girl. He'd be a strong male figure in her life. She'd compare her young men to him and take only those who measured up. Which would be darned hard to do.

Rational; she had to be rational. She had very little money. She really needed the job. Besides, she couldn't leave until her father was found. And until she decided what to do about Melanie and Kane. Kane thought she was being selfish about Melanie, but he didn't know the half of it.

"Maybe I'll take the job," she began tentatively.

He looked so taken aback, it was almost comical...if she'd felt like laughing.

"Until I find my father. That should give you time to find someone else." A lightness stole into her, as if something deep inside wanted to assure her she'd made the right decision.

"And have to train her," he muttered.

"I'll stay for a week after you get someone new. It doesn't take a rocket scientist to run an office." She was aware of his thigh close to hers, with only a couple of inches and a sheet between them.

She glanced down, puzzled. There was only a sheet between them! A new fear ate into her. She was drawing a complete blank on the evening. How and when had she gotten into bed? And most important, *why?*

"I don't remember taking off my clothes," she said. "I don't remember anything."

"When you fell asleep in the chair, I carried you to bed—"

"Is this your bedroom?"

"Yes—"

"Why didn't I wake up? How could I sleep—" She broke off as the implications became clear. "That pill. It knocked me out."

He nodded. "It should have merely relaxed you, but you've obviously been doing too much. You're exhausted and stressed out. I recognized the symptoms. As a doctor, I thought you needed some rest, but it wasn't my intention to put you to sleep."

"I see," she said slowly. "But did you have to undress me to the bare...bones?" She gave him a troubled glance.

"I thought it best, yes. You were so tired, you should have slept until morning." One dark eyebrow rose quizzically. "Perhaps, instead of medicine, you need to go to church. They say confession is good for the soul. You seem to have a load on yours, if that nightmare was indicative of your dreams."

She couldn't meet his eyes after that last quip. Taking a deep breath, she pushed the sheet off her legs and swung them out of bed. "Where are my clothes? I'll go back to the cabin."

"Oh, hell," he said. "Stay. I'll leave if you're so damned uncomfortable with me in the house."

For a second, she was speechless. "Where would you go?"

"What do you care as long as I stay out of your life? You seem to resent every breath I take, not to mention what happens when I venture an opinion or show any concern about your family."

He stalked across the shining oak floor.

"Kane, wait," she called. She swung her legs into bed and covered them with the sheet.

He paused at the door.

"If you stayed, where would you sleep?"

"In the guest room. The bed wasn't made up in there when you went to sleep, so I brought you in here, then made up the other bed for myself. Only I went to sleep in the recliner in the study and never made it to bed."

She weighed the insanity of staying there against heading out into the night like a virgin chased by a werewolf. "Then, if you don't mind, I'd like to stay. It's late...."

The hall clock struck the hour at that moment. She counted the strokes. Ten...eleven...twelve.

Midnight.

"The witching hour," she said.

"Yes."

He stayed a moment longer, their eyes meeting and holding until neither could look away. She trembled as longing grew in her. It would take so little for her to fall in love with him all over again. She gasped at the thought.

With another oath, he walked out, closing the door behind him. She didn't get up and lock it, but she felt better. Any barrier was better than nothing. They were both too close to the edge. She didn't know where they would land if they went over.

* * *

Kane was already at work when she woke the next morning. After she washed and dressed, she went to the kitchen and found a note on the table telling her to help herself to whatever she wanted for breakfast.

She poured a cup of coffee, grabbed her purse and jacket and headed for her car. When she reached the cabin without seeing anyone she knew, or who knew her, she felt as if she'd scored a victory. If Lily Mae knew she'd spent the night at Kane's place, she'd spread the news far and wide. That would be all Moriah needed to complete her stay in Whitehorn.

After dressing in a skirt and blouse—her office gear— she returned to town, parked in the drive behind Kane's house and went into the office.

It was total chaos.

Patients were grumpily waiting their turn. Two mothers sat with screaming children on their knees. The nurse was trying to figure out someone's bill. The telephone was ringing like mad.

Moriah went into the small office, tossed her purse on a file cabinet and picked up the phone. "Dr. Hunter's office," she said.

The nurse looked at her in surprise.

She put her hand over the mouthpiece. "I'm the new secretary," she announced.

"Thank God." The nurse laid the bill down and walked out of the office. "Mrs. Rivers," she called.

A woman got up and walked down the narrow corridor after her. Moriah checked the appointment book, wrote the patient's name in it, hung up the phone, then turned to the waiting man with a calm smile. Four people lined up behind him, each looking to her for an answer to their particular problem. Moriah didn't have a minute to think the rest of the day.

At six, the last patient walked out the front door. The nurse locked it behind him and turned to Moriah. "You must be Moriah Gilmore. I've heard Lily Mae mention you. I'm Sandy Mason."

"As in Mason's Jewelry?"

"Married to the son. Clark runs things now. His dad comes down every day and makes sure he's doing it right." She grinned. "Allow me to compliment you. I've never seen anyone take over an office the way you did today and get it shipshape in no time."

"That's kind of you to say, but I'm afraid nothing is in order. It's just stacked in neat bunches so people will *think* there's a plan."

They laughed together.

Kane appeared at the door. "Dinner, anyone?" he asked. "My treat."

"I've got to go home, but thanks anyway," Sandy replied.

Kane looked at Moriah.

She hesitated, then nodded. They had to discuss the trip to Great Falls tomorrow and her employment—the hours and salary.

"I'll change and be with you in a minute." He disappeared up the stairs.

Moriah looked through the filing drawers while she waited. She needed to familiarize herself with the procedures used in this office. The files were a mess. Well, that certainly simplified the priority list. Straightening everything out came first.

"Ready?"

She closed the file cabinet and looked around. Kane had changed to a casual outfit. He looked frighteningly handsome in black boots and jeans with a red flannel shirt open over a white T-shirt. "Yes," she murmured.

"Do you want to go to the cabin and change first?" He locked the door behind them and led the way to his car.

"Where are we going?"

"There's a place south of town on Highway 191 that has the best fried shrimp in the state. It's relatively new. I thought you might enjoy going there."

"Is it very far? I have to get some things together for the trip to Great Falls—"

"You won't need anything. The trip doesn't take more than an hour at the most by plane."

"Yes, but I think I should drive my car and stay—"

He whipped around so fast that she nearly walked into him. "I thought you were taking the job, that you were moving here."

"Well, I have to do something with my furniture and close the apartment." She couldn't afford to keep the place if she wasn't using it. She would put her furniture in storage until she returned to the city. "I thought that, while Melanie was out of school, she and I could get all that done, then drive down on Tuesday."

She rubbed her forehead. There were so many things to do. Maybe moving to Whitehorn wasn't such a good idea.

"I know some people there. We can get it done in a day."

"A day?"

"Sure." He smiled. "You can get anything done if you know the right people. Would you rather eat at the Hip Hop? It's closer than the other place."

"Yes, that would be fine." She walked along the street with him, not sure what she'd consented to, but feeling like she'd committed herself to some undefined future.

At the café, he told Lily Mae that Moriah was moving back to town...and that she was his new secretary.

Moriah felt the speculation in the widow's eyes and in

the glances of the people around them who'd heard the announcement.

"It's temporary," she said quickly. "Just until I find my father." She looked at Kane defiantly. She wasn't going to be stampeded into another mistake because of him.

However, when they returned to the office, she called her old boss and told him she wouldn't be back. Her hand trembled when she hung up. A brief, wild excitement beat through her. What was her future now? She hadn't a clue.

Nine

Melanie was at the airport when Moriah and Kane arrived on Saturday at nine. "Jessy's mom dropped me off. They were going shopping," she explained. "You don't mind that I came out to meet you, do you?"

Moriah noticed her daughter asked this of Kane, not her, but she spoke before he could. "No, it's fine."

"Did you talk to Grandma?" Melanie asked.

"Not yet. I'm going to see her before we leave." She and her mother had had one confrontation when she'd taken Melanie and moved out. There would be another today.

She sighed, which earned her a glance from Kane as they went to the rental-car counter. They hadn't talked much on the trip. Melanie's bright chatter helped cover the silence at present.

Soon they were on their way. At the apartment, Kane put in a call to a moving company. He arranged for her furniture to be put in storage. Yes, they could come out Monday, and yes, they'd get the key from the landlord.

Moriah called the apartment manager, who agreed to let the movers in and to take care of everything else. By noon, everything was done. She had Kane drop her off at her mother's shop while he and Melanie went to lunch. She would take a cab to the airport and meet them there, she told him.

"Do you want me to come with you?" he asked quietly.

She shook her head. "I can fight my own battles," she said grimly.

"Give her hell." He gave her an encouraging smile that glowed in her heart long after he and Melanie—who had a hand over her mouth to stifle her laughter—drove off.

Moriah entered the discount store and went into the office without knocking. Her mother glanced up with a frown at being disturbed, then looked surprised...and uneasy.

"I have some questions to ask you," Moriah said.

She closed the door.

Moriah was oddly calm as she settled in the cab for the ride to the airport. The discussion with her mother hadn't taken long, but it had proved illuminating.

When Moriah had confronted her with Kane's disclosures about the calls and letters, Joleen didn't deny her interference, but had insisted she'd acted in the best interests of all concerned. She was furious that her daughter would question her motives.

"What about the letters from my father?" Moriah had asked. "Was making me think he had totally abandoned me in my best interests? Or Melanie's, to never know her grandfather?"

Joleen had had the grace to look ashamed for a moment. Then she'd flown into a rage against Homer and White-horn and all the man and the town had stood for. They'd held her back, none of them believing she was capable of running her own business. She'd schemed and planned for years to show them. And she had.

Moriah had looked at the office and realized it represented her mother's world. The store was the most important thing in her life. With that had come other realizations.

Her mother was possessive, but not loving. She'd used Moriah as an excuse to do what she'd wanted to for years—leave Whitehorn. She'd also used Moriah as cheap labor in starting the store, but she'd never offered her a part of it.

Knowing her mother would never admit her actions had been anything other than for her family's sake, Moriah had stood and walked to the door. An infinite sadness had washed over her. They could have been friends, but Joleen had never seen that.

Her mother needed no one. She had her heart's desire.

Moriah watched the passing scenes from the cab window without really seeing them. The whole picture of her past had fallen into place that afternoon. It was a painful one.

Thinking she'd been abandoned by the men in her life, Moriah had been grateful for her mother's help and advice. In return, she'd worked hard to make the dress shop a success…for free.

For those years of work, she'd received nothing when she'd moved out and started a life of her own, nothing but Joleen's fury.

She'd trusted her mother, had believed her lies about Kane and her father, but it had been Joleen who had used her, not Kane.

It was hard to accept. Considering her own love for Melanie, Moriah had never questioned her mother's motives.

"Why did you marry Father?" Moriah asked before she left.

"I was born on a hard-scrabble farm in the hills. You should try that if you want to know what real work is like. Your father came along. He was fun, charming and full of promises, which he didn't keep once I married him."

Moriah had never known the depths of her mother's bitterness and anger at Homer. "He didn't live up to your ambitions," she said slowly. "He had his own dreams."

"He was a fool. Look at his life, then look at mine and tell me who failed and who succeeded."

Moriah had eyed her mother's fashionable dress, her coiffed hair and smooth makeup. Joleen looked expensive and important. The two things she wanted in life, Moriah realized.

"I hope you enjoy your riches," she'd said. She'd opened the door. "Melanie and I are moving to Whitehorn. I don't think we'll be back." Even if she left Whitehorn later, she wouldn't want to be near Joleen, not now and not for the foreseeable future. She didn't think she could forgive her.

"You're making a mistake," Joleen informed her.

"Maybe, but it'll be made without lies and subterfuge." Except for the lie to Kane and Melanie about their relationship. She didn't know how to make that right.

"Don't come running back here expecting me to take you in when you get in trouble again."

Moriah's face had flamed, but she'd managed to retain her dignity. "I won't." She'd paused, then realized there was nothing left to say. "Goodbye, Mother," she'd murmured, walking out.

Kane was loading supplies into the plane when Moriah arrived. Melanie was helping. He left the teenager at it and came across the tarmac. "You okay?" His gaze searched over her as if looking for visible wounds.

"Yes." Moriah gazed at him, feeling dazed and cut off from reality. "I've made so many mistakes."

"We'll talk about it later."

"My father—" She couldn't go on.

"We'll find him. Come on, get in." He led her to the plane and helped her inside. She felt like an invalid.

He was being kind. He felt sorry for her for being such a fool all these years. She felt sorry for herself, for the young girl who'd given her love and trust to the wrong person. The problem was she wasn't sure who the right person was. She no longer trusted her own judgment.

They were soon airborne. Moriah's doubts about her decision, now that it was irreversible, escalated with each mile. It was so hard to know if this was the right thing.

Melanie had no doubts. "I can't wait to get there. Where shall we stay?" she asked, peering around the front seat, where Moriah had insisted she sit, to look at her mother, her eyes so bright and eager for this new life.

Moriah swallowed hard. If they stayed in Whitehorn, if anyone noticed Melanie's eyes had a dark green circle at the outer edge of the iris like Kane's, what would she say?

"At the cabin," she answered.

Melanie looked distressed. "Oh, but that's so far from town. The ranch where Keith works is in the opposite direction."

The complaint hardly registered in Moriah's conscious mind. Several truths were becoming clear to her. If they stayed, she would have to tell Kane about his daughter…before someone like Lily Mae figured it out and blurted it all over town.

But not now. She didn't think she could take any more

confrontations in the immediate future. Later, when she felt more secure, when things settled down, she would tell him.

She *would*, she promised him silently. When life didn't seem so hard. When her way was clearer.

"Your first concern isn't to see Keith, is it?" Kane asked Melanie pointedly. "Finding your grandfather—isn't that the first priority?"

"Oh…oh, yes. Of course it is." Melanie sighed, then smiled at Kane. "I sounded like a selfish brat, didn't I?"

"Just a tad," he admitted, giving her a wry smile in return.

Melanie turned toward the back once more. "I'm sorry, Mom. I know you're worried about your dad and the move and everything."

"That's okay."

"We'll find him soon," Melanie said with great assurance.

Moriah hoped so. She felt time was running out and that something terrible was going to happen. She just didn't know what it was or when it would occur.

Melanie looked around the cabin. "We're going to stay here—with both of us in one room?" She obviously couldn't believe this was her mom's intention.

"This is it," Moriah confirmed as cheerfully as she could. She set her suitcase and box by the bunk she'd been using. "We need to bring in the groceries."

Melanie put her things by the other bunk and went out to the car to help with their supplies. She was quiet.

Moriah felt defensive regarding the cabin. She also felt guilty for bringing Melanie to this sparse environment, even though the girl had wanted to come.

Perhaps she should have explained where they were going to stay until she found out what apartments cost in

Whitehorn, assuming there were any and how much she could afford to pay.

She and Kane hadn't discussed her salary, and now she felt too embarrassed to ask. How did she get herself into such situations?

Her mother would have been glad to answer that.

For the first time in twenty-four hours, Moriah was able to smile, although it was wry and brief. After Kane dropped them off at her car yesterday, she and Melanie had spent the night in town, then stopped by the grocery on their way to the cabin.

She picked up two bags of canned goods and headed back inside. It was midafternoon. Soon it would be time for supper, then bed.

"But how will we get calls? There's no telephone in the cabin," Melanie reminded her, giving her mother a look of tragic disbelief that they were to live this Spartan life.

"I know," Moriah said, taking a breath and preparing for a barrage of questions about how soon they'd be getting one.

Melanie said nothing.

Moriah turned to observe her daughter. She caught a look of disappointment and despair on her face before Melanie realized she was being watched. Then she smiled as if she were the happiest person in the world.

Moriah went back to her task. She tried not to think of the charming house in town where Kane lived. She had deprived her daughter of that life.

Dear God, please let me find my father before it snows, she pleaded desperately, and then let me find another job and leave here before Melanie finds out the truth....

What would happen in that case, Moriah couldn't even begin to guess. And Kane—what would he do? They would both hate her....

For a moment, she thought she might come apart at the seams, then she gathered her courage and said with a lightness she didn't feel, "Shall we go on a hike before we start dinner?"

"Sure." Melanie came over and helped stack the groceries on the wall shelves. "When will we go to town? I need to call Keith and tell him I'm here."

"When we get back from the hike?" Moriah suggested, accepting the inevitable. "In fact, we can eat at the café. There's a pay phone outside. You can call Keith from there."

An hour after they returned to the cabin from town, Keith Colson drove up. He and Melanie sat in his truck and talked until ten o'clock, while Moriah stayed inside the cabin and read.

On Monday Moriah got Melanie registered and in classes, then reported for work a little after nine. The office was full.

"Thank God you're here," Sandy Mason said to her. She handed Moriah a stack of charts. "These are to be filed. We opened early this morning. The flu bug is going around."

It was, and with a vengeance.

By noon, the appointment schedule was hopelessly behind, as more and more patients dropped in to get something for their aches and fevers. Moriah called the Hip Hop and asked them to send over food for the three of them.

She ate with one hand and answered the phone with the other. Once, looking up, she spotted Kane watching her from the open door of his office. He flicked her a pensive smile. It gave her an odd, tingly feeling inside, sort of warm, sort of achy.

Melanie came by after school. Moriah closed the sliding glass panel between her office and the waiting room and took a fifteen-minute break to talk to her daughter.

Kane stopped by the office. "Hello, Melanie, how did the first day go?"

"Great. I've been put into the calculus class and I've already got a job on the school paper." She smiled.

"Hmm, are you going to be a doctor, a news correspondent or a famous mathematician?" he asked, his teasing gentle, his interest sincere.

She wrinkled her nose in a charming grimace. "It's hard to decide. There are so many options."

"Yes, we all have to make choices." His dark gaze flicked to Moriah, making her feel the impact of every decision she'd made in the past sixteen years.

"Well, I have homework to do. Oh, by the way, I need a job after school to help pay for my Christmas dress. Can you use an extra file clerk or something?" she asked Kane.

"I sure can. My office is a mess. I'll pay you to get it in order. Under your mother's supervision, of course. She's the office manager and has the final word."

Kane and Melanie turned to Moriah. Flustered, she nodded and murmured, "Yes, of course. There is a lot to do. I mean, the filing, the office…" She floundered as she realized she was about to insult his and the nurse's efforts at order.

"Exactly," Kane said dryly. He spoke to Melanie. "You're hired," he said, and named a generous hourly wage.

"Wow," Melanie exclaimed. She gave her mother a big grin. "I asked Keith if the school sponsored a dance at the end of the semester. He said yes…and asked me to be his date."

Moriah had to smile as Melanie gave in to inner excitement and threw her arms around her neck for a spine-snapping hug. She hugged her daughter back and wished this moment could last forever.

When Melanie released her, Moriah glanced up at Kane. She was startled to witness an expression of… yearning? loneliness?…on his handsome face. Then it was gone.

He smiled and gestured at the desk stacked high with work. "You're handling the office very well," he said, complimenting her. "Several patients have commented on your calm efficiency and your charming personality."

"I told you Mom was great," Melanie reminded him.

"So you did." He looked at Moriah for another second, as if trying to understand something about her that eluded him.

"Well, we'd better get back to work," she said, nervous under his scrutiny, yet feeling the familiar tingles his nearness caused.

"One more thing—I'm having a cellular phone delivered today. It's for you, since you don't have one at the cabin and it costs too much to run a line out there."

Moriah tried to protest.

"As part of my staff, you'll have to be available in case of an emergency. I may need to get hold of you." He turned back to Melanie. "You may use my study for your homework. That takes priority over the filing. If your grades drop, I'll fire you."

"Yes, sir!" Melanie gave him an impudent salute.

He smiled and returned her salute. "Drinks and snacks are in the refrigerator, if you're hungry when you get in from school. Help yourself. You, too," he said to Moriah. "Have we covered all the bases?"

She nodded, feeling dazed by his acceptance of them in his life. Melanie gathered her books and went across the hall to his private quarters.

Kane looked at her. "You didn't tell me how it went with your mother. Are you all right?"

His concern reached right inside her and set a chord to humming. "Yes. Let's just say we agreed to disagree on our basic view of life and leave it at that."

After a second of delving into her eyes, he returned her smile, which she hoped looked saucy and insouciant. "Right." He went to his next patient.

Moriah sat there for a moment, comforted by his support and sympathy...by his caring.

On Tuesday, Moriah and Sandy had the office to themselves while Kane attended the clinic at the reservation. On Wednesday, he took a half day off and went on some mysterious errand of his own. She heard him on the telephone before he left. He was ordering lumber.

The rest of the week was so busy, she caught only glimpses of him coming and going from the examining rooms or dashing over to the hospital. He and Melanie didn't see each other at all.

When Melanie arrived at the office from school on Friday, Moriah decided they should do something about Kane's office. It was a mess, and he was out again, called to the hospital for an emergency surgery. Moriah had rescheduled his appointments.

"What should we do first?" Melanie asked, looking doubtful about sorting through the stacks of debris.

"Put all the books in the bookcases," Moriah directed. She pointed out the different types of medical books on the shelves and had Melanie put them in order, including the volumes stacked around the room on various surfaces.

By five, all the books were neatly shelved and all the papers were sorted into piles for filing or whatever.

"Let's clean the furniture now that we can see it," Melanie suggested. She eyed the papers. "I'll do it while you take care of those, if you'd like."

"Good idea." Moriah checked Kane's desk drawers, then made up file folders for the papers that stayed and took the rest to her office. She put items needing Kane's "keep or toss" decision in the In basket on his desk with a note to that effect.

At six, Moriah got up off her knees in front of the file cabinet, groaned and stretched her back carefully.

"Mom, come look," Melanie called.

She went to Kane's office. The furniture gleamed like new. The straggly philodendron was neatly clipped, dusted and watered. Melanie had placed it on the oak credenza by the window. Recently issued medical journals were stacked on either side of the plant.

"It looks wonderful," Moriah said, complimenting Melanie.

"I agree," a baritone voice said behind her.

Moriah looked over her shoulder. Kane propped his hands on the doorjamb and peered over her head at the shining office. He was close enough that she inhaled the warm, masculine scent of him when she breathed and felt his body heat on her back.

"Such labor deserves a reward. How about dinner on me?"

"Hurray!" Melanie cheered. She rubbed her back. "Boy, I'm tired. You must be dead, Mom. You've worked at this all day."

Kane dropped his hands to Moriah's shoulders. He massaged the tense, achy muscles with great skill. It reminded her of the night in his kitchen. He'd rubbed her neck and forehead then. After giving her a knockout pill. Then he'd undressed her and put her to bed, as if she were a kid.

She tried to be indignant about that, but she didn't have the energy. Remembering the way he'd looked at her, she knew he didn't think of her as a child.

"Thanks for all your work," he murmured close to her ear. "This was above and beyond the call of duty. I'll have to give you a raise."

"Speaking of raises, you haven't told me how much I'm going to make," she ventured, moving from the door and his nearness. She flicked an imaginary piece of dust from the desk.

He told her.

It was more than she'd made in Great Falls. She was sure it was more than the going rate in a small town like Whitehorn.

"That's too much," she protested. She didn't want anyone finding out her salary to think he was paying for more than secretarial help from her.

His jaw tightened stubbornly. "Not for an office manager."

"Who am I managing?" she demanded. "Myself?"

"And Melanie for now," he asserted coolly. "Later, we might need to add a full-time file clerk."

They fought a visual duel while Melanie glanced from her to Kane and back, puzzled at the tension between them. Moriah sighed and backed off. "We'd better go," she told Melanie.

"Yeah," Kane agreed. "The café will be sold out of the specials if we don't get there soon."

Melanie fell into step beside Kane. Moriah brought up the rear. She listened to their conversation on the way to the café.

"I'll be able to get my dress out in a month." Melanie pointed to the boutique as they passed. "Did you see it? It's just the most beautiful thing ever!"

When they entered the café, Melanie caught her breath. "There's Keith," she whispered in an aside.

Kane spoke to the man and woman at the table with the

cowboy, then introduced Moriah and Melanie to Luke and Maris Rivers and their son. Moriah remembered the woman from her visit to the office earlier that week.

Moriah didn't mention that fact when she said hello. A visit to the doctor's office was confidential.

Both Luke and Maris were tanned and fit looking. When she found out they raised cutting horses, she figured they must spend a lot of time outdoors. Maris was very pretty, a no-nonsense type of woman who didn't wear makeup and probably never had to diet. Their son, Clay, was a little over a year old and looked a lot like his father.

Keith was cut from the same mold, a rawhide-tough, lanky young man who looked older than his years. They were celebrating his birthday, it turned out. He was nineteen.

A year older than Kane had been when he'd come home from college for Christmas vacation. Seeing the exchange of glances between her daughter and the young man, Moriah experienced a sinking in the vicinity of her heart. She knew how compelling love could be.

The Rivers family made room at the table for the new-comers. The talk was merry during the meal. Moriah learned a lot about horses as Melanie, with her inquisitive mind, asked a thousand-and-one questions.

Sitting there between Kane and Melanie, chatting with Keith and the other couple, Moriah had a sense of home-coming, as if she belonged. She was intensely aware of Kane at her side—almost like a husband, a traitorous part of her mind whispered.

But he wasn't.

It was probably a good thing their paths rarely crossed at the office, she admitted. When he was near, her mind went into a trance that was both sensual and filled with yearning.

When they were finished, and everyone had eaten a slice of Keith's birthday cake—including Clay, who obviously adored his "big brother"—the young man cleared his throat. "I have my truck. Would it be okay if I took Melanie home?"

All eyes focused on Moriah. It was such an innocent request, delivered with courage in front of four adults. She consented.

Melanie smiled happily. Keith grinned, too. His ears turned pink. Maris gave Moriah an approving glance. She obviously thought Keith was pretty special.

"Have you heard any more on your father?" Luke asked.

"No. I'm thinking of hiring someone with tracking dogs," she said, mentioning this thought aloud for the first time.

Kane approved. "That's a good idea."

"Keith has one of the best trackers in the county," Luke told her. He turned to the cowboy. "What do you think about taking Blackie for a trial run? You can have the weekend off. With pay," he added, smiling.

"Sure," Keith said.

"Oh, that would be wonderful," Melanie exclaimed. "Wouldn't it be neat if you found my grandfather?" She gazed at him as if he were three or four superheroes rolled into one.

Keith's ears turned bright red this time, but there was a gleam of pride on his face as he looked at the girl, his dark blue eyes adoring. He was already in love with Melanie.

Moriah's heart ached for him. Had she ever been that young and in love? Oh, yes, she certainly had.

"I have to go," she said rather abruptly. "It was nice meeting you." She touched her daughter's shoulder. "I'll see you at the cabin in an hour."

"An hour?" Melanie questioned. "It's Friday night. There's no school tomorrow."

"I'll have her home by ten," Keith promised. "We'll take Blackie out about seven in the morning, if that's all right."

"Yes, thanks." She said farewell to the couple.

Kane paid their bill and left, too, escorting her to her car behind his office. "I'll follow you home."

"There's no need for you to drive out, then back."

He smiled wryly and walked off without another word. She quickly climbed in and started the engine. When she pulled out onto the street, Kane's ute fell in behind her. He stayed with her all the way to the cabin drive. There he turned around and headed back toward the main road.

Standing on the porch a moment later, she watched a fuzzy white cloud drift across the moon and let herself really think of Kane instead of avoiding the subject as she'd done all week.

An acute awareness existed between them. It didn't matter that they avoided each other. The attraction lingered in the air like the low notes of a bass viol, low and throbbing, felt more than heard, long after they'd spoken or glanced at each other.

Watching him with his patients didn't help, either. He was remarkable with them—calm and caring, with a ready smile and word of encouragement. No wonder they all loved him. She swallowed hard as emotion rose in her.

All the things she'd loved in him years ago were fulfilled in the man. He'd achieved his goals. His vision included a better life for his people on the reservation and for the town as well.

The irony of the situation struck her. Her dreams of working with him were also fulfilled, but in a way she'd never imagined—as his employee, not his wife.

A darkness settled on her spirit. He'd once told her she

was the light of his soul, but that was so long ago, it seemed another lifetime. He didn't think that now. Besides, there was another factor—Lori Bains, the woman who was obviously perfect for him.

Troubled, Moriah went inside and prepared for bed, afraid of the feelings she couldn't control, afraid of falling in love with him—with the man, not the boy she'd once known and loved, but Kane, as he was now, mature and serious and wonderful.

Keith arrived promptly at seven the next morning. He had a big black dog with him that was aloof until Melanie dropped to her knees, scratched her ears and crooned over her. Then she melted in a puddle of adoration at her feet.

Moriah returned Keith's wry grin. Neither man nor beast was immune to Melanie's charm.

In a few minutes, the youngsters—after letting Blackie sniff a shirt belonging to Homer—were off on the trail with bag lunches and snacks to get them through the day.

Moriah declined to accompany them, since she'd already been over the nearby trails more than once. She watched the couple and the dog bound out of sight, her feelings toward them tender.

Going inside, she cleaned the cabin and straightened her father's books and journals. Later, she heard a vehicle in the clearing. She went outside.

Kane parked his sports ute and climbed out. He was dressed in jeans and boots, a long-sleeved green-and-red plaid shirt and a red fleece vest. He wore a gray Stetson that showed much wear.

He was slender hipped and tight muscled, a sleek, powerful man of perfect proportions in her eyes. When she stepped onto the porch, he slammed the ute door and crossed the sparse grass.

"Did Keith arrive?"

"Yes. He and Melanie and Blackie have already left. You're too late."

He shook his head. "I came to see you." He stopped on the step just below where she stood, their eyes on the same level. She stared into his, at the green flecks in the valleys, the brown striations radiating through the irises, the dark green circle at the outer edges.

A low thud like waves crashing on a rocky shore hit her ears. She realized it was the sound of her pounding heart and pressed a hand to her chest to still the erratic beat. An impulse to move forward one tiny step goaded her beyond reason. If she did, she'd be in his arms.

"Oh? Why?" She tried for nonchalance, but her voice came out reedy and breathless instead.

"I figured you needed a break. The past week has been pretty frantic at the office." He gestured toward his ute. "We could go for a ride."

Words of refusal rose swiftly to her lips.

"I thought we'd take the logging roads and see if we spotted anything that might lead us to Homer."

Put that way, she couldn't think of a reason to refuse. "I need to change—"

"You look fine," he told her.

Her hair was in a French braid that Melanie had done for her after breakfast. Her slacks and shirt were old and faded from many washings. She wore no makeup. Not that it mattered. The purpose of the trip was to look for her father. It wasn't a date with the town's favorite bachelor.

"I'll change my shoes."

He nodded and sat on the porch to wait. She ran inside the cabin, kicked off her loafers and slipped into socks and hiking shoes, in case they decided to search along a trail.

After leaving a note for Melanie, she rejoined Kane on

the porch. He walked her to the ute, but let her get in by herself. She was relieved.

They drove along the old Baxter road until it ended in a circular clearing. From there, Kane followed a rough logging road that had once divided the Baxter ranch from the prosperous Kincaid spread. She kept a sharp eye out for signs of Homer, but saw nothing to indicate he'd come that way.

Shortly after noon, they bounced out of the trees onto a graveled ranch road. "Where are we?" she asked.

"On the reservation. This used to be grazed by the Kincaids, until the lease expired. The tribe uses it to raise beefalo."

"I remember there was a fight about the lease. I read about it in the papers. The Kincaid attorney tried to claim squatter's rights or something like that."

"Yeah." Kane smiled. "The Indians won this time."

She smiled, too, glad that justice had prevailed. When Kane turned onto a county road, she wondered if they were going to the tribal headquarters. At the main road that ran by the entrance to the reservation, he turned right instead of left.

A few minutes after that, he turned right again into a lane covered with pine needles. A quarter mile beyond that, he pulled up in front of a partially built house and turned off the engine.

"Would you like some lunch?" he asked.

She nodded, somewhat hesitantly.

Kane watched her reaction carefully. She was startled by his invitation, but he saw no signs of fear in her. Looking into those soft brown eyes, he found he wanted to reach for her and kiss her until she closed them and melted against him. He didn't.

Instead, he got out of the ute and motioned for her to

follow him to the house. This was part of his plan—to let her get to know him again, to give them some time alone.

It was impossible to hold a private discussion at the office. The demands on his time wouldn't allow it.

Neither would his patients, he reflected sardonically. They flocked to Moriah like ducklings to their mama, asking advice, expecting her to straighten out their appointments, their insurance, their bills and anything else that arose. She was a miracle of quiet efficiency.

A miracle in his life? Once he had thought so, but the intervening years had taught him differently. No, bringing her here was a logical decision. He was following Lori's advice.

"Whose house is this?" she asked, studying it with a bright, curious expression.

"Mine. I'm building it in my spare time," he explained when she cast an inquisitive glance at him.

"Oh," she murmured, obviously surprised. "I heard you ordering lumber one day."

"Come on in," he invited, leading the way. "The outside is basically finished. I'm working on the inside now."

The floors and wall studs were in, but not the wallboards. He found he was curiously anxious about her opinion when he showed her the layout. "The master suite is downstairs," he said. He led the way up the steps. "There are four rooms on the second floor for guests...or for children."

"Children," she echoed, a flush invading her cheeks.

For a moment, he thought he saw intense sadness in her eyes, then she smiled and glanced around. "It'll be a lovely home when you finish."

"Yes." He leaned against the framing and observed her closely. Her fingers disclosed a slight tremor when she brushed a strand of hair out of her eyes and tucked it into the long braid hanging down her back.

She looked about seventeen—young and full of hope and terribly vulnerable. It did something to his insides....

He cursed silently. She wasn't a sweet innocent. She was the woman who had said she loved him, but who had doubted his love at the first obstacle, even knowing how her mother had disliked him.

But there was passion between them. Was that enough to build a relationship on? That's what he wanted to find out.

"I suppose..." she began, then stopped.

The breeze through the open window brought her scent to him. An ache speared into his groin as desire at once went to flash point. "Yes?" he said, his voice dropping to a husky level.

"Has Lori picked out the colors yet?" She smiled brightly, but didn't look at him.

He could feel his pulse pounding through his body, hot and urgent. He almost forgot the question as his gaze was drawn to her slender outline in front of the window. "No," he finally said. "Lori and I...we're not seeing each other anymore."

The words sounded stark. Color flared in Moriah's face, then receded, leaving her delicately pale. She toyed with a button on her shirt. He wanted to replace her hands with his, to unfasten the buttons one by one and watch her silky flesh become visible.

"I'm sorry." Her voice was almost a whisper. "Was it because of—of me and...what happened between us?" Her teeth sank into her bottom lip, which trembled ever so slightly.

"Partly," he admitted. "She and I were friends, not lovers. It was time to go on or end it."

He thought of how it would feel to run his tongue over that tortured lip, to taste the honeyed warmth of her mouth. He moved toward her, unable to resist.

Her eyes met his. A startled expression flashed through them before she turned and rushed for the steps. "This will be lovely," she said, going downstairs. "We'd better be going."

He followed and headed her off before she reached the door. "I have lunch in the kitchen." He took her elbow and guided her down the short hallway and into the kitchen, which was the only room with walls and furnishings. It was almost finished.

Moriah gasped with delight. The colors were green and white, with shades of mauve in accent pieces. A skylight over the cooking area brightened the whole room. A table made of oak held place settings for two. In a daze, she took the seat he indicated.

The wide bay window framed a panoramic view of the mountains to the west. She could see cattle grazing on the lush pastures in the far reaches of the valley, and higher up, sheep gamboled on the steeper terraces. The golden stubble of wheat straw beckoned like treasure laid out for the taking.

His words rang through her head. He wasn't seeing Lori. They'd been friends, not lovers. She was afraid to think what it might mean...or why he'd brought *her* to his house.

"What about your house in town?" she asked, seeking a safe subject. "What will you do with it when you finish this one?"

"Keep it for my office. Perhaps rent out the other rooms. It would be best to have someone in the building."

"Oh, yes, of course."

He removed bowls from the modern side-by-side refrigerator and filled their plates with Chinese chicken salad. He added a wooden bowl of bread sticks and glasses of iced tea before taking the chair opposite her.

"This will be my home, where I'll raise my family."

She set the glass of tea down without taking a sip. "Your family," she repeated.

"Yes." He bit off the end of a bread stick and chewed thoughtfully, his eyes on her, but his gaze on some inner vision that only he could see. "I want children, at least two, maybe more. I'll have to discuss that with my wife."

"I see." Her throat felt raw and aching.

His eyes narrowed as he looked at her. "You're lucky to have Melanie. She's a delight. You did a good job of raising her."

Tell him. Tell him now.

She opened her mouth, but the only words that came out were a wan, "Thank you."

He talked of his plans for the house and the acres he owned, which numbered several hundred. He'd planted trees each spring for the past five years, until this year, when he'd started the house.

She managed to choke down the food. When the meal was over, she helped him with the dishes, standing beside him at the shiny white sink and drying the plates after he laid them on the rack.

The scene was too domestic. It invoked too many longings for things she'd dreamed of for years—having a home of her own, sharing it with a husband who loved her with all his heart as she would love him, raising their children together.

She sensed the passing of time as if her life were on fast-forward. She was thirty-four. If she were to have more children, it should be soon.

Kane loves babies.

Yes, she could see that. He was building this house for his family. Tears clogged her throat. She had to tell him about his daughter. God help her, she had to....

"Moriah," he murmured, suddenly close. His hands settled on her shoulders. He tossed the dish towel on the counter. He looked grimly determined, almost angry as he leaned over her. "I've been wanting to do this for hours."

His lips settled on hers, warm and firm and sensuous. She couldn't breathe, then she did, inhaling the faint scent of after-shave lotion on his skin. It was so wonderful, she went dizzy.

She grasped the lapels of the red fleecy vest and held on as his tongue initiated a foray into her mouth. The world disappeared under the onslaught of his passion, and she was helpless to fight him or her own tumultuous feelings.

He moved his hands over her, rubbing along her back, over her hips, then lifting her against him and fitting them together like two pieces of a puzzle, two halves of a whole.

Oh, yes, she thought. He was part of her. And she of him. She loved him...loved him...loved him.

The phrase beat over and over through her mind, a litany of hot desire and need. *Her love...her only love...*

"Kane," she whispered, "we have to talk."

"No." He shook his head, kissing along her neck, opening buttons as he went lower on her chest. "Talk never gets us anywhere. This is how we communicate best."

He unhooked her bra with a quick gesture, then pushed it up while his mouth went unerringly to one taut nipple. She closed her eyes as pure ecstasy flowed through her, over her, around her. She couldn't think...but she had to.

With a thousand caresses of his mouth and hands, he showed her his pleasure in her. He was right. They had this. It had to be more than the means of satisfying a driving hunger.

"Kane...when you touch me...I can't think," she confessed, pulling him closer, feeling his hand close over one breast and repeat the actions his mouth performed on the other.

He raised his head and stared into her eyes with a burning regard. "How could you share *this* with me, then go to the arms of another man and have his child within a year?" he demanded, shocking her with the tortured pain in his eyes. "Did his touch please you as much as mine? Did you give those sharp little cries of pleasure that drive a man right over the edge?"

"No," she protested. "There's so much you don't understand—"

His lips cut her off as he kissed her quick and hard before speaking. "I've changed my mind. I don't want to know. The past is gone. Let it die. There's only now, this moment, you, me...."

Before she could answer, he kissed her again, devouring her in the hot need that sprang up like wildflowers when the spring rains fell on the meadows in the valley. He caressed her with his tongue, with his hands, with his body, until all thoughts fled.

His hands went to her jeans and tugged the snap open. He slipped them and her briefs over her hips. It wasn't until he lifted her to the tiled counter that she realized his intent. He was going to make love to her there, at that moment.

"Kane, no, we can't," she panted, wanting him more than air, but knowing she couldn't accept the gift of pleasure from him at this moment. "Passion isn't enough—"

He stiffened in her arms, then lifted his head from where he'd been planting wet, thrilling kisses along her neck. The passionate intensity left his eyes, and his face stilled until he looked as if he'd been carved out of sandstone.

"You're right," he said, his voice as devoid of passion as it had been filled with it a moment ago. "Passion wasn't enough before. Why did I think it would be this time?"

He lifted her down, then stepped back as if he couldn't bear to touch her. She felt like weeping at the loss, but she knew they had to talk.

"About Melanie," she said, adjusting her clothing.

He spun from her and crossed the room in long, angry strides. "Not now. I don't want to hear about her now." He glanced at his watch. "I'll take you home. I have to be at the hospital in an hour."

Looking at his face, she realized he wasn't ready to listen to anything she had to say. He was angry with her, but she wasn't sure why. She thought she'd hurt him, but she wasn't sure how.

But there was their daughter. Before they could go forward, she knew they had to clear the past. "Please," she said.

He turned a closed countenance to her, but before she could blurt out the truth, a beeper shattered the silence between them. Kane withdrew a cellular phone from his pocket and answered. "Just a moment," he said. He held it out to Moriah. "It's for you."

When she answered, she heard Melanie's excited voice on the other end. She listened, her heart speeding up at the news, then hung up and handed the phone back to Kane. He folded it and stuck it in his pocket.

"Melanie and Keith found a backpack," she told him, dazed by the news. "There was a journal inside. They think it belongs to my father. She called the sheriff. He's going to organize a mounted rescue team. I have to go."

"Of course." He led the way outside, locked up behind them, then headed for Homer's place.

Ten

Kane sipped from the hot mug of rosehip tea and watched Winona Cobbs. In her hands, she held a shirt of Homer's.

The old prospector had been missing five weeks. The search-and-rescue team had worked the woods and scrub for a half mile around the place where the backpack had been found. No luck.

Other than the old journal, there wasn't any evidence that the backpack belonged to Homer, no name or anything in it, so it could have been a false lead.

That's why he was here.

Winona, with her psychic ability, had given valuable insights into cases in the past. Just last year, she'd picked up the vibes of a tourist's child who'd wandered away from a roadside picnic and gotten lost. She'd called the sheriff's office and told Judd where the kid was before he'd even gotten the report that the boy was missing. She might be able to give them a clue…or at least tell them if the old codger was still alive.

Kane shifted restlessly. He was tired of the whole thing, of the search for someone who probably didn't want to be found, of feeling guilty for something that had happened years ago, of Moriah tensing up every time he came near and continually seeming to live on the edge, now more than ever.

And yet, there had been those moments of incredible sweetness between them. He wanted her…as the woman in his life. Did he love her? He felt a harsh tightening inside. Ah, God…

Winona opened her eyes and gazed at him. He realized she was locked in to some inner vision.

"There are things you will discover," she said at last. "You must act with great wisdom or lose something close to your heart. Don't let anger control your actions. Guard your words."

He noticed her hands clench on the shirt. Was she talking about him or referring to Homer?

The psychic sighed, then laid the shirt aside. "I don't think Homer is dead," she said, her eyes narrowed as if focused on a distant place. "I see him in a cave."

"A cave?" Kane set the mug on the table and leaned forward. "He usually explores the old mines in the mountains. Do you think the cave might be a mine shaft?"

"Yes, it could be." She frowned. "But there's a gate… with a padlock on it. And the two-faced woman."

"What?" Chills slid along his neck at the portentous words.

"I've seen her before. Wait, something is coming.…" Winona closed her eyes. Her hands clenched now on the folds of the long skirt she wore. "A hospital…pain…the two-faced woman. No, someone else. She's hurt…"

Kane waited as patiently as he could while Winona sighed, opened her eyes and glanced around, needing to orient herself after her vision. "Are sapphires valuable in medicine?" she asked.

He was surprised by the question. "There's a new technology where they're used in laser surgery. It's just been approved. How did you know about that?"

"I saw a hospital room. A woman was in the bed, her face smashed. Two nurses were talking about using sapphires for some procedure and how valuable they would be when the news got out."

Winona shook her head as if troubled. She looked pale to him. He took her wrist and felt her pulse. It was fast, skipping some beats here and there.

"Let it go," he advised, worried about her. She always seemed hale and robust, but still, he knew her to be close to eighty.

"It's the strangest thing. For a moment, I saw the two-faced woman. I've been getting images of her for over a year. She has one body, but two faces, one superimposed on the other." She stopped suddenly, her eyes narrowing.

"There used to be an old sapphire mine in the county. I remember hearing some cowboys talking about it when I worked at a ranch one summer." Kane tried to recall what he'd heard. "The mine was on Kincaid land. I think."

"It was on Baxter land," Winona corrected. A startled look crossed her face. She pressed both hands to her chest.

"Winona, what is it?" He reached for her hand again, but she drew back, refusing to let him touch her.

"The Baxter girl…no, the Baxter ranch…Homer is near there. I can't tell where…mountains all around, high country, rough. But houses…log houses… It's gone." She sighed. "For a moment, I thought I had something."

"He's probably traipsing around the hills, not a care in the world, while we worry ourselves to death about him."

Kane gave a grimace of disgust at the whole situation. He'd like to walk away and never come back.

"Now for you," the psychic said, turning a determined gaze upon him.

"Me?" he inquired with sardonic humor.

"Yes." She was serious. "Give me your hand."

He laid his hand in hers, palm up. She scanned it for several minutes. He began to feel a bit edgy.

"You will soon make a startling discovery, one that will leave you confused and angry," she said softly. "Don't let the anger take control. Be very, very careful, Kane. This will affect your entire future."

"What is it?"

She released his hand and rose. "It isn't for me to tell you." She poured fresh tea into their cups and drank deeply of it. Her fingers showed the slightest tremor.

He found himself impatient with her mysterious secret. "Then who will?" he demanded.

"Soon you will know. Before the weekend is past, I think." She picked up a cat and began to stroke its fur. It was almost as if she'd shut him out of her thoughts now that she'd delivered her warning about this mysterious thing he was supposed to discover.

It was Sunday. He sighed in frustration, but knew Winona well enough to know he'd get no more out of her. He'd have to see what the next few days would disclose.

"I saw Tracy earlier today," Winona said. "She says she and Maggie have a bet on who goes into labor first. Any clues?"

He shook his head. "Babies have their own times."

A vast, unexpected wave of emptiness hit him. He'd delivered twins at the res in the wee hours of the morning. Then he'd spent several hours at the hospital. God, but he was tired. And lonely.

Recalling Lori's advice about courting Moriah made him laugh. She was about as friendly as a porcupine—a nervous porcupine. If he got too close, he was lucky to get no more than a verbal barb from her. After their episode at his house, she seemed even more nervous around him. He couldn't figure her out.

However, she was a damned good office manager. She and Melanie had his desk and files shipshape. The front office was neat, too. All the records were in place, the insurance claims filed and a method to keep order instituted.

Melanie was pulling the records of patients who had died or hadn't been in for more than five years and was putting them in the Closed files set up in the unused butler's pantry.

Moriah had opened up the turret room of the old Victorian and had made it into a children's waiting room, which was working out great. He'd been skeptical at first.

She'd also initiated "well baby" day, holding appointments on Wednesday mornings for mothers to bring children in for routine shots and checkups. That had speeded up the process and helped keep healthy children separated from the sick ones.

Winona broke into his thoughts. "You still love her," she said softly. "Go to her. Tell her. Now, Kane, before it's too late." She spoke with a sudden urgency.

He gulped the last swallow of tea and stood. "It's already too late. Sixteen years too late."

Grabbing up the shirt, he thanked her for her help and headed out. Winona walked him to the door, a worried expression on her face. Halfway across the cluttered front yard, he remembered something he shouldn't have forgotten—the goats.

One butted him in the back of his knee.

His leg buckled. He went down cursing.

"Baa-aa-aa," the goat called from on top of an old station wagon. It sounded like a laugh to Kane.

"You'll be goat stew if you come down from there," he snarled, getting to his feet and gingerly limping to his sports ute. He drove back to town in a sour mood.

In his study, he sat in his recliner, put on his reading glasses and tried to get through some of the medical journals that had piled up during the past six months.

His life got busier and busier, it seemed. He stubbornly clung to his Wednesday afternoons, when he could work on the house. That was his one relaxation and recreation for the week. Hell, for the year.

He woke to the shrill ring of the telephone. For a second, he thought about ignoring it and letting his answering machine pick it up. But it might be an emergency.

"Hunter," he said into the mouthpiece.

"Kane, this is Moriah."

His heart went into double time. He glanced at the clock and saw it was almost one in the morning. He'd fallen asleep in the chair every night for...he couldn't remember how long.

"Yeah?"

"Have you seen Melanie?"

The question made no sense. "No. Why?"

"She was supposed to be home by midnight. I wondered if you'd seen them. They were going to an arts-and-crafts fair on the reservation with some of Keith's friends."

"Yeah, it's a money raiser for the tribe," he said while he considered the situation. "I didn't attend."

"Have you heard of any wrecks or anything?"

He heard the near-panic in her tone. "I'm sure she'll be home soon. They probably forgot about the time."

Dead silence.

"Look," he said soothingly, "you're being overanxious. Keith is a good kid. He'll take care of her."

"The way *you* did, taking a young girl's trust and betraying it?" There was a moment of stunned silence. "I'm sorry. That was untrue and uncalled for." She hung up.

For a moment, he thought of calling her back…or maybe going out there and facing her head-on. He wanted to know what she'd meant by that nasty crack. He'd been as hurt as she had by their past.

By Mrs. Gilmore's deceitful actions, he amended. He took a breath and calmed down. Maybe the woman had acted for the best. The way things now stood between him and Moriah, they'd have been divorced before they got to their sixteenth wedding anniversary.

He sighed and paced the floor. He could understand her worry about her daughter. It was normal.

He picked up the phone and called the night dispatcher at the sheriff's office. She had no report of a wreck. He asked her to pass the word to be on the lookout for Keith's pickup. He called the hospital just to be sure they weren't there. They weren't. He couldn't think of anything else to do. He tried Moriah's number and found the line busy.

Carrying his boots, he padded upstairs in his socks. When he'd undressed, brushed his teeth and was about to drop into bed, the phone rang again.

He answered quickly, wanting to hear Moriah's voice even if she were to bawl him out. "Hunter."

"Kane, this is Lori. There's been an accident. Can you meet me at the hospital? You'll need to scrub for surgery."

"Sure." He reached for his clothes. "Where? Who? How bad?"

"Keith Colson. Apparently a car sideswiped his truck. It

went off the road into a ditch. I happened to spot the pickup on my way home from the hospital. I'll bring them in—"

"Them who?"

"Keith's date. Moriah Gilmore's daughter."

God. "Is she hurt?"

"No, mostly shaken up. Keith has a piece of metal in his chest. It looks bad."

"See you at the hospital," he said, and hung up.

He jerked his clothing on and headed out into the night, his mind concentrated on the task ahead, planning the surgery, thinking of possible complications.

At the hospital, he parked and went in through the Emergency-Room doors. "Heads up," he called. "Lori's bringing a car-wreck case in. The upper chest is involved."

The trauma team were assembled when Lori came barreling into the hospital drive. A sheriff's deputy was leading the way, his siren sounding like a scream in the night.

Kane saw Moriah's daughter climb out of the back of the utility vehicle. There was a bruise on her forehead. A wave of relief went through him. At least he wouldn't have to call Moriah and report that her daughter was badly hurt.

A medic dashed around and opened the rear door for the stretcher team. Lori stood by and directed them in lifting Keith out.

Kane winced when he saw a piece of chrome trim sticking out of the boy's chest. He'd bet ten years of his life they'd been drag racing. He was disappointed in Keith.

Melanie, standing to one side while a trauma nurse looked at her head and took her vital signs, whimpered at the sight.

"Put her in a room for the night," he said when the stretcher came in the door. "Have someone look at her if she needs it. Otherwise, I'll see her in the morning. Call her mother."

He did a cursory check on Keith, started the IV's and nodded toward the operating suite. "Let's go, team."

It was going to be a long night.

At four, Kane walked down the hall. His surgical mask hung around his neck. He flung it into the bin, pulled off the gown and tossed it in, too. He rubbed his eyes, which felt as if he'd been walking into a sandstorm for most of the night.

His stomach rumbled. Instead of heading home, he went into the cafeteria and ordered breakfast. A police officer sat at a table, drinking coffee and filling out a report. Kane joined him with his tray.

"How's the kid?" the policeman asked.

"He'll make it." He explained about Keith's injuries.

The officer told him what he knew of the accident. "I got a report from the girl. She said they were hurrying home because she was late, when a car came up behind them, going fast. As it passed them it swerved over and hit the truck's wheel, making the Colson boy lose control. The truck hit a mailbox, crossed the ditch and slammed into the corner post of the fence. That's what did the real damage."

Kane finished his meal and sipped the hot coffee.

The officer stood. "I'm off. I still have another two hours of patrol." He shook his head. "Never a dull moment."

"'Night," Kane said as the man left. He, too, was tired and wanted to go home. He'd check first to make sure Melanie was okay, that the nurse had called Moriah to reassure her her daughter was fine. Then he'd head in.

To sleep in the chair?

The night Moriah had slept in his bed haunted his dreams. Maybe that's why he didn't sleep there anymore. When he climbed between the covers, he imagined all sorts of things—that he could still smell her perfume on the sheets, for one. Which was impossible, for he'd changed them before he'd slept there again.

After he finished his coffee, he went to the nurse's station. He nodded to the night nurse at the desk and picked out Melanie's chart. He'd better take a quick peek at her, then be off.

He looked over her vitals while he walked down the hall. He noted her blood type was B positive, the same as his.

Outside her door, he paused, a frown on his face. The information on the chart couldn't be right. It listed her birthday as last month…sixteen years ago!

He stared at the date. Moriah had said the girl was fifteen. He'd wondered briefly if she could be his, but Moriah had said…

Everything in him stopped functioning. He couldn't draw a breath. He couldn't think. Doubt, suspicion and disbelief held him suspended. It couldn't be….

His mind switched back on, racing furiously.

Moriah…nervous as hell around him, in a tremor all the time. Melanie…with the same blood type as his.

Dark hair, like his. Dark eyes, darker than the golden brown of her mother's. With green flecks circling the perimeter of the irises. He'd noticed the color the day she'd cleaned his office. His eyes were similar.

And her birthday. From December, when he and Moriah had been together, to September, when Melanie had been born, was nine months. Nine damned months!

No wonder Moriah had sneaked out of town at spring break. She'd been four months pregnant. With Melanie. With his kid.

The shock of it hit him, rolled over him like a tidal wave, leaving him limp and unable to believe the evidence before him. He slumped against the wall.

Melanie…*his!*

God, he had a kid, a sweet-faced, smart-mouthed girl. His.

And Moriah's.

He had a few things to say to *her.* He bit back a round of curses so strong they'd have shocked a sailor. Instead, he silently walked into the room…and stopped dead.

Moriah was there, asleep in a chair. He clamped his mouth shut against the things that rushed to his lips and went over to the bed. He stood looking down at the sleeping girl in the bed.

Her hair lay in long, straight strands over the pillow. Without the sun to pick out red highlights, it looked as black as night. As black as his.

His. The child he'd never known. The child he'd have claimed. The child he'd have loved.

The anger started then. It grew to blazing heights. He recalled the psychic's warning.

Don't let anger take control.

Was this what Winona had seen?

Well, it was too late. He was already angry. And he was going to get some answers to some pretty important questions in the very near future.

He walked over to Moriah and touched her arm. She opened her eyes with a start, then smiled when she saw him. He didn't return it. He nodded toward the door, indicating she was to follow him.

He walked out, left the chart at the desk and gestured toward the empty cafeteria when Moriah paused beside him.

She wore the blue sweat suit he'd seen the night he went to her house in Great Falls.

"The nurse said Keith will be okay," she said, with a question in her eyes.

He nodded. He noted she looked terribly tired, vulnerable and emotionally drained. His heart seemed to clench at the sight.

He wasn't going to feel sorry for her. Whatever had happened, she'd brought it on herself by denying him a place in her life...in his child's life. The anger surged anew.

"Let's get some coffee," he said for the nurse's benefit. She was watching them curiously. Moriah nodded and followed him down the hall. He got them each a cup of coffee and selected a table in the far corner.

He sat in the chair opposite her and studied her for a long minute. "I saw Melanie's birth date," he said softly.

A minute or an eternity swept by. Moriah tried to think. Nothing came to mind. She'd been trying to tell him all week, afraid of this very thing, but she hadn't found the opportunity. They were never alone at the office, and Melanie was with her after school until it was time to go to the cabin.

"Also her blood type...which is the same as mine, in case you didn't know," he added.

She shrank from his anger, so cold and carefully controlled that she found it more frightening than if he'd raged at her.

"Kane..."

What could she say? One look at his face told her he wouldn't forgive this wrong no matter what she said. She straightened and faced him.

"Why the hell didn't you tell me?" he demanded.

"How?" she asked, resigned to the confrontation. "I called and got no answer...none that I knew of," she added at his hard glance. "I wrote. Was I supposed to take out an ad?"

"Your mother—" He broke off, as if the anger was

more than he could contain. He looked as if he'd like to hit something.

"Yes, my mother," she said sadly.

"I can see how she might have intercepted my letters, but how did she stop yours from getting to me?"

Moriah smiled and felt the bitterness all the way to her soul. "I put the letters in our mailbox. It never occurred to me that she'd remove them. I trusted her."

"Yes, her, not me," he said. "I keep reminding myself that you were young, scared, but it doesn't wash. The problem was you didn't trust me, the man you supposedly loved. You didn't think I could take care of you and the baby—"

"You couldn't," she said, gripping the cup with icy hands. "You had no money. You were on a scholarship. I thought you'd hate me if you lost it."

She crossed her arms over her chest. Her heart seemed to ache with each beat. She was tired of the worry and anger and tension between her and this man.

"But you didn't ask me…*me,* the father of your child. My child. I never had a choice. I never knew her, still wouldn't if it hadn't been for your father's disappearance. God, do you have any idea what this does to a person?"

"Yes." The rage and frustration on his face were plain to her. There were other emotions—pain, she thought. And perhaps something akin to grief. Oh, yes, she knew them all.

He heaved a deep breath of frustration.

"What will you do?" she asked finally. She ventured another glance at him when he didn't answer. "About Melanie?"

He pushed a hand through his hair. The waitress started another pot of coffee, filling the room with gurgling noise. It grated on her nerves while she waited for an answer.

"I don't know." He closed his eyes and pinched the bridge of his nose. "I just don't know."

Moriah realized how tired he must be. First she'd disturbed his sleep, then he'd dashed to the hospital and operated on Keith, and now…this.

She wanted to apologize, but she didn't know how. She wanted to explain the past, but surely he knew how frightened she'd been at that time—pregnant and ashamed and scared out of her wits when she couldn't contact him.

The coffeepot stopped gurgling. Moriah got up and refilled their mugs. Their fingers brushed when she handed it to him. Both of them jerked as if burned. She returned to her chair. "Are you—do we have to tell her? I mean…"

He stared at her as if he couldn't believe what she'd said. "You're damned right we have to tell her."

"I meant right away. I'll need some time—"

His face was suddenly close to hers. "Twenty-four hours," he said. "That's all you've got. You've had her for sixteen years."

It was what she'd expected, but… "Will you let me do it? I'd like to explain the situation to her."

"Get your licks in first, you mean." He looked as if he'd refuse to let her see Melanie at all.

"No, I won't," she quickly protested, wondering if he could refuse her admittance to Melanie's room. No, he wouldn't do that.

She knew him well enough to know he was speaking in shock and anger at the present. Later, they could talk sensibly. "I won't say anything to disparage you," she promised. Her voice quavered. She swallowed against the pain in her throat.

"You're damned right you won't. I'll go with you. We'll both explain our view of what happened."

"Kane, please," she whispered. She didn't think she could face Melanie and him together. They'd both be against her….

She pressed a hand over her mouth. She was afraid. The future looked bleak…dark, so dark…so *alone*.

"Are you going to cry?" he demanded gruffly.

She shook her head. "No. I did that years ago. It's too late for tears."

He gave her an unreadable look and drank the coffee. She sipped from hers, grateful for the heat it produced. She was cold inside. She might never get warm again.

"All right," he conceded in weary tones. "When are you going to tell her? I want to see her right afterward."

"Will she be allowed to come home today?"

"Yes."

"Then I'll try…" At his glance, she started over. "I'll explain when we get home…at the cabin."

She didn't know where her home was. No place was comfortable. She belonged nowhere. Don't start feeling sorry for yourself, she warned sternly. She was an adult. She could face whatever had to be faced, as she had years ago. She may have made the wrong choices, but she had made them…and lived with the consequences.

He heaved a deep breath, then nodded. "I'll come over after supper." He paused. "Or I can bring a pizza. Does she like pizza?"

It was the oddest thing—to be talking about food when her life hung in the balance. Well, not her life, that was a bit dramatic. But her future, hers and Melanie's.

"Yes, with peppers and onions. Where will you fit in?" she asked quietly, drawing on reserves she didn't know she had.

"What do you mean?"

"What will you expect in regard to Melanie?"

He gave her such a look, she lost track of what she was saying. He hated her, truly hated her. She didn't think anyone had ever hated her before. It was unnerving.

"I expect you to let me and Melanie make our own

decisions. We'll determine our relationship. You're out of the loop."

"I won't let you have her. I'll stop you—"

He swung up from the chair and loomed over her. "Try it," he warned. "If you refuse to let me see her, I'll have you in court so fast your head will swim."

She refused to be cowed by him. "You'll have to prove paternity," she said, not sure of this or the law, but taking a brave stand. "Until you do, I'm still her mother. She's a minor, and I'm still in charge."

"Paternity is a snap these days."

"DNA testing," she murmured.

"You got it." Kane forced himself to sit again. The adrenaline was pumping. He wanted to go to court today, this minute. He wanted his daughter.

He looked out the window and watched the sun rising on the far horizon. The earth seemed new and bright all at once. A kid. He had a kid. He felt himself relax for the first time in hours. A smile settled on his mouth.

Melanie. He liked her as a person. To have her for a daughter… There were so many things to catch up on.

Movies to see. Books to discuss. The new house. He'd take her to see it. She could pick out the room she wanted, help build it if she wanted to, select all the colors and furniture. God, there was so much to learn about each other.

He experienced an intense regret for all the things he'd never seen—her first smile, her first step, her first word. He'd lost out on all those.

The anger rose again. He glared at Moriah, ready with a string of demands. The words died in his throat.

She sat huddled in the chair. She looked as if her world were coming to an end. He found he couldn't hurt her. He hardened his heart. He wasn't going to be a softy in this case. She'd had her time with Melanie—sixteen years of it. Now it was his turn.

"I want joint custody," he said, suppressing the sudden, stupid need to go to her and hold her...just hold her.

She rubbed her temples. Yeah, she probably had the granddaddy of all headaches this morning. He looked away before he melted.

"What time can I take her home?" she asked, ignoring his last statement.

"At nine. I'll check on her during my morning rounds and dismiss her." He glanced at his watch. Time to go home, shower, change and get to work. He had a full day at the town office ahead of him, then he'd have to plan his talk with Melanie. He couldn't begin to think of words for how he felt.

God, his daughter! He still couldn't believe it. He'd wake any minute, at his house, alone in the chair in the study.

He glanced at Moriah. If he was dreaming, she was having a nightmare. She looked like hell. Which she deserved, but still, as a doctor, he knew about pain and despair. She looked about at the end of her rope.

"You'd better get some sleep this morning. You need a few hours rest before you talk to your...our daughter."

She looked at him, then away, at his change of words. There was fear in the depths of those golden eyes. The wounded-doe act.

"How will we share custody?" she asked.

"Melanie is old enough to make her own choice as to where she will live, and with whom."

She grimaced. "You know she'll pick you. You're new and handsome and exciting and different—" She stopped as if choked by grief.

A knot swelled in his throat. He wasn't as tough as he thought he was where she was concerned. Ah, hell...

An idea came to him—crazy, sure, but it was an answer to the dilemma. "We could marry," he heard himself say, "and provide a real home for Melanie, the one we should have given her years ago."

Eleven

Marry. Marry. Marry.

The word echoed in her mind like the distant sound of tom-toms, warning of danger yet to come.

"Marry," she repeated. "We couldn't."

His eyes directed a challenge at her. "Why not?"

She saw that, having made this preposterous statement, he wasn't going to back down. His finely modeled mouth curved in a mocking smile. There was no love in his expression, no affection, not even tenderness or sympathetic understanding of the shock he'd just delivered to her system.

Pressing a hand to her chest—her heart felt as if it would leap right out at any second—she shook her head. As a seventeen-year-old, she'd shyly asked him if he loved her. She couldn't do that now. She couldn't take the answer. Right now he looked as if he hated her.

"I can't," she said on a quieter note. "Not without…" She shook her head.

"Not without love?" he questioned cynically. "Is that what's missing? I suspect many marriages have begun on the basis of passion." His brooding gaze raked over her, reminding her of the caresses they'd shared. "My main concern is Melanie's future at the present. That, by necessity, includes you."

Moriah winced at the words. "You can bring the pizza around six," she told him, knowing it was inevitable.

He didn't answer, but stood there watching her for a long minute, as if trying to figure out if there was some trick she was pulling that he didn't see. At last he nodded and went to the door. There he paused and said, "I don't want to hurt you over Melanie. I'm not going to take her away from you. That would be wrong. I just want my share of her time and affection."

Kane waited until she nodded, then he left. He stood in the parking lot, watching the dawn spread over the sky in golden arcs. He was half-angry with himself for softening at the last minute and reassuring Moriah about his intentions toward their daughter.

Their daughter.

A lump formed in his throat at the thought. He got in his vehicle and drove home, wondering why he'd suggested such an outlandish thing as marriage. Moriah had obviously thought he was out of his mind.

Maybe he was, but the more he considered it, the less farfetched it seemed. They had a child in common. They had shared the most incredible lovemaking either had experienced. They were certainly compatible at the office. A wry smile formed. He took care of the patients; Moriah took care of everything else.

It was as good a foundation to build on as most marriages had. He could give her a good life.

What about love?

The question was so real, he glanced at the passenger seat, almost expecting to see someone sitting there.

Love? he mocked. What's that?

Once he'd loved Moriah with everything in him. He wouldn't put his heart and soul in her keeping the way he'd done as a youth. He'd learned better. However, he did want a family. With Moriah, he'd have one, ready-made. Yeah, marriage was the solution.

He took a deep breath and admitted the truth. He was a fool, but it was the solution he wanted. He'd have to convince Moriah.

"I can't believe it," Melanie said for the twentieth time. She sat on the bunk bed, her back against the cabin wall. Her eyes sparkled in spite of the black bruise that partially surrounded one of them. She'd taken the news of her paternity with unfettered delight. "Kane Hunter—my father!"

Moriah added another log to the stove. The day was turning progressively colder as a storm came in. Indian summer was at an end, it appeared. She returned to the chair, feeling old and creaky as she sat down and stared out the window. It was hard to look at the happiness on her daughter's face. Each exclamation of delight was a stake in her heart.

"I'm an Indian," Melanie muttered, as the realization hit her. "Half-Indian. Jessy is going to simply die when I tell her. She'll turn green if she ever gets to see Kane—Father—Dad…. Heavens, I don't know what to call him. Mom, what should I—"

The purr of an engine stopped the one-sided conversation.

Moriah turned an apprehensive gaze toward the door. Hearing Kane's step on the porch, she tried to rise, but found she couldn't move. Her legs simply wouldn't support her.

He knocked once, then opened the door. When he stepped inside, the aroma of pizza filled the small room. He glanced at the two females. "Supper," he announced.

For the first time, Moriah noted a hesitancy in his manner. He was as unstrung by his newfound fatherhood as she was. When his gaze shifted from Melanie to her, his face hardened and the uncertainty disappeared. His feelings for her were clear.

Melanie rose from the bunk. Kane set the package on the table and opened his arms to her. She leapt into them.

"Daddy," she said in a tearful murmur against his neck. "Oh, Kane, I can't believe you're my father. It's so wonderful."

Moriah watched while he held his daughter, his cheek pressed against the black hair that was so like his own. He kissed the top of Melanie's head. They turned as one, his arm around the girl's shoulders, and together they faced Moriah.

Her breath caught at how incredibly handsome they were. A piercing loneliness left her desolate and afraid. She didn't blame Melanie for loving Kane. How could she? Every time she herself looked at him, she was overcome by feelings she couldn't control—by her own love for this man, her first love, her only love....

"Mom told me everything," Melanie said, looking at him with adoration in her eyes.

Moriah felt a moment's sympathy for Keith. The young man had temporarily been supplanted by a more-powerful male. She met Kane's questioning gaze and nodded.

"Everything?" he asked softly.

"Everything," Moriah echoed. "Including my mother's part."

"That was mean of Grandma, refusing to let you talk to Mom when you called," Melanie said indignantly. Her eyes snapped with righteous anger, but she subsided at a look from Moriah.

"The proposal," he said. "Did you tell her about that?"

Moriah gasped and could think of nothing to say. She hadn't taken his mention of marriage seriously. He'd been sarcastic when he'd uttered that preposterous suggestion.

"Proposal? What proposal?" Melanie demanded, high color riding her cheeks as she gazed from one adult to another. "Are you going to be married?"

"I—"

"We're discussing it," Kane cut in smoothly. His gaze was a dark challenge that shook Moriah to her soul.

She clenched her hands, helpless even as she denied it. An invisible force pulled her toward a fate she couldn't possibly accept. To marry him, not for love, but for her daughter's sake... No, she couldn't. She wanted so much more....

A sigh pushed its way out of her. "It's impossible," she whispered, her throat aching with all the things she couldn't say.

"I think it would be great," Melanie said, showing no qualms at all about the situation. "We'd be a family. We'd live together." She stopped and peered at Kane. "Is there enough room for all of us at your house?"

That she wanted to live with him was so obvious, it was like a knife in Moriah's heart.

"Of course." He smiled. "There are two rooms on the third floor that would make a nice bedroom and study for you now. Maybe by next year I'll have the new house finished—"

"What new house?" Melanie interrupted.

"The one I'm building." He launched into a detailed description of the home he was constructing himself. "You can help me pick out the colors. I'm not so good on that part."

"Oh, we will," Melanie promised fervently. "Mom and I are super at decorating."

Moriah thought of the tasteful colors at the Victorian. Lori had helped him there. Grimly, she blocked the images this idea suggested and arranged plates and napkins on the table for their supper. She didn't know if she could get the food down.

After preparing glasses of lemonade from fresh spring water, she moved her chair to the table. "We should eat," she said.

Melanie scooped out a piece of pizza and returned to the bed with her plate and glass, leaving the two chairs for the adults.

Kane sat opposite Moriah. He served her, then himself. Lifting his slice of pizza, he wolfed down half of it. His eyes stayed on her. She thought she saw amusement in them. He knew she'd already lost the battle concerning her daughter...their daughter. Melanie was obviously enchanted with him. He also thought he could win the one about marriage, too.

She'd tried to figure out why he'd suggested it. It made no sense. There was the passion, of course, but he seemed to resent the feelings she aroused in him. She sighed. If only he could love her again the way he once had, the way she loved him now! For a moment her heart leapt at the thought.

"This is my favorite food," Melanie said after a spell.

"So your mother told me."

"When did you see her?"

"This morning at the hospital," he explained. He flicked Moriah a hard glance. "After I saw the birth date on your chart and realized you were mine."

Melanie looked from one parent to the other, her face solemn, but her eyes sparkling. "What should I call you?"

He shrugged. "Whatever you like."

"Daddy sounds odd," she confessed. "Father sounds sort of stiff. I suppose...do you think...Dad?"

"Yes."

They smiled at each other, father and daughter, so in tune it broke Moriah's heart. They were drawing closer together as they explored this new relationship. Her own threads to the girl seemed to be breaking, one after the other.

"Dad, are you going to the hospital tonight?" Melanie asked.

"Yes." He looked at his watch. "I have to leave soon."

"I haven't visited Keith except for a few minutes before Mom brought me home this morning. The nurse let me into his room for a sec, but he wasn't awake. I was wondering if I could go with you."

"Of course. In fact, he was asking for you earlier when I stopped by. I assured him we weren't withholding the news of your demise from him. It would probably be better for his peace of mind if he saw you for himself." He turned to Moriah. "Is it all right if she goes into town with me?"

She was completely surprised by the question. "Yes, I suppose so. If you think she should...I mean, if Keith needs..." She trailed off, not sure what to say.

"Good. You can ride in with us. I have some things to go over with you. We can discuss them while the kids visit."

She nodded and finished the piece of pizza, which she usually loved, but which tasted like mush tonight. After the meal, she freshened her lipstick and combed her hair, while Melanie changed into jeans and a warm sweater. Kane waited outside for them.

During the drive to town, they all sat in the front seat, Melanie in the middle. "Just like a family," the girl said, giving her mom a smug grin.

Moriah saw the matchmaking gleam in her daughter's eye. So did Kane. He gave her a knowing glance, then turned his attention to the highway. At the hospital, he studied the charts before taking Melanie to see Keith. The boy's employers, Luke and Maris Rivers, had just left, the nurse told him.

Keith's room held a large vase of flowers and a small box of candy. The candy was from Melanie, delivered earlier in the day when she'd tiptoed in to see him before leaving for the cabin.

"Thanks for the candy," he whispered, his eyes flickering open at their entrance. It clearly hurt him to breathe.

"Oh, Keith," Melanie exclaimed softly. They clasped hands and gazed into each other's eyes.

"I'm fine," the cowboy murmured. "The doc fixed me up good." He grinned at Kane, who laid the chart aside and came to the bed.

After examining the bandage and asking a few questions, Kane motioned for Moriah to leave the room with him. "We'll let the kids have a few minutes alone. Do you want to wait in the cafeteria while I make the rest of the rounds?"

She nodded and turned down the hall, aware that he watched her go. She didn't breathe freely until she rounded the corner.

The cafeteria was nearly empty when she arrived. She bought a cup of coffee and took a table in the back. Leaning her head against the wall, she closed her eyes and rested.

The plunk of a cup on the table woke her. She sat up, startled, then met Kane's eyes as he sat opposite her.

"You look like hell," he said.

She stiffened her spine at his forthright opinion. "It's nothing a night's sleep won't cure."

"Yeah." He sipped at the steaming cup of coffee, his

dark gaze never leaving her face. "Melanie wants to stay in town so she can visit Keith. I said it was okay with me, if you agreed."

The bottom dropped out of her world. "Kane, don't take her away from me," she pleaded, not meaning to beg, but unable to give her daughter up so easily.

His jaw clenched as if he was biting back the words he wanted to say. "You're welcome to stay at the house, too."

She gasped as if shocked.

"Damn it, Moriah," he began in a low growl. He stopped, visibly taking himself in hand, then started over. "I've thought about us, the three of us, all day. I meant what I said."

She stared at him, trying to decide which conversation he was referring to. "About joint custody of Melanie?"

"About marriage."

A tremor ran all the way through her. Marriage with Kane. Her dream come true. But too late, way too late.

"Oh, Kane, what chance would a marriage between us have? It would be a failure from the start."

"Why?" he demanded. His eyes glided over her face, down her body, then back up. "I told you I wanted a family. This way I get one immediately. And there's Melanie to think of. She needs a father."

"She needs you," Moriah corrected softly, accepting the truth. "If she wants to stay with you, I won't object. That will free me to look for my father. I can go out every day. The weather is changing fast now." She lapsed into silence as she thought of snow and freezing cold.

"You still work for me," Kane said sternly.

She gazed at him in surprise. "Everything is changed—"

"No, it isn't."

He smiled, surprising her even more until she saw the determination in his eyes. It had been the same when he talked about making it through medical school years ago. Kane had made up his mind and that was that.

"You're the best office manager I've ever had. I expect you at work in the morning." He drained his cup and rose. "Come on. I'll take you home, pick up some clothes for Melanie and come back for her before going to the house."

His gaze softened as he took in the distress she couldn't hide. "I'm not stealing her away. You can come, too," he said huskily. "If you want."

Her head jerked up at his tone. His gaze ran over her, as hot as heat lightning. She saw the desire he wouldn't or couldn't try to hide. She also saw something akin to tenderness in his eyes.

She wanted to question him, but he headed for the exit. She followed him to the parking lot, feeling as if she were in a surreal landscape where nothing was quite what it seemed. It wasn't until they were almost at the cabin that she realized she hadn't said goodbye to Melanie. But she'd lost her daughter the moment Kane had found out Melanie was his.

She swallowed hard. She had no one to blame but herself. She knew she shouldn't have come back to Whitehorn.

Moriah sat on the porch of the cabin and lifted her face to the soothing rays of the sun. She'd declined Kane's offer to stay at his house. She hadn't gone to work that morning, either. She needed some time to herself.

She surveyed the rugged hills and ravines around the cabin and wondered if her father was beneath the rubble of a cave-in.

The day seemed darker as she realized she might never see him again, that he might not have a chance to know his granddaughter, or for Melanie to know him.

Restless, she stood and paced across the clearing.

She'd go for a walk, she decided. The quiet solitude of the mountains had brought her comfort before. Maybe it would this time, too.

She'd started for the ridge trail when she heard a noise and stopped. She felt her scalp tighten as she noticed the silence of the squirrels and birds.

A shuffling rustle came from the path above her, then a figure became visible through the bushes. The person walked slowly along the trail. When he rounded the bend, he became fully visible.

For a moment, Moriah didn't recognize the tottery old man who stood fifty feet from her, peering through the foliage at her. His hair, mostly gray, with only a few russet strands left, streamed out around his shoulders in an unkempt halo. His beard touched his chest. He stared at her from sunken blue eyes.

"Father?" she said, unable to believe this hermit was the man she'd last seen sixteen years ago. He seemed... ancient.

"Moriah," he said. He reached out a hand and tottered forward a few feet before sinking to his knees.

She ran forward. "Daddy," she whispered, kneeling beside him and feeling for his pulse.

In the silence, she could hear her father's ragged breathing. "Pneumonia," she murmured, noting the fever spots on his gaunt cheeks. "We've got to get you to town."

Kane. She had to find Kane. He'd know what to do. He'd take care of her father.

Her father stirred. "Found it," he said. He looked around suspiciously. "In my pocket. Found what they were looking for, but...didn't tell them...anything."

"Who are you talking about?" she asked, supporting him with an arm around his waist. She led him toward the clearing and her car.

He clasped her hand in a painful grip and pulled her close. "The aliens. They're here. I didn't tell them anything. Got the proof…in my coat." He swayed alarmingly.

"Hold on," she ordered. She helped him into the car. He rested his head, eyes closed, on the seat back while she strapped him in. Feeling hard objects in his coat pocket, she removed three rocks. She studied the crystals embedded in them, recalling all he'd taught her years ago about rock formations.

"Sapphires," she murmured. "Veins of sapphires."

Moriah leaned against the wall of the hospital corridor. Melanie stood close by. Kane was in the room with Homer, who had been in the hospital since Tuesday. It was now Sunday night.

"We're done. You can come in now," a lab technician said, then walked away at a brisk pace with her vials of blood.

Kane stood by the bed, talking quietly with the old man as they entered. Her father looked much better than he had when she had brought him in, but in her eyes he still looked unbearably old and ill.

He'd had a bath, and someone had trimmed his beard. His hair was braided into two long plaits that hung over his shoulders. The fever spots had left his cheeks, and his skin resembled leather that hadn't been tanned correctly. Deep wrinkles scored his face.

Judd Hensley, the sheriff, came by to interview Homer. He didn't change his story: he'd been kidnapped by an alien. He was sure there were others, but he'd only seen one at a time. He wasn't sure if it had been the same one or not. The aliens wanted the sapphires. That's why they had kidnapped him.

"But I didn't tell them a thing," Homer confided.

After the lawman left, Moriah questioned him further. "Where did you find the sapphires?" she asked, showing him the ones she'd found in his pocket.

He picked the stones up and peered at them. "I don't remember," he said, looking confused and anxious. He'd found his treasure, only to lose it when the alien had knocked him out. He couldn't remember where he'd been.

Moriah felt sorry for him, while her daughter, true to form, was delighted with her grandfather. He told her wonderful stories of his explorations and mysterious ones of his capture and escape.

He'd been held in the former jail of the abandoned mining town. The jail was a shallow mine shaft that had played out. An iron gate with a padlock had kept the prisoners in.

Homer had fooled the aliens. He'd worked at the rusty hinges with a sharp stone until he'd broken through and escaped. He'd gotten mixed up for a while and lost his way, but finally, after a night in the woods, he'd found the path to the cabin. That's where Moriah had found him.

Kane had met them at the hospital and taken over. Homer had been suffering from a severe case of the flu plus pneumonia. He was out of danger now and recovering rapidly since the antibiotics had taken effect and he'd had some decent food. The aliens had kept him on a starvation diet.

"Isn't Dad a wonderful doctor?" Melanie asked, taking her grandfather's hand. "I'm going into medicine, too."

Homer had taken the news of a grandchild with equanimity after the first shock. Moriah had explained everything to him before letting Melanie visit, including Kane's presence in their lives.

He looked from Kane to Moriah, then at his granddaughter. "That sounds like a wise choice." He listened to a tinny banging from the hall. "Is that supper? I'm hungry as a spring bear."

Moriah laughed with her daughter, then sighed, realizing the crisis was truly over. It was time to take up her life again.

Kane gave her a sharp glance. "Are you coming back to work tomorrow?" he asked.

"I haven't really thought about it." She'd stayed with her father the past few days. It came to her that she'd used him as an excuse to avoid the office, where she'd see Kane every day.

"We really need you, Mom," Melanie chimed in. "Dad can't find a thing, and Sandy is threatening to quit because he's so grouchy. If you two married, we could live there and keep everything in perfect order, couldn't we?" She grinned impishly at the two adults.

"Enough," Kane said to his daughter. "Let's go get some food while Homer has his dinner. Keith wants you to eat with him," he mentioned to Melanie, who immediately kissed her grandfather and darted out and down the hall.

He took Moriah by the elbow and guided her from the room before she could protest. She looked as if she might faint.

"Does the thought of marriage to me bother you so much?" he asked when they were out of hearing.

"I...no... I haven't really thought about it at all." She stuck her chin up in the air as she told the blatant lie.

An unexplainable bout of tenderness assailed him. She tried to be so tough, but everything she did—from overseeing her daughter's life to caring for her father to working tirelessly with his patients—indicated a warm, loving woman.

The one he wanted.

Yeah. That was no secret. From the moment he'd seen her again, she'd filled his thoughts. His dreams, too. He shook his head wearily, then smiled as he met the sheriff coming down the hall with a bouquet of flowers for his wife.

After Judd spoke and passed on by, he told Moriah, "The Hensleys had a girl this morning at six. Tracy had a miscarriage last year, so we were keeping a close eye on her. Lori said the delivery went well."

Moriah nodded, but said nothing. She wasn't giving away the slightest emotion where he was concerned. He wondered if she'd really dismissed his proposal. That's what he wanted to talk about, since everything was out in the open between them.

They went through the cafeteria line and selected their dinner. Ignoring various other diners he knew, he chose a table for two in the back corner, partially hidden by a rubber plant.

When he finished eating, he refilled his coffee cup and waited for Moriah. She mostly picked at her food.

"Have you thought about us?" he asked, growing impatient at her dawdling.

She raised her beautiful, golden-toned eyes to his, then looked back at her plate. "What about us?"

As if she didn't know! He bit off the anger that formed and tried for patience. "Marriage. Melanie. A family."

Her fingers turned white on the fork, she held it so tightly. Damn, you'd think he'd mentioned mass murder or something, the way she reacted to every suggestion from him.

"No."

Just the one word. A denial. "No, you haven't thought about it, or no, you aren't going to marry me?"

She carefully put the fork down on the plate. "Why are you doing this?" she asked in a choked voice. "Isn't life hard enough without—" She broke off and shook her head.

For a second, he felt guilty. She looked as if she might

cry. Was the prospect of being with him that awful to her? He kept his fist in his lap to keep from bringing it down on the table as hard as he could. Venting his temper in juvenile ways wasn't how to convince her he was right.

"This isn't a spur-of-the-moment decision," he assured her. "I've thought it out these past few days. It would give Melanie the home she wants. It would give you some peace of mind."

She jerked, glanced at him, then looked away again.

When she didn't speak, he went on, relentlessly laying out the facts before her. "I can provide for both of you. The house I'm building…I thought you liked it."

"Would I have a room of my own?"

He was taken aback at the low-voiced question. It seemed like an insult, as if she couldn't bear the thought of being close to him. Anger flamed, and it was a moment before he could trust himself to speak.

"How long do you think we could live in the same house and not cohabitate?" he demanded. "Not long, I think."

Moriah gasped at his bluntness. She pictured them in the new house he was building. It would be a beautiful home with its oak floors and giant fireplace of natural stone. Outside, the walls were stone and red cedar. And the view! The verdant greens of the hills and valley were spectacular.

"If we marry," he continued, ruthless in his determination, "I'd expect to share a room with my wife. And a bed."

She thought of sharing a house, of working together at the office and coming home together at the end of the day. Of making love in his wide, comfortable bed. Of worrying over Melanie together, of laughing at the teenager's irrepressible humor.

"I—I don't know," she whispered.

He bent his head toward her. "Do you remember what we shared at the cabin? We'd have that every night. I'll be gentle with you," he promised. "I'll wait until you want me."

She felt the impact of his words right down to her toes. Wild heat dashed into her cheeks, making her face feel as if it were on fire. She remembered every beautiful, aching moment of the brief interlude in the cabin.

Inside she felt her body soften, preparing for him. The warmth spread outward in great circles of need and desire. Oh, yes, she remembered. But were passion and a lovely daughter enough to cement a marriage? Melanie would go off to college in a couple of years, and desire would cool.

"Think about it," he advised. He touched his lips to her temple. "The scent of your hair reminds me of apples, fresh and crisp and tasty. I want to taste you again."

He turned her face to his and kissed her on the lips, a quick kiss, but ardent, she realized as he drew away.

"I want you," he said.

She was so shaken she couldn't speak. As they left the cafeteria, questions buzzed in her brain. Could they make a marriage out of bits and pieces stitched together from passion, a daughter and one month of memories? What about feelings?

"It seems so impossible," she said. She tried to figure out why he wanted marriage. He could seduce her easily.... It occurred to her that he felt responsible for her as well as Melanie.

"Sleep on it." He took her arm and led her into the corridor again. "Bring your clothes and some of Homer's. He'll need care and a warm place to recover. You can stay at my house."

Moriah sighed, closed her book and stared into the fire. Her father was upstairs in bed. Melanie was visiting Keith at the No Bull ranch—strange name, that. Kane had gotten in late from hospital rounds and was in the shower.

Their supper was bubbling in the oven, a beef stew with vegetables. Her father had eaten an hour ago and was drifting asleep watching the news on TV. She'd put his dishes away and decided to wait a while longer for Kane.

It was Friday night, the prime dating night in a small town. The city, too, she supposed. The few nights she'd stayed at Kane's house, she'd shared a room on the third floor with Melanie.

Kane's proposal preyed on her mind. The truth was, she wanted to marry him, but she was afraid. The temptation was there to take all she could get and never look back, but…she wanted more. She wanted to tell him of her love and ask for his in return. Was she wishing for the impossible?

Twelve

When Moriah heard Kane's step on the stairs, she went into the kitchen, her heart thrumming nervously. Placing a trivet on the table, she set the ovenproof bowl on it and laid the ladle on the plaid tablecloth she'd found in the pantry.

Kane came in, bringing a whiff of soap and shampoo and after-shave with him. His hair waved attractively back from his broad forehead. His nose was an arrogant blade in the middle of his face, and his mouth—his mouth…

Her heart went into a nosedive. He was so incredible—tall and proud and self-assured. Brilliant. Capable. Considerate. All the things a person could hope for in a mate.

She turned from him as an ache pierced her soul. With quick, shaky motions, she set out a hot skillet of corn-bread and poured glasses of nonfat milk. Crackers went into a wooden bowl carved with Indian designs. Fruit compotes were ready in the refrigerator for dessert. Fresh coffee was perked.

Kane pulled out her chair and waited until she sat down before he took a seat. His fingers brushed her shoulders, sending tingles of awareness through her.

"This was worth coming home to," he said with a dazzling smile in her direction, digging into the simple meal.

The words poured over her like warm honey. It was nice to be complimented on her efforts. Her mother was such a perfectionist. She'd always found fault. Moriah noticed that Kane looked for the good points in any situation. It was very satisfying to watch him devour the dinner she'd prepared.

"Maggie Hawk had a boy this afternoon," he mentioned when he was almost finished. "Did I ever tell you she's a distant cousin of mine?"

"No, I don't think so."

"Her grandmother, Annie Little Deer, belongs to the same clan my grandmother does, we discovered. I want to introduce Melanie to her Indian family as soon as possible." He shot Moriah a hard glance, as if expecting an objection to his plans.

She nodded. He sat back in his chair and watched her as she tried to finish the meal.

"Jackson did fine during the delivery, but he told me later he wondered how women ever forgave men after going through that." His voice softened. "But women always do."

Their eyes met above the brightly printed tablecloth. There were questions in his. *Did you have a hard time? Will you ever forgive me for not being there?*

"Melanie was a wonderful baby," she murmured.

"Was she?"

Moriah heard the wistful note in his voice, saw the longing in his eyes. She found she wanted to share those early days with him, to give him his daughter's childhood.

"Oh, yes," she said, forcing a light mood. "I thought she was a gift from the fairies, she was such a good baby. She seemed to love life from the moment she was born. And she never saw a stranger. I worried about that—her trust in people."

An expression of pain crossed his face.

Instinctively she reached out and touched him, then withdrew. "Kane," she said helplessly, knowing he was recalling her cruel words about trusting him and feeling betrayed.

"I'd give anything to be able to go back…to be with you." His voice was low, husky, conveying regret so deep it touched her soul. "I'd give anything to have been there to coach you through the long hours, to see our child come into the world, to share the miracle of life with you."

Moriah put her fork down, unable to take the last bite. To her horror, she realized she was about to lose her composure in front of him. For the third time. First there'd been her tears at the cabin, then her uncontrollable laughter. Now…now she felt as if she were melting inside, as longing for a past that would never be overcame her.

"I wanted you," she said, "so much I thought I would die." Her voice shook, and she could hardly get the words out, but she couldn't hold them back. "I was so lonely…and then Melanie was born. She filled all the empty places." She stopped as she realized this wasn't exactly true. "Most of them."

"I know about the loneliness," he said.

Looking into his eyes, she knew he did.

"Going back to school that spring was like having my soul ripped to pieces. One of those pieces was with you, wherever you were. I often wondered if you were happy, if you'd found someone else. Even when I finally dated, I wondered about you."

She clenched her hands together to keep from touching him again. "I didn't think you'd miss me at all," she managed to say on a lighter note. "All those college girls— bright and beautiful and poised—"

"None as beautiful as you," he interjected.

Their eyes met. They smiled, tentatively at first, then more easily. A weight lifted from her, and she felt strong and in control once more.

"Not one of them knew how to make fry bread," he added in mock complaint. "You made it for me one snowy afternoon. It tasted like ambrosia, better than my grand- mother's. Speaking of which, she'll have my hide if she hears I have a daughter from anyone but me. She'll take her cane to me." He paused. "I told her about you that spring break when I came home and you'd left."

"Me?" She tried to imagine what he'd said.

"Yes. She knew I had the sickness of the heart. I told her everything. She said only time could heal this wound, but she gave me a special medicine to help me hang on while I got through it."

"I wish I'd had someone like her," Moriah said, recall- ing her mother's anger with her and the problem she'd caused.

"I'll take you to meet her when Melanie and I go out. She lives far back in the mountains and collects herbs in case anyone needs an old-fashioned healing. She'll want to look you over before we're married."

Her breath caught. She laid a hand against her throat. "You're moving too fast. I haven't said—"

"Yes," he supplied for her. "But you will."

She wanted to. Oh, yes, she wanted to!

"You will," he repeated softly.

Suddenly he was standing beside her. He took hold of her and practically lifted her from the chair. They stood face-to-face, their quick breaths the only sound in the room.

"K-Kane," she stammered.

"Yes?" His voice was deep, husky. He stood so close.

She had only to lean forward an inch to close the gap between them. Invisible electricity arced from body to body, a torch of need and desire that had never been appeased.

His hands settled on her shoulders. With gentle, circling motions, he soothed and massaged her doubts away. Her world focused on the warmth of his hands, large hands, gentle in their touch. He'd always been so gentle with her.

A sob lodged in her chest, growing bigger and bigger, until the pain caused her to gasp. His lips were there, on hers, catching the sob before it was uttered.

It was the gentlest of kisses.

She leaned into him, unable to resist. The days had been endless, the worry of looking for her father and shielding her daughter from the wayward past too much. She wanted to dive into his strength and never come up.

The kiss became a thousand, traced in tender arcs over her face and neck, so that she lifted her face to his, wanting more.

His breath quickened. So did hers.

"Come with me," he invited in a hoarse growl that caused a blizzard of feelings to run along her nerves.

"Kane," she whispered, a last grasp at sanity. "This is madness...*madness.*"

"I know."

"We can't—"

"Shh."

"I think—"

"Shh."

When his hand trailed down her arm to her waist, then upward until he cupped her breast, she closed her eyes, unable to fight it a moment longer.

The ringing of the telephone shattered the golden moment. She jerked from his arms, as embarrassed as a teenager discovered by her parents.

With a low curse, he went to the wall phone next to the kitchen planning area and answered gruffly. After a moment, he said, "You'll have to have your mother's permission."

Moriah went forward when he held the instrument out to her.

"It's Melanie," he told her, and stepped aside.

"Yes?" she said, taking the receiver from him. When he walked away and began to collect their used dishes, she stifled her regret at the loss of closeness.

"Mom, Mrs. Rivers has invited me to spend the night. She's going to teach me to ride tomorrow. Is that okay with you?"

The eagerness in her daughter's voice made Moriah smile. The city kid seemed to be taking to small-town and ranch life like a duck to water. Perhaps she had deprived the teenager of her natural inheritance.

Moriah glanced at Kane, who stood by the sink, rinsing their bowls and plates before putting them in the dishwasher. There was so much for Melanie here—her father and grandfather, the young cowboy who'd apparently captured her heart at first glance, the friendliness of the town, the beauty of the mountains....

All the things *she* liked. "All right," she said. "Have a good time."

"I'll be really polite," Melanie assured her with feigned seriousness. "And I'll help with the dishes."

This last was a private joke between them. In teaching Melanie how to get along with her grandmother, Moriah had told her to help with the dishes. It always softened Joleen up. The older woman hated doing dishes.

Moriah hung up, a smile lingering on her face. Until she looked at Kane.

He'd finished the dishes and now stood with his hands in the back pockets of his tan cords. He wore the red flannel shirt she'd seen before, his favorite, she guessed. His T-shirt formed an enticing triangle of white in the open wedge of his shirt collar.

He watched her with an introspective frown on his handsome face, his thoughts unreadable.

"Thank you," she said simply. When he raised his brows in question, she continued, "For letting me make the decision about Melanie spending the night."

"Did you think I'd barge right in and take over, playing the heavy father to make up for lost time?"

"No," she admitted. "I know that isn't your way. You're a fair and honorable person. And kind."

His eyes held hers. "Is that truly how you see me?" he inquired softly, a smile hovering on his mouth.

Before she could reply, he turned and walked out of the pleasant, homey kitchen. She heard him on the stairs, going to his room. Mystified, she wiped up the few crumbs on the table and countertops, deciding to check on her father, then go to bed.

She found Homer sound asleep. On an impulse of affection, she kissed his cheek, then clicked off the TV and turned out the lamp on the bedside table. She left, closing his door behind her.

For a moment she stood in the hall, wishing things were different, wishing she dared grab what Kane was offering.

Except she wasn't sure what it was. Marriage. Melanie. His bed. But where was his heart? And what was she going to do with the overwhelming love she felt for him?

She shook her head, helpless against the tide of emotion

that swept through her like a tornado. During the month she'd been in Whitehorn, she'd seen so many facets of him—as a concerned friend to her father, as a doctor to the people of the town, as an exquisite lover, as a surprised father. As a husband...

Not wanting to think about that, she hurried down the dim hall. His door was open. She couldn't help but glance in when she passed. He stood by the window, gazing out at the night. He'd taken off his long-sleeved shirt and tossed it on a chair.

The solid masculinity of his back dissolved her intention of hiding in her room for the rest of the night. She was aware that they were alone for all practical purposes, with Melanie gone and her father lost in the restful sleep of convalescence.

As if sensing her stare, he turned. His dark eyes met hers. A blaze seemed to leap to life in them. She felt the tremors start deep within her. She wanted him. Yes. *Yes.*

Without looking away, he crossed the flower-strewn oriental rug and stopped by the door. Then he waited.

She took a step. Then another. And another.

Kane felt the tension increase with every step Moriah took. Finally she stood in the doorway. He waited, schooling himself to patience the way he had years ago when he worked the local ranches, breaking young horses to the touch of a man.

The moment stretched out like a lazy cat taking her time before deciding where she wanted to sleep.

The wide, golden-brown eyes flicked over the room, then to him. He held her gaze, letting her see into his soul.

He loved her, he realized. He'd always loved her. He could no longer hide it from himself. His heart pounded so hard it hurt when she stepped inside.

He closed the door and pushed the button that locked it before she could change her mind. She looked as if she might bolt at any moment…like a doe who feared she was targeted in the cross hairs of a hunter's sights.

For a moment, he wished she would come to him joyfully and without doubts, knowing that what they shared was right and natural.

The way she once had?

The consequences of her trust had been severe for a young girl. No matter what the circumstances, he hadn't been there when she'd needed him. It would take time to overcome that.

"It's all right," he murmured, taking her hand in his. "I'm here. I'll always be here." It was a vow he intended to keep.

She looked at him, puzzlement in her gaze.

He smiled slightly. She didn't understand, but gradually she would come to trust him again. He'd show her, every day in a thousand ways, that she was safe with him, that he'd be there for her in the future…for all their lives.

Her lips parted. He saw her chest lift as she drew a deep breath and let it out. It sounded shaky.

"I'm shaking, too," he said. "I've wanted you for so long. All my life, Woman-with-Eyes-Like-a-Doe."

Her eyes widened, and he knew she remembered him calling her that long ago, giving her an Indian name important only to them. She reached up and caressed his lips with the tips of her fingers.

He fought the need to sweep her into his arms and claim her for his own for all time. The love he'd once felt burst from his heart, refusing to be locked away any longer. She was the only woman he'd ever loved. He knew that without a doubt.

He picked up a blanket his grandmother had given him

and swung it around his shoulders. Then he held it open, inviting his woman inside to share its warmth, in a custom as old as the Montana hills. Would she remember it was the Indian way of expressing love?

She hesitated. A smile formed at the corners of her mouth and she took the necessary step to bring her within its folds.

He enclosed her in his arms, the blanket hiding all but their heads from view. A groan was wrung out of him at the feel of her body against his. His own responded with a harsh pounding of blood and a sharp ache in his nether regions. He was ready for her in an instant.

Moriah felt the shudder Kane couldn't control and wrapped her arms around his waist. The rigid tumescence against her abdomen told of his hunger. She, too, was ready. The feel of the blanket against her neck reminded her of the significance of this ritual. Kane was asking her to be his woman.

She searched his eyes, trying to discover if there was love as well as passion in those stormy depths.

He tightened his arms around her. The elation returned, making her dizzy. She couldn't think when he made her feel like this. "I want…"

"Yes?" He picked up on the words at once. "Say it. Tell me what you want."

But she was too reserved now. At seventeen, she'd been open and honest with him, but she'd learned to hold herself in check.

He gazed into her eyes. "Me," he said, clearly shaken by the need she couldn't hide. "You want me."

"Your hands," she murmured in a wild confession, "on me. Your lips…all over…making me…making me ache."

He dipped his head and stopped her words with his mouth. He savored her every taste and texture with his lips, his tongue.

"Don't say things like that," he warned when he finally drew away from her a tiny space. "It makes me crazy."

She laughed then as something like joy rushed over her. He attacked her neck with a low growl, nibbling down to her throat until he reached the barrier of her gold-hued sweater.

He frowned, tossed the blanket onto the chair and grasped the hem of the garment. "Let's get out of these."

"Yes," she agreed, only too eager to comply.

With a flick of his capable hands, he removed the sweater. It joined his shirt and the blanket on the chair. Their shoes fell silently to the rug. Her gray wool slacks followed, then his faded cords, the material soft from many washings.

"Ah," he breathed, stopping the disrobing to gaze at her with eyes flaming with hunger.

He cupped her breasts and ran his thumbs over the smooth satin of her bra. Her nipples beaded into hard, visible points beneath the fabric. He pressed upward, then kissed the mounding flesh above the lace edges.

When he ran his tongue over the same spots, she grew weak and had to clutch at his shoulders to keep from collapsing at his feet. Like magic, her underclothes disappeared. He bent to her again, taking the pebbled nipple in his mouth and rolling his tongue over it until she moaned in ecstasy.

"You like that, do you?" he teased, pleased with her response.

For answer, she clasped his T-shirt and tugged it upward and over his face. She left him blindfolded by the cotton and dived into his bed, hiding under the cover.

She waited for him to join her. A moment sped by, then another and another. She stuck her head out to see what kept him…and then was still.

He stood by the bed, waiting for her, a tiny smile

playing about the corners of his mouth. He was a wild, beautiful savage without a stitch of clothing on his tall, elegant form.

"Kane," she said, shaken by the sight. "You are...I used to dream..."

"So did I...of you, every night." His gaze roamed over her as the sheet dropped from her shoulders to pool around her waist.

She held out her arms. "Come to me."

He sat beside her and hooked a finger under her chin so he could gaze into her eyes. "You used to say that to me, inviting me into your bed and your arms."

"Yes."

He skimmed his fingers over her, down her throat and onto her torso, making her shiver with delight. "Tell me how you feel," he demanded. "Are you as hot as I am? As wild?"

"Yes," she cried softly. "You make me feel larger than life and yet part of all creation. I want—I want..." She closed her eyes. "I want it all, the way it used to be."

His mouth paved her chest with wet kisses. He pressed her down into the bed and hovered over her. "Each time with you is like the first time all over again. It blows my mind. Exciting and so hot...so very, very hot...."

He sucked at her long slender nipples until they turned from pale to hot pink. She writhed under him, unable to lie still.

Running her fingers through the light furring on his chest, she whimpered as heat filled her deep inside. Restless, she ran her hands over his back, his hips. She explored the line of his spine and followed it between his buttocks until he bucked against her as she touched a sensitive spot.

"Much of that and it'll be all over for me," he chided, shifting so she couldn't touch him quite so intimately.

"I want to explore you as thoroughly as you've explored me," she explained breathlessly, enchanted by this sweet, aching play between them.

He turned them suddenly, so that she was above him. He reached up and gripped the bed frame. "Then have your way with me. I'll try like hell to hold out."

His smile flashed white and sexy against his tanned skin. She laid her hands in the center of his chest and noted the contrast of her pale flesh to his swarthier tones.

She kissed the middle of his chest, then each small, beaded nipple hidden in the black curling hairs. Sitting back on her heels, she stroked down until she reached the phallus rising from the thatch of dark hair.

"I loved your body from the first moment I saw it," she confessed. "It seems rich and dark and mysterious, like the earth. A place of nurturing. A place to grow."

She brushed her fingers along the hard length of him. The muscles stood out along his ribs as he fought visibly for control while she touched and explored him to her heart's content.

When she dropped forward on her elbows and used her mouth to explore him further, to detect taste as well as texture, Kane swore softly and released his hold on the bed. Pushing himself upright against the pillows, he ran his fingers into her hair, dislodging the band that held it at the base of her neck.

It sprang out around her face and shoulders, falling over his abdomen and thighs like waves of fire that warmed but didn't burn.

She'd been his first love, the dream that wouldn't die or leave, no matter how hard he'd tried to forget her.

When she stopped her tormentingly light touches and took him into her mouth, he clenched his teeth and held on. Then, unable to stand it, he cupped her head in his hands and pulled her to him.

She fell onto him, landing with a soft thud against his chest. He brought her face to his and took her mouth in a kiss of rampaging hunger.

"The first time, all over again," he murmured, reaching blindly for the bedside drawer and the packets he kept there.

Moriah opened her eyes with an effort. When she saw what he was doing, she stopped his search with a hand over his. "I'm on the pill. I became so irregular, the doctor put me on hormones to help straighten things out."

"I've never indulged without protection," he said. "Do you trust me enough to take me that way?"

"Yes."

The glow in his eyes warmed her clear through. "You trusted me once before. It wasn't so safe for you then, was it?"

"We tried to be careful," she reminded him.

"That first time," he said softly, "I'd carried the packet for so long—at least a year—that it was foolish to trust it. I didn't know that then."

She nodded and smiled. "All boys do that, I think."

He traced the line of her lips with one finger. "Are you sure?" he asked. "You're not afraid to take me…bare?"

"No. You said there'd been no others, not without…" Heat rushed into her face. It seemed odd, but right, to be talking about this. A measure of honesty, she thought. And trust.

"There haven't." He took a breath, held it and let it out carefully. "I'm about to come undone just thinking about it. That's what you do to me." He shifted closer to her. "I want you like that…with nothing between us but the hot honey…."

He captured her roaming hand and brought it to his lips, kissing her in the center of her palm and on each finger. His other hand moved over her, touching her breasts, her tummy, then sliding down to cup her intimately.

She laid her head on his chest and pressed the side of her face against his warm, hard flesh as he began to stroke her. His touch called forth every ounce of passion in her. When he slipped a finger inside, she, too, nearly came undone.

"Now," she whispered. "I want you now."

The world spun until she was lying against the mattress and he was over her, nestled between her thighs. He entered her in one sure stroke of pleasure.

"Like that?" he asked, low and hoarse, straining at control. "Is this how you want me?"

"Yes, oh, Kane, yes!"

"Move against me," he whispered raggedly. "Take what you need, and I'll try to hold on."

She thrust upward while he rocked back and forth, each stroke fueling the fire that bound her to him. With lightning speed, she came apart under him, unable to stop the wild convulsions and the cries of ecstasy. He rode the storm with her, and, as she regained her own senses, felt his release deep inside her.

She lay in his arms, breathing deeply, as contentment eddied through her inch by inch.

"The best, the very best ever," she heard him say.

A great swell of pride suffused her entire body. She felt languid and voluptuous and incredibly beautiful. Sexy. Daring. Exciting. Feminine.

All of those.

She woke some time later to his movement beside her.

"I'm hungry," he said.

A smile played around her lips. She couldn't chase it away. "Me, too. There's fruit and cookies in the kitchen."

"Let's go."

He found her a robe to wear and pulled on his cords. She slipped into her socks. When they started out, he dropped an arm across her shoulders. It felt right.

In the kitchen, they sat at the table and ate the fruit compotes and the cookies from the bakery. This time she sat in his lap. He wouldn't let her out of direct contact.

"I'm afraid you'll disappear again," he confessed with such candidness it brought tears to her eyes, but she managed a smile.

As long as they were like this, just the two of them, drowsy and content after their lovemaking, she had no doubts. If only they could stay this way forever.

"Are you going to marry me?" he asked when they were finished and she had curled up against his chest. "Are you convinced we're good together?" He chuckled. "Good, hell, we're the best!"

She swallowed hard before she could speak. "Yes."

His arms tightened around her, then he let out a whoop of surprise and hugged her until she was dizzy. She gave a gasp of protest, which he ignored. He kissed her speechless, then breathless.

When she'd regained her senses, he looked at her solemnly. "That was 'yes, I'll marry you,' wasn't it? You weren't merely agreeing we were the best lovers in the world, were you?"

"No. Yes. I mean…" She felt a shiver of uncertainty. She wanted to ask if he loved her, but pride wouldn't permit such a show of weakness. "I will marry you."

He sighed, grimaced, then gave a resigned smile. "Oh, lordy," he said, "my grandmother will declare a tribal-ceremony day when she hears I'm getting married." He grinned at Moriah. "Even if you are a doe-eyed white woman."

Thirteen

Word of the engagement spread fast, especially when Kane mentioned it to Lily Mae when he and Moriah saw her at the Hip Hop Café the next day. After seeing to her father's lunch, she and Kane had taken a long walk, then stopped in for pie and coffee in the late afternoon.

"Mother was right. Lily Mae would have told everyone in the county that I was pregnant if she'd known." She realized what she was saying and shut up. That was the past.

"I wish someone had told me," he said, taking her hand and swinging it between them.

"I'm sorry—"

"No," he cut in sharply. He pulled her to him as they walked up the steps to the house. "I didn't mean to put a guilt trip on you. You did the best you could under the circumstances. Perhaps if we'd both had a little more faith in each other, we would have tried harder. Anyway, it's the future that counts now."

She kept sneaking little glances at him as she prepared supper. He read a medical journal at the table, wearing a pair of dark-rimmed, businesslike glasses. She smiled.

He looked relaxed and happy. Because of her? Because of the passion they'd shared more than once during the night?

Melanie came bouncing in before dark. She was starved, she told them. "Be right back." She dashed out to shower and change for dinner.

Homer came to the table for the meal. Moriah glanced around the group. Melanie chatted eagerly to her grandfather about the horses she'd ridden at the ranch. Homer nodded his head at each pause and sometimes gave a piece of advice about animals. Kane observed it all with a smile lurking at the corners of his mouth. When he caught her looking at him, he winked.

The meal was nearly finished when he spoke up. "Melanie," he said casually. When he had her attention, he continued, "Did your mom tell you we're to be married?"

Her eyes widened. A huge smile broke over her face. "Super!" she said. "When?"

Moriah and her father had the house to themselves on Sunday. Melanie was taking a riding lesson with Maris Rivers and visiting Keith. Kane was at the hospital.

"I found your letters," she said to Homer. They'd been discussing the past and bringing each other up to date on their lives. "Kane showed them to me. I thought you'd forgotten about me after Mom and I left."

He gave her a sad-eyed look. "That first year was the loneliest of my life. I finally got used to it, though. A person has to adjust."

"Yes."

He rubbed his hands together as if they were cold.

"Your mother and I...we weren't suited from the start. I knew it, but I thought in time she'd come to love living out here with the mountains all around." He make a sweeping gesture. "But she never did. She was a city girl at heart."

"You and Mom never mentioned your anniversary, but I saw your wedding certificate one time. I was cleaning out a closet. I was born seven months after the marriage."

He shook his head. "We weren't forced into it," he said, correcting her impression. "You came two months early because of nature, not us. We eloped on our third date."

She was astounded by this information, unable to imagine her mother being that impulsive. "She said you were her ticket to a better life, or so she thought."

"It was a mismatch from the first. We probably should have given up long before she took you and left."

"You know why we had to leave," Moriah murmured, embarrassed.

Homer gave her an understanding smile. "Yes, your mother would have thought it was the end of the world to have to face a town full of gossip. She was proud. And ambitious. I never paid much attention to her talk of owning a store. I had my own plans for striking it rich." He shook his head. "A fool's dream. Your mother's was much wiser."

The regret in his voice pained her.

"I could have helped her," he went on. "I could have steadied down and saved enough for her to start her own place. But I never did. I always thought I'd strike it rich... just one more season, one more mountain to explore."

"You found the sapphires," she reminded him. He had finally remembered where the new vein was located.

"They're on Kincaid land."

"Well, you're entitled to a finder's fee. Or maybe more, if the state retained the mineral rights. I'll ask Kane to check."

He would be home from his rounds soon. A frisson ran over her. Each day her love for him grew, until it felt as if her heart couldn't contain it.

"Don't throw away your life like I did," Homer advised with sudden intensity. "You have to talk to the other person. Share your dreams. Listen to his."

Moriah considered her father's unexpected advice. Marriage to Kane would fulfill all her dreams, but what about his? Was he marrying her for Melanie's sake, giving up his dreams in order to have his daughter? He seemed happy....

"Joleen and I both had to have our own way. We couldn't find a middle ground," Homer continued. "Tell Kane what you want, then let him tell you his wants. You might be surprised at how similar they are."

"He wants a family," she confided. "He wants Melanie."

"You love him," Homer deduced. "Have you told him?"

She shook her head. It would be too humiliating if he didn't love her in return, if he was only marrying her because it was so obvious that Melanie wanted them to be together.

"Tell him," her father urged. "Tell him."

"I...tonight," she said. "I'll talk to him tonight."

Tonight she would face Kane and ask him what he really wanted, Moriah thought that evening. She was dressing for a party she and Kane were to attend at the Kincaid ranch. The invitation had surprised her. She knew Dugin Kincaid by sight, of course, but she hadn't been in his circle of friends while growing up there.

Neither had Kane, but as one of the town's few doctors, he'd been invited to ranch doings in the past. Since Dugin had married—to a librarian, Kane had said—they entertained more often at the ranch.

Moriah was interested in seeing the inside of the local

landmark. The house was a two-story mansion complete with a good-sized ballroom. She'd once seen the layout in a magazine.

"Ready?" Kane entered the bedroom, which they now shared. He came to her and held out a jeweler's box. "Here, this should make it official."

She opened the box. It held an engagement ring. "Oh, Kane, it's beautiful." She cast him a worried glance. "It's so large. What if I lose it?"

He laughed at her fears. Lifting the ring from the satin, he slipped it on her finger. It fit perfectly. "I always dreamed of showering you with jewels when I became a great and famous doctor."

"I still have the necklace you gave me," she murmured. "In the little velvet case it came in."

"Wear it," he requested.

With shaking hands, she retrieved the necklace. Before she could put it on, he took it from her and slipped a pendent on the slender chain. He fastened it around her neck.

She stared at the engagement ring, then at the matching diamond in the pendant. "Kane," she breathed, and couldn't say another word.

He kissed her. "Come on," he said huskily. "We have to go."

They went to the study, where Melanie and Homer were watching a game show. "Mom, you look beautiful. Let me see your ring. Oh, it's gorgeous. I helped pick it out. Do you like it? And the necklace? Were you surprised?"

"Thank you. Yes, and yes," Moriah responded, laughing at her daughter's excited babble. She felt like Cinderella on her way to the ball. With a bright smile, she put on her warm coat and waltzed out the door on Kane's arm.

An hour later, she waltzed in his arms to dreamy music played by a small band in the Kincaid ballroom. The night was magic, like a dream…one that was coming true for her just as it had for the heroine of the fairy tale.

"I'm almost afraid to blink," she said, nestling her head against his shoulder.

"Afraid that it will all disappear?"

She was surprised that he understood. "Yes."

"I feel the same." He tightened his arms around her. "I'm afraid if I let you go for an instant, you'll return to some land beyond the beyond and I'll never find you again."

He sounded so sincere, so…loving. Her heart did flips and other silly things, speeding up, stopping, then racing again.

She relaxed and let herself enjoy the moment. Soft laughter close to them drew her eyes to her hostess. She was dancing with a tall rancher whose name Moriah couldn't remember.

The librarian who had snagged the county's richest bachelor seemed to be enjoying herself. Dugin's wife was pretty. She had a soft, fluttery manner. Moriah could envision her as a children's librarian, reading stories in her girlish voice, her eyes going wide at the scary parts.

Just the way they'd done when Moriah had described how she had discovered her father in the woods, looking like an apparition from hell when he'd appeared on the path. Mary Jo Kincaid had been very interested and had asked several questions.

"Aliens?" she'd said when Moriah had come to that part of Homer's tale. Instead of laughing, she looked sympathetic. "Poor old dear. He must have been frightened out of his wits. Oh, I'm so sorry…I didn't mean—"

"That's okay," Moriah had said, stopping her hostess's

embarrassed apology. "He's doing fine now. He can't recall much about the episode."

"Hungry?" Kane asked, breaking into her musing.

"Yes."

At his knowing grin, she blushed. She was always starved after they made love. He'd teased her about it last night.

They went to the refreshment table, then joined Luke and Maris Rivers at one of the tiny tables scattered around the edges of the ballroom. "Keith was disappointed Melanie couldn't visit," Maris told them. "He said she had to grampa-sit."

"She volunteered," Kane said. "Makes one wonder what mischief she's up to, doesn't it?"

They laughed at his suspicions. "You'll have to get used to having a very attractive daughter," Luke advised. "Keith really has a case on her."

"Yeah, I know." Kane gave Moriah a look she felt clear down to her toes.

The band struck up a new song. She remembered some words from it. *So in love, so much in love.* Oh, yes.

After the repast, they left the table to dance again. The night wafted by on gentle wings. She smiled, realizing she was waxing poetic, or perhaps just maudlin.

Kane was called aside by a rancher. Moriah returned to the table. Luke and Maris were talking to their host, she saw. Dugin Kincaid was much as she remembered—a tall, lanky, diffident man who was never sure where he fit in. She hoped his marriage had made him happy.

She patted back a yawn. She was tired. They had worked hard in the office all week. She'd cooked and looked after her father on top of that, and then, last night and the night before, she and Kane had turned to each other, hot and eager and demanding.

Glancing around the ballroom, she saw Kane was still talking. She'd go to the ladies room and freshen up, she decided. In a dreamy fog, she drifted along the hallway to the rest room. Coming out, she paused to admire the Indian artifacts arranged in glass cases along the wide corridor.

There were baskets, pottery, full costumes, ceremonial masks—a veritable museum. In fact, most of the pieces were better than those she'd seen at the Native American museum in town.

She moved farther down the hall, examining the contents of each lighted cabinet and reading the cards that explained the meaning of each relic. One case held a display of shamanic wares.

It contained several medicine pouches and gourd shakers, she noted, plus an impressive headdress and mask made from a buffalo skull, with the hide still attached. It would cover most of the face, shoulders and torso of the medicine man. Fringed buckskin leggings and a beaded breastplate completed the outfit.

"Horrible, aren't they?" Mary Jo asked. "I've been trying to convince Dugin to get rid of the old things."

Moriah glanced up. "Well," she hedged, "I would guess they're quite valuable. They look like museum quality."

"Oh, do you think so?" Her hostess peered at the items as if assembling their value, then murmured an excuse and disappeared down the long hallway.

Moriah returned to the ballroom. Across the way, Kane was conversing with Lori Bains. They were smiling, talking with the ease of old friends. A fierce jealousy arose in her.

Kane had said they weren't lovers. Moriah believed him, but it was hard to watch him with the woman. Lori was beautiful, smart and poised. The perfect wife for him in many ways.

If not for her and what had happened between them at the cabin, Moriah wondered if he would be engaged to the lovely midwife by now. They were so well suited. But Kane, with his sense of honor, would feel responsible for her and Melanie.

Back at the table, she accepted a glass of champagne from a waiter and drank half of it. It didn't relieve the parched feeling she had inside.

Maris Rivers returned to the table to say they were going home. She leaned over to peer at Moriah's hand. "Your ring is lovely," she said, admiring the brilliant stone. "When are you and Kane getting married?"

"Soon," he answered.

Moriah glanced around. He stood behind her, looking so incredibly handsome in his dark suit she wondered why the other women didn't swoon when he walked by.

He gave her a level glance, then smiled at Maris. "By Christmas, I think."

"Good. Tracy Hensley wants to give you a shower."

"She has her hands full with the new baby," he said, obviously thinking as a doctor.

"Umm-hmm. Winona Cobbs and Maggie have volunteered to help. So did I. We're looking forward to an excuse to get together." With a grin and a wave, she left.

Moriah trembled when Kane laid his hands on her shoulders.

"How about another dance?" he suggested.

She nodded, feeling that events were moving much too fast. She needed time to think, to sort things out. But when he took her into his arms, her mind stopped working altogether.

Kane surreptitiously studied Moriah as they danced and chatted. Worry ate at him. Never talkative, she was unusually quiet tonight. Had someone hurt her feelings while he'd been away from her? Perhaps she'd overheard some snide remarks about them and their daughter.

Gossip was rampant in the town. He knew that. But he thought most of it was of the merely interested variety. No one had reason to be malicious. Still, some people could be cruel just for the hell of it. He'd experienced that during his youth.

When the evening was over and they were on their way home, she was even more withdrawn. At the house, he dropped an arm around her shoulders as they walked inside and up the steps to their room. He felt he had to hold on to her, that she was slipping away.

The house was silent, the other two occupants asleep. In the privacy of their room, Kane observed her while he slipped out of his clothes and pulled on a pair of cords. She stood by the window, gazing out at the moonlight.

The night had turned cold, and frost glittered on the lawn and shrubs. Winter was fast approaching. He felt its chill breath on his neck and sensed disaster.

"Tell me what's bothering you," he requested.

She held her hand up so the diamond sparkled in the lamplight. "This. Are we doing the right thing?"

The question hurt, he found. He wanted her to be happy about a future with him. When she was in his arms, she seemed to be, but when she wasn't, she became pensive. Her doubts made him angry. Wouldn't she ever believe in him?

"Yes," he said. "It's right for me and for Melanie…and for you, if you'd only see it."

"But if it doesn't work?" She turned a troubled gaze on him.

He didn't want to talk. Backlit by the full moon, she was once again the beautiful, ethereal creature who'd taken his heart and not given it back almost seventeen years ago. He wanted to make love to her and claim her for all time.

She was his, damn it! When was she going to realize it?

"It will work," he told her.

Her chin took on a defiant tilt. "You've made up your mind, so it has to be the way you've decided. Life isn't like that. Right now we share passion and a child, but passion cools and children grow up and leave home." She shook her head. "It isn't enough. I want…more."

The cool logic of her tone set him on edge. He was the one who was supposed to be rational. But he wasn't. He was in love, and God knew, there was no reasoning with that. "What?" he demanded. "Tell me and I'll get it." *Or die trying.*

Moriah ignored his statement. "By the time we realized our mistake and divorced, you might have lost the woman you really could love. She might have married someone else by then. We can break our engagement—"

"What are you talking about?" He glared at her as if she'd lost her mind. "What woman?"

It took more courage than she'd thought it would, but she said it. "Lori Parker…Lori Bains. The midwife," she added when he looked totally confused.

"Lori," he repeated with a frown. "I do care for her…as a friend. She's a wonderful person."

"Yes, she is. Of course you love her. I don't blame you," she quickly added, as his face took on an expression she couldn't read. His gaze seemed to pierce right through her.

"So you think I'm in love with Lori," he mused. "Maybe that explains it."

She watched him, wary of his changing moods. "Explains what?" she finally had to ask.

"Why you're closed and withdrawn now when earlier you were warm and loving." He gave her a narrow-eyed look. "We're not breaking our engagement. I'm not in love with Lori. I never have been. You're the woman I want."

"Want," she repeated. "It isn't enough."

"Then perhaps you'd better tell me exactly what is. In simple words, please. I'm a man of simple tastes and needs."

She knew she'd have to explain the whole thing for him to understand. "I was wrong about you," she told him. "Years ago. I know you wouldn't have abandoned me when I needed you."

He gave a snort at that. "Do go on," he invited when she stopped. A tiny smile had formed at the corners of his mouth. She couldn't tell if he was being sarcastic or not. The growing blaze in his eyes confused her.

She cleared her throat as she reached the hard part. "I know you love and want Melanie." Her breath came and went in jerky stops and starts. "And I think you feel responsible for me."

"Yes, I do." His gaze didn't waver when she glanced at him. He gave her a look so intense she nearly forgot what she was trying so hard to explain. She just wanted to go into his arms and stay there forever.

Reining in her thoughts, she nodded. It was just as she'd suspected—he felt he had to take care of her.

"Since coming back to Whitehorn and seeing you with your patients, I realize you're a caring person…very caring and kind and—and honorable."

"Right," he agreed. "The noble savage."

She blinked at this display of arrogance, a trait she hadn't noticed in him previously.

He strode toward her like a demigod—powerful and

filled with purpose, finely controlled energy crackling around him like lightning. He stopped no more than a foot from her.

"But there has to be more between a man and a woman for a marriage to succeed," she said through a tight throat. She removed the ring and held it out to him. "I want love as well as passion. I'll not settle for less. Neither should you."

The muscles stood out in his jaw, and he looked dangerous. "I don't intend to. I admit I was thinking of marriage to Lori, but then another woman came into my life, one I fell in love with—not the girl I loved long ago, but a woman, mature and compassionate. I fell in love so far, so deep, that I'll never get out. I don't want to," he added in a rough purr.

She stared at him.

"Don't you know?" he murmured. "Can't you tell? I live for you, only you."

"But you said…" She couldn't remember exactly what he'd said. "You and Lori were at a point… Then the night at the cabin happened and…"

He touched her lips with his fingertips. "If I'd never met you, maybe I could have married someone else. My life might have been simpler, with none of the heartbreak, but maybe none of the joy, either. None of the wild delight that rushes through me when I see you. None of the fiery passion of our lovemaking. None of the fierce contentment I feel afterward in your arms."

"Kane," she whispered, hardly daring to believe what he was telling her, and yet, his eyes… That glow…

He leaned into her, sliding between her thighs to gather her close. "None of the hope that fills me when I think of our future, working together to build a strong, healthy community, with you keeping my life and my office straight and sane…except when we go crazy together in each other's arms."

When he pressed close, her body responded, her nipples peaking, her skin flushing at his nearness. The blood became a roar in her ears, almost drowning out his words.

"I do want more." His lips touched hers lightly. "Say you love me," he said, not sounding quite as certain as he had, "the way I love you."

Her eyes widened. "Do you really love me?"

He kissed her again. "Oh, yes, I do." He gave her a stern look, part amazement, part exasperation. "Surely you knew."

"How could I?"

"Why do you think I forced the engagement? I thought with the passion we shared and with Melanie's influence, you'd come to love me…to trust me again."

"I do."

His voice dropped to a whisper. "I've never forgotten how you came to me that first time, the trust you gave me. I want it like that again, with no doubts, with nothing between us but a love so great, it never died." He drew back a little. "Did it?"

He was asking for confirmation from her, she realized. She saw the need in his eyes, the love he didn't try to conceal. It was all there.

She realized it had been each time they had made love, including that night at the cabin, if she'd only trusted him and her own instincts. His love was hers for the taking.

With a glad cry, she reached for him.

Fourteen

The wedding of Moriah Gilmore and Dr. Kane Hunter took place the day after Thanksgiving. After rain during the night, the day dawned bright for the ceremony. Moriah had asked for a quiet exchange of vows with only relatives present, but Kane had told her there was no way. He was right.

They ended up having two ceremonies—one at the church in town and one at the reservation afterward, where the reception was held. His grandmother and aunts had prepared a huge feast.

Moriah wiped the last bite of fry bread through the honey on her plate. Before she could get it to her mouth, Kane caught her hand and brought it to his. He ate the sticky treat.

"Beast," she said.

He leaned over and kissed her.

"When am I going to get a brother or sister?" Melanie demanded, watching the play between her parents with delight.

"Soon," Kane promised. He gave his wife a smoldering look. "Very soon."

To everyone's delight, Moriah blushed bright red. She glanced around the table. She had a large family now, she realized. The entire tribe, it seemed. If the people Kane introduced to her weren't blood relatives, they were honorary aunts, uncles or cousins. She particularly liked Jackson and Maggie Hawk. This was their first outing with their new baby, who had slept soundly throughout the reception.

"We'll have one like that," Kane whispered to her.

She turned to look into his eyes. He looked happy. Because of her, she realized. Joy glowed inside, warming her to the outer limits of her soul. She lifted her head proudly.

Kane made her see herself in a different light. She'd never felt that she was more than average in looks or intelligence, but he made her feel beautiful. He praised her efforts in the office, telling her they couldn't get along without her. Sandy, his nurse, echoed that sentiment. He made her feel wanted and needed.

That's what every person requires, she realized. She glanced at her mother, who, dressed in a designer suit, was listening to her ex-husband tell of his weird captivity in the mountains. Her smile was a bit fixed, but she'd been polite throughout the festivities.

Joleen had her faults, but she was Moriah's mother and Melanie's grandmother, as Kane had pointed out. They might never be close, certainly they'd never be friends, but, well, there were some ties that couldn't be severed.

Homer looked nice. He was clean-shaven, his hair neatly braided. He had decided to move to town and live in the Victorian as a sort of caretaker and night watchman, since Kane and Moriah and Melanie were moving into the new house. He was also a partner with the Kincaids in the mining venture.

Moriah smiled with affection as she heard him expound on his enthusiastic plans for discovering more sapphire veins. He liked the hunt more than the treasure.

Looking at Melanie, who was dancing with Keith, she realized how blessed she'd been. She'd tried to be a good mother to Melanie, to appreciate her daughter's talents without demanding that the girl conform to some ideal in her own mind. That was the best anyone could do.

She looked at her husband. Kane did that instinctively with everyone. He liked others for what they were, not what he wanted them to be. If she had loved him for nothing else, she would have loved him for that quality alone.

But she loved him in many, many ways…as he loved her. She sighed, pleased with life and with herself. Part of her problem in not trusting him had been her doubts about herself. Thanks to his love, those were gone.

Later, after a youthful band set up their drums, guitars and electronic keyboard, they danced. It was almost midnight when Kane asked Moriah if she was ready to leave. He kissed her temple and nuzzled her with his nose.

"Do I need to drive you two home?" Melanie inquired. "I'd hate for you to get arrested for not paying attention to the road and have to spend your wedding night in jail."

"I can manage," Kane told his impudent offspring. "Just make sure you don't cause a riot at the res over the weekend."

Melanie was staying with her great-grandmother at the cabin deep in the woods of the reservation. She wanted to learn about herbs and medicines to use in her medical practice.

Suddenly, Moriah wanted to be alone with her handsome husband. She needed to touch him, to have him caress her. He took her hand and squeezed it gently. "Let's get out of here," he said huskily.

They dashed away into the night, needing only the magic of each other. "I came here to find my father," she murmured as they drove toward the new house that awaited them just a short piece down the road and where she'd elected to spend their honeymoon, working together on their dream home. "Instead, Melanie found hers, and I found…" She ran her fingers through Kane's silky black hair. "I found my very own love."

"Again," he added, stopping in front of the house. They walked to the door. He lifted her in his arms in a masterful sweep. "We found each other. I'll never let you out of my arms this time."

"I'll never want to leave them."

He stepped over the threshold into their new home, into a new life…together.

* * * * *

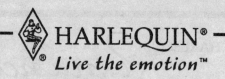

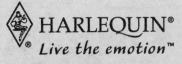

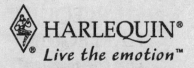

HARLEQUIN®
INTRIGUE®

BREATHTAKING ROMANTIC SUSPENSE

Shared dangers and passions lead to electrifying romance and heart-stopping suspense!

Every month, you'll meet six new heroes who are guaranteed to make your spine tingle and your pulse pound. With them you'll enter into the exciting world of Harlequin Intrigue— where your life is on the line and so is your heart!

THAT'S INTRIGUE— ROMANTIC SUSPENSE AT ITS BEST!

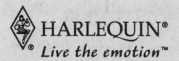

HARLEQUIN®
Live the emotion™

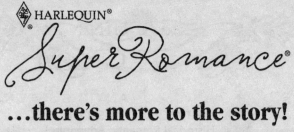

HARLEQUIN®
Super Romance®

...there's more to the story!

Superromance.
A *big* satisfying read about unforgettable
characters. Each month we offer *six* very different
stories that range from family drama to adventure
and mystery, from highly emotional stories to
romantic comedies—and much more! Stories
about people you'll believe in and care about.
Stories too compelling to put down....

Our authors are among today's *best* romance
writers. You'll find familiar names and talented
newcomers. Many of them are award winners—
and you'll see why!

If you want the biggest and best
in romance fiction, you'll get it
from Superromance!

Exciting, Emotional, Unexpected...

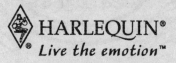

HARLEQUIN®
Live the emotion™

Harlequin® Historical
Historical Romantic Adventure!

Imagine a time of chivalrous knights and unconventional ladies, roguish rakes and impetuous heiresses, rugged cowboys and spirited frontierswomen— these rich and vivid tales will capture your imagination!

Harlequin Historical . . . they're too good to miss!

HHDIR06